BRUMBACK LIBRARY
3 3045 00093 3586

D0327336

THE COUSINS

RONA
JAFFE

THE COUSINS

A NOVEL

DONALD I. FINE, INC.
New York

 Published in the United States of America by Donald I. Fine, Inc. and in Canada by General Publishing Company Limited.

Library of Congress Catalogue Card Number:

ISBN: 1-55611-465-6

Manufactured in the United States of America

10 9 8 7 6 5 4 3 2 1

Designed by Irving Perkins Associates

Also by Rona Jaffe

AN AMERICAN LOVE STORY
AFTER THE REUNION
MAZES AND MONSTERS
CLASS REUNION
THE LAST CHANCE
FAMILY SECRETS
THE OTHER WOMAN
THE FAME GAME
THE CHERRY IN THE MARTINI
MR. RIGHT IS DEAD
THE LAST OF THE WIZARDS (FOR CHILDREN)
AWAY FROM HOME
THE BEST OF EVERYTHING

1

ON A CLEAR, bitingly cold New York winter morning, Olivia Okrent hurried through the noisy, littered streets, ready to start her real day and looking forward to it. She was a beautiful woman, both slender and voluptuous, tall, and with a style of her own. She was forty-five but looked younger, with brown hair that this year was a warm red, a toned body she had dragged unwillingly to the gym for twenty years, large hazel eyes that in some lights were almost topaz—and that too often betrayed her by giving away her thoughts—and a child's grin men had told her lit up the room. She was wearing a big fluffy fake-fur coat, pale green with Mickey Mouse stenciled all over it. When people asked her what it was made of she always said: "Bathmat."

As soon as she entered the house she lived in with Roger Hawkwood, the outside world disappeared. They had been together for ten years. She loved that house and her life in it. It was a townhouse they owned together in the East Seventies, with their clinic downstairs. She and Roger also did surgery there, if the patients didn't have to have it done in a regular hospital, and after an often frantic day it was wonderful to climb the stairs of her house and enter her sanctuary. Upstairs were pale cream walls, oriental rugs, good paintings, books, music, fresh flowers and tranquillity. There was a state-of-the-art kitchen where she could really cook on weekends, when she had time. There was a sand-colored marble bathroom with a tub big enough for two, with a Jacuzzi. The bedroom had a king-sized bed with a television set in front of it that was as big as the footboard and was hooked up to their stereo sound system and a VCR, where they could watch a rented movie on a Saturday night like an old married couple, their dogs cuddled beside them.

She smiled at the receptionist. "Where's Dr. Hawkwood?"

"Examining a patient."

"Okay, I'm going to surgery now."

Olivia scrubbed and got dressed in her surgical greens. The familiar ritual always calmed her, made her feel the most like herself. She went into the clean, glistening operating room like a goddess: Carrie already asleep and ready for her, her assistant Terry close at hand. She worked swiftly and efficiently. She liked to talk to the patients while she was operating on them, because she was sure they heard her, even though the anesthetic made them forget everything.

"Don't you worry, Carrie," Olivia said. "You're young, and you have a wonderful life ahead of you. When I get finished with this you can go out and have a *good* time." She smiled and looked down at the beautiful face of the peacefully sleeping German shepherd. "Spaying is a piece of cake, kiddo."

She tied the last stitches and left Terry to finish up. Tonight Carrie would sleep in a cage in the downstairs recovery room, and tomorrow she would walk in the garden, and the day after that she would go home.

The family thought her career was just one more too unconventional thing about Olivia. They called her cousin Kenny the heart surgeon "the doctor," and Olivia "the vet." At first she had thought this was the old guard's attitude towards women, but after she went into practice with Roger they called him "the vet" too. Never was either of them referred to as a doctor. Their chosen profession was one step too close to the barnyard for the fastidious Miller clan.

When she was a child her mother had said animals were filthy and refused to let her have a pet. Olivia had always adored animals—they were so unquestioningly loving, so forgiving, and they couldn't really tell you what hurt. For years she had brought home every waif and stray that seemed to need her, and her mother had tossed all of them out. There had never been a veterinarian in the family.

"You keep the clinic in the house?" her aunt Myra had said, looking squeamish. "Don't they bark, and uh . . . go to the bathroom?"

"The same as anybody's pets," Olivia said cheerfully. "And some of them miaow."

Three more surgeries, and that was over. She passed Roger in the hall and they winked at each other and grinned. She looked at her watch. Now there would be patients to see, for hours, because people had to come after work, too. Their days were as long and crowded as if they had been taking care of humans instead of animals, except there was less money in it. But then if there were no emergencies she and Roger would have the end of the evening together. She rolled her shoulders, working the stiffness out of them, and thought about their Jacuzzi . . . the two of them in it, maybe making love, maybe sending out for Chinese food later. She was so lucky.

On her third try for a lasting relationship with a man, she'd finally gotten it right. She'd met her first husband, Howard, in college, and they'd gotten married right after graduation, at Mandelay, the family summer estate—the long white gown, the *chuppah,* the happy family, the works. If they had stayed together, as they'd expected they would, they would be looking at their twenty-fifth anniversary now! She couldn't even imagine it. They had been lovers and best friends, but after two years they both knew they were careening in different directions and they didn't know what to do to stop it. It was fortunate they hadn't had a baby.

It was the late sixties, people were trying to "find themselves." She knew she wanted to go to vet school, she'd wanted that since she was a little girl. Howard decided he wanted to travel through America and maybe Europe and be a photojournalist. The world was changing so fast and he wanted to be a part of it. His parents had thought he was going to go to law school. So had hers. Their parents were more upset at the failure of their marriage than they were. She and Howard, although they were very sad, also felt it was inevitable, that they were being realistic and mature, that they had escaped a great mistake.

After the divorce they saw each other from time to time, talked all night and smoked grass and drank a little wine, and then made love as if each of them had met an amazingly compatible stranger. There always seemed something forbidden and exciting about this, but after a few more years they stopped seeing each other, then he stopped sending postcards, and then she didn't even know where he was. She supposed they could have found each other if they'd really wanted to. She had always kept her maiden name and stayed in New York. It was so strange to know there was a man out there to whom she'd once been married and that they would probably never see each other again for the rest of their lives.

She met husband number two, Stuart, the respectable lawyer her parents were so delighted to have in the family, when he came to her in tears, carrying his dog who had been hit by a cab. The fact that it had happened outside her office seemed to be kismet. The dog died of internal injuries. Afterward he asked her to have dinner with him. It was the first and last time she went out with a client.

The marriage lasted three years, but it should have been over right after the honeymoon when he started seeing other women. They were always models, always foreign. She pictured him standing at the airport waiting for planes that would bring those skinny insecure French girls into his life, panting to whisk them away and be their first romance in New York. But of course it wasn't that way; he met them on blind dates when Olivia was working. She wondered when *he* ever worked. Apparently he gave them the impression he was waiting for his divorce.

And he told her. He admitted nothing had ever lasted for him, that he was unable to make a connection. He said he liked her very much, but he didn't really love her, that if he did get to love her he would be able to have sex with her again, but as things were it was just easier to have it with women he didn't much like or respect. It was the freewheeling seventies, and for a while Olivia didn't realize how crazy he actually was. She didn't want another failed marriage, she wondered if there was something she wasn't doing right. In her loneliness and pain she became anorexic trying to look like those models, but she couldn't get him to change, and finally one night when she looked at herself in the mirror it was for the first time with horror; and a week later she started the proceedings that would make her twice divorced by the age of thirty.

What a record. Her family didn't discuss it in front of her, but she knew they were appalled, and that they did talk about it behind her back.

By the time she met Roger she had decided exactly what she wanted in a man. She wanted a comfort level, something like what she'd had with Howard, but she wanted him already to be what he was going to be so she would have no bad surprises. Attractive, of course, and there had to be strong chemistry, but she also wanted a best friend. Roger was warm and cute and cuddly and affectionate, with dark auburn hair, hazel eyes like hers that were sometimes topaz, and a wonderful smile. They could almost be taken for brother and sister. He was three years older than she was. The fact that he was also a veterinarian was the sheerest good luck.

They met in a movie line, at an art theater that was showing a revival of *Two for the Road.* They had each gone alone. They left together. She told her parents they had met on a blind date.

He didn't mind that she didn't want children. He did ask her why not, and she admitted that she had always been secretly afraid she would be a bad mother. He said he was sure she would be a wonderful mother, but children were not really a priority for him at that moment. He didn't even mind that she didn't want to risk getting married again. He seemed relieved. He'd survived a bad marriage and he said they could always change their minds later.

The senior members of the family from time to time made it known that it would be more acceptable if she married him. He wasn't Jewish, but at this point in her life none of them cared anymore. But after she and Roger had bought the building together and moved in together and merged their practices, they seemed to themselves as wedded as anyone could be. Once in a while, after a particularly romantic evening, one of them would turn to the other and say, "What do you think? Should we get married?" And the other would invariably answer, "I thought we already were."

* * *

When they finally closed the clinic for the night and she had gone in to check on Carrie and the other patients who were staying over, Olivia's afternoon thoughts of potential sex were only a memory. She was so exhausted she knew she and Roger would have their Chinese food *in* the Jacuzzi and be lucky to stay awake.

Roger rubbed her shoulders in the hot, bubbling water, and she leaned against him with a sigh. She had lighted some jasmine-scented candles, and the white takeout cartons of Special Chicken Fried Rice and Buddha's Delight were lined up next to them on the Jacuzzi's rim. Their two dogs were lying on the cool tile floor: Wozzle, hers, and Buster, his. Wozzle was the product of a chance encounter between two free spirits—Olivia thought one had been a giant schnauzer—and her black hair stuck out all over the top of her head as if she was surprised. Buster was a pedigreed golden retriever. The Modern Jazz Quartet was playing on the stereo, softly, peacefully.

"I wish you'd change your mind and come with me to Aunt Julia's funeral tomorrow," she said.

"But one of us has to attend to the patients."

"It's just for two hours!"

"I can't cancel everyone at the last minute. You know that." She didn't answer. "It's not that I didn't like your aunt," he said. "I neglect my own relatives too."

"Well, it would be better if you were there. I always have the feeling my aunts and uncles are looking to see what's wrong with me."

"You'll be able to see your cousins," he offered gently. He knew she always looked forward to that. They had grown up together in a large, close-knit family, and now they were scattered all over with lives of their own.

"Yes," she said. "That will be nice."

"You won't even notice I'm not there."

"I will, and so will they." Then she decided to let the issue drop. She was too tired to get into an argument about it now, and besides, it was useless.

"I do love you," Roger said, massaging her back.

"I know." There was really so little about Roger that she could complain about. "I love you, too," she said. "I don't know what I'd ever do without you."

"You won't have to," he said.

She relaxed into his touch, his presence. Safety, she thought, was the most important thing in life. Once you had it you could do anything else. She had never understood why people looked for danger.

The funeral was at Frank E. Campbell's on Madison Avenue, elegant, impeccable, nonsectarian. Years ago Grandpa and Grandma Miller had their funerals at Riverside, the traditional Jewish choice, but eventually they had all gravitated to Campbell's and were used to going there. The first thing Olivia did when she entered was rush to the ladies room to comb her hair. Then she slipped into the room where the service was to be held. It was small, with rows of folding chairs; not a chapel, just a room. When she saw the coffin she started to cry. Whenever people die it's like a whole chunk of my life goes away with them, she thought.

Julia Miller Silverstone had been the oldest member of the family, in her mid-eighties, and very ill for a long time. Her grandchildren, Grady and Taylor, here from California, had been the ones to plan the funeral, because not only had she outlived her husband, but, much worse, she had outlived her only child, her son Stan. That was tragic, not normal, but neither had his death been normal. The old guard, who thought Grady and Taylor were a little strange because they weren't Jewish, were waiting with mild curiosity to see what the service would be like.

The flowers Grady and Taylor had chosen were blue, Aunt Julia's favorite color, and the music playing softly over the loudspeaker was a Charleston. There were none of Julia's contemporaries here at all; they were either dead, or too fragile, or gone to live in a warmer climate. Poor thing, I should have gone to see her more, Olivia thought guiltily. But she never complained about me. I hope I don't have to be like that, old and alone, having to pay somebody to stay with me and push my wheelchair, who probably doesn't even like me.

She looked around. Right in front of her was Uncle Seymour,

the silver-haired patriarch of the Miller family, who still ran the store even though he was eighty-one; and his wife, Aunt Iris, who had been a great beauty. Their son Charlie the Perfect ran the store with him, and was not here today because he was in Europe on business, but their daughter Anna the Perfect was, in her tight little suit and her neat little haircut just like her mother's. How the other girl cousins had resented, growing up, hearing from their mothers how perfect Anna was!

"Anna is taking dancing lessons," Olivia's mother Lila had said in that smug voice she saved for comments about the family, "and she's such a *beautiful* dancer they asked her to teach."

"Mother," Olivia said, "it's aerobics."

Never mind—it was Lila's family and it was *Swan Lake.*

Uncle Seymour turned to look at Olivia and gave a little nod, glancing around for Roger. Of course his daughter Anna the Perfect's husband was there, a dutiful family member, even though he and Olivia had gone through entire parties without exchanging a word, and sometimes she thought he didn't recognize her.

From the next row of chairs Kenny the chubby heart surgeon, here from Santa Barbara, turned and smiled at her, although his eyes were grave. Olivia smiled back. Looking at Kenny was like looking at an age-progression drawing someone had superimposed on his baby face—it was unreal, imaginary. He would always seem the same to her. He had lost some hair, his nose was bigger, and there were lines, but she still saw the sweet and slightly fey kid she had played with during the long country summers of their childhood.

She remembered how at her mother's funeral he had hugged her and then unexpectedly said, "You're my sister." She had been touched because they were both only children and she hadn't known he felt that close to her. Now they met only at events of family significance, and occasionally he would call her from California, but she also knew he had been to New York many times to theaters and museums with different girlfriends and never called to say he was in town. Maybe that still meant he was like a brother, maybe that was how some brothers behaved. He did, however, always stop by to pay his respects to Uncle Seymour, which was how she had found out he was there.

Down in the front row she recognized, with a rush of love, her cousin Jenny's dark curly mop of hair, like a berserk chrysanthemum. When she was young and conflicted about whether or not she ever wanted a child, she used to carry Jenny's baby picture in her wallet and pretend Jenny was hers. But Jenny was too close in age to be her child—she was more like a little sister. Like Olivia and Kenny, she had no siblings. Their family bred late and infrequently, but Jenny was making up for it, with five children under the age of twelve. Jenny Cooper was the only cousin who had a full-time career and children too; she wouldn't have it any other way. She and her husband Paul, a professor, were here from Cambridge, Massachusetts, for the day with their oldest two.

The music had changed to something very soft and classical, and then faded away. The small room was full. Their cousin Grady, Aunt Julia's grandson, got up to deliver the eulogy. Olivia had known him and his younger sister Taylor since they were babies, sent back East from California every year to spend those crowded family summers at Mandelay, when everyone was still alive.

Grady Silverstone was thirty-four, a stuntman, as his father Stan had been; handsome, well built, broad-shouldered, strong and wiry. But there the resemblance ended. Stan had looked like a cowboy, but Grady looked like a Marine. Perhaps Stan would be different today, if he had lived, but it was the way she remembered him. Grady had the posture of someone who had gone to military school, and even though he was a superb athlete there was always something held back and rigid about him. His curly little smile held secrets.

"When Julia was a little girl," he said, "her mother would dress her up in a beautiful clean dress, with a big bow in her hair, and Julia would disappear. Where she wandered on her adventures no one knew, but every day she came home bedraggled and dirty, no matter how she was scolded. She felt there was so much in the world to do and see. When she was older she was a flapper. She liked to sing and dance, and her dearest ambition, although it was never fulfilled, was to be an actress. All her life she was so alive, until her long illness. Her mind was always there; it was only her body that betrayed her. But now her lively spirit can at last fly free. Fly, Julia. Fly and be happy." Grady sat down. Olivia was crying.

In front of Olivia, Uncle Seymour turned in confusion to Aunt Iris and whispered, "What is he, some kind of life-after-deather?"

Taylor got up and went to the front of the room. She had been deaf since she was seven, and over the years her speech had deteriorated into the nasal tones they were now all used to. She was terribly pretty, and as golden as Grady was dark. Sometimes strangers took her for a Scandinavian person speaking in some foreign accent. Most deaf people Olivia had seen had very expressive faces to enhance their communication, but Taylor always had a look of forced calm, except when she was talking to Grady. She had learned to wear a mask—they both had.

"I love you, Grandma," Taylor said. "You took care of us, you were always there. I will miss you very much. I love you." She sat down. Her husband Tim leaned over and touched his cheek to hers.

It was over. Short and simple. Outside, the cousins hugged hard.

On the way to find the limousines Olivia saw a woman who looked familiar, but she couldn't remember who she was. She was a large woman with gray-streaked fair hair and a face wrinkled and puffy from years of obvious dissipation. There were faint signs that she had once been very pretty, and Olivia tried to picture her as she had been in the past; it was annoying not to know, some memory nagged at her. The woman was hanging back diffidently, being ignored. It was as if she knew no one liked her, that they were annoyed that she was there.

Then suddenly she knew. It was Earlene—Big Earl, as Grady called her behind her back, Grady and Taylor's mother. Stan's widow. Aunt Julia's daughter-in-law. Olivia had heard that she was living in Santa Fe now, but no one ever saw her but Grady and Taylor, and they as infrequently as possible. Olivia didn't know why Earlene had made the long trip, since she didn't seem to even much like Julia.

When they all finished piling into the limousines to go to the cemetery, Earlene had disappeared.

Olivia had not been to the family's cemetery in years, in fact none of them had, except when they had to bury somebody. It was so far away, in Queens. The family paid for Perpetual Care. When Julia's coffin had been lowered, Olivia wandered around, looking at the weathered gravestones that belonged to their clan. She supposed there was a space for her somewhere if she wanted it. She turned around to see that her cousin Melissa had detached herself from the others and was now walking with her.

In every family there is the Pretty One—in theirs it had been Olivia, and later Melissa. When Melissa was growing up she looked uncannily like Olivia, but now that she was grown they looked quite different, although Melissa was still a beauty. She was very thin, nervous, intense; she never ate. She was now Melissa Ardon, a well-dressed suburban Houston, Texas, wife and mother of three young children; she was very sweet, and she would never be caught in a bathmat coat with Mickey Mouse on it.

"How do you feel having your parents buried in two separate cemeteries?" Melissa asked sympathetically. "It must be strange."

"It's awful," Olivia said. She remembered how she had hated leaving her father in that big empty plot all by himself. "But it was what Grace wanted. She said since it was a second marriage for both of them, neither of them could be buried with their first spouse; they had to get a new place. She said it was a religious law."

"What law?"

"I don't know. I can't decide if I want to be buried with my mother or my father, so I'd rather be cremated and have my ashes scattered in the ocean."

"Maybe you'll get married again."

"I doubt it."

"Well," Melissa said cheerfully, "you've been with Roger longer than with either of your husbands."

"Longer than the total of the two of them," Olivia said. "I think that was the point of our arrangement."

They walked on in companionable silence. Her mother had died of cancer when her father was already quite old, and when he had remarried people were at first surprised. Her mother had spent the final years of her illness teaching her father how to make his own meals, and it had never occurred to her that when she was gone he would prefer to find a younger woman to dine out in restaurants with him. Grace immediately got rid of all the furniture Olivia's parents had had for over forty years, and tried to throw out all the family photographs. "You'll never look at them," she had snapped as Olivia adamantly carried them away.

How could anyone be so heartless as to destroy a family's history? How could she not want to keep the childhood picture of her mother Lila with her ruffled dress and solemn face, of Aunt Julia with the big bow in her hair . . . Olivia remembered reading about how some Holocaust survivors had kept pictures of their parents hidden inside the soles of their shoes through all the horrible years until the Liberation. But second wives, and their husbands, had been obliterating the existence of first wives for centuries. It was probably part of nature. As for Grace, after Olivia's father's death she had gone back to her children from her first marriage, and she and Olivia had not been in contact in two years.

"I think I want to be buried here," Olivia said. "With my mother and the grandparents. Some sense of continuity. Will you remember?"

"It won't be for a long time," Melissa said.

"So?"

"Okay." Melissa looked uncomfortable. Her own mother was buried here, with a place waiting for her father, Uncle David, but like all the other cousins who had moved away, Melissa and her husband had bought a family plot in their hometown. Jenny and her husband had done the same, as had Kenny.

The mourners were walking to the limousines, and Melissa headed back, but Olivia stood for a moment looking over the neat rows of headstones lined up into the distance until they finally disappeared into the low mist of the damp, darkening winter afternoon. Many, many generations ago there had been only one cemetery, and everyone was buried there. Now there was no room, and even if there had been, people had gone away. The past seemed so simple. It made her feel sad.

Back at Aunt Julia's apartment the relatives were eating ravenously from a buffet. Olivia wasn't hungry. She looked around.

There was the covered silver candy dish from the living room in Mandelay, and the four antique side chairs with needlepoint seats, which the children never sat on because they were itchy. And there next to the phone sat the TTY with its computer screen and keyboard, which Julia had used for her long-distance talks with Taylor.

In the living room Aunt Myra, Jenny's mother, the youngest of the aunts, who had no sisters anymore, was sitting close to her two older brothers and her sister-in-law, looking small and vulnerable. The "girl" cousins were talking about their children and schools, the "boy" cousins were talking about the family business (because even though most of them had chosen other occupations, the whole family still got money from it) and no one was discussing the departed.

Grady and Taylor were sitting by themselves in a corner, conversing rapidly in sign language, their faces bright and animated, the way they were only with each other. Her graceful hands flew like two tan birds. What were they saying? They had had a habit since childhood of signing instead of speaking when other people were around, mischievously hiding in their private, secret world. A world none of the others had tried hard enough to enter. . . .

Olivia remembered how, during those long summers at Mandelay, after what the family referred to as the Tragedy, all the cousins had tried to learn sign language so they could continue to talk to Taylor. They had approached it with the brief enthusiasm of children, and afterward, when they all grew up and scattered, they had forgotten most of it. Taylor had been their little pet, their toy. Olivia remembered Jenny at fourteen, sitting so patiently and setting Taylor's silky flaxen hair into curls, because while Jenny was always trying to straighten her own dark tangled mop and look like Taylor, Taylor wanted only to look like Jenny. In her own way Jenny had spoken to Taylor through the language of her fingers, even then practicing to be the mother she now was.

But now Jenny was at the door, her husband and two older sons in tow. "We have to catch a plane," she was saying. "I have a baby-sitter."

Kenny, still chewing, embraced Olivia. "I have to go too," he said. "I have a quintuple bypass tomorrow morning."

He'd better stop eating all that junk or he'll have one of his own, Olivia thought.

"Come visit us," Jenny said to Olivia with a wave.

"If I can get away from my patients," Olivia said.

"And you can visit me," Kenny said. But they knew nobody visited anybody.

They left. Olivia went around the room hugging everyone goodbye. Then she rode down in the elevator alone. She wondered why the aunts and uncles still made her so anxious. When she had been a child they had all adored her, the bright and cherished little niece. Maybe her mistake had been to grow up. But they were all totally unaware of how they affected her, and probably would have been surprised. She was, after all, the independent one, the untamed.

2

Olivia was very young when her cousin Stanley Silverstone graduated from high school and left for Hollywood. She remembered growing up hearing about him—he was different, he didn't like to study, he was unusually athletic, physical, even wild. The family said he was a daredevil. It was the fifties. People wanted security, not adventure. The family department store, Julia's, named after Stan's mother, had been intended as a great, glittering career opportunity for the men in the family, and an income for their sisters. If Stan didn't feel it was for him, well, then he could become a lawyer, or even a doctor like his father, secure and respected. But everyone knew early on that Stan wasn't interested in a normal life. He wanted to become a stuntman. Who had ever heard of such a thing?

Stuntmen came from rodeos and carnivals, from Hollywood stuntman families and little towns with names like Rabbit Jump; they rode horses and motorcycles and dirt bikes, they had fights, they dove from tall buildings and through plate-glass windows, they crashed cars and staggered from these crashes engulfed in flames. This did not seem like any kind of world for a Jewish boy from New York City who had gone to private school.

He rented a little house in Topanga Canyon, a Western landscape of scrub and chaparral and big trees. His few neighbors were beatniks and artists and reckless young men who dressed in black and rode big black Harleys in packs. While he honed his skills and tried to make contacts to break into the closed world of stunt people, Julia sent him money. He hung around bars called the Palomino and the River Bottom, where he got into fights and drank and made friends, and eventually one of these stuntman friends got him a Guild card so he could work.

It was hard getting work, like trying to be an actor. Once you were a star you would have jobs all the time, but in the meantime . . . Stan kept on practicing, getting better. He learned the importance of safety and planning. Julia kept sending checks. He was likable, talented and lucky, and by the time he was in his mid-twenties he was someone who, while not yet anywhere near being one of the big boys, could at least make a living. Julia was proud of him.

He met Earlene Taylor on a movie, where she was hanging around with the crowd watching them film. She wanted to be an actress, but so far she'd only been waiting tables. She was a big, very pretty, twenty-three-year-old blonde from a small town in Mississippi, who had come to Hollywood to become famous. She had been hoping someone would see her on the set and maybe let her be an extra. Stan did the motorcycle gag that had become one of his specialties, where he slid it under an eighteen-wheeler and came out the other side, and when the director yelled "Print," Earlene ran up and asked for his autograph. Nobody had ever asked him for an autograph before.

When he brought her back East to Mandelay, to introduce her to his family as his future bride, none of them much liked her, but they tried to be as nice as they could. They thought it was typical of Stan to bring home this unsuitable *shiksa* of limited sophistication, who drank as much as a man. Earlene was completely stunned by the wealth she saw: the rolling hills covered with manicured lawn and huge neatly pruned old trees, the formal gardens, the swimming pool, the tennis court, the twenty-seven-room Gothic mansion which even had an elevator in it that looked like a cage, although the caretaker had disabled the elevator because the parents were afraid the children might try to play in it and get hurt. The family money made Earlene uncomfortable, and discomfort made her hostile.

Olivia was only ten, but she was very perceptive and picked up on all of this. She was rather in awe of Stan, who had become her childhood hero. He was wearing his hair longer than any man she had ever seen, and he had a handlebar mustache and a deep tan, and was dressed like a cowboy. He had cowboy boots and a turquoise bracelet. He didn't even move like any man she had seen; he was quick and fluid like a snake. He rolled his own cigarettes when he thought he was alone under the trees, and they smelled different from the cigarettes other grownups smoked.

"Why is this place called Mandelay?" Earlene asked Stan, on the cool porch with the vista of what seemed like heaven. She was drinking iced tea laced with bourbon she had found in the bar.

"My aunt Lila named it. The store was named after my mother, so my grandfather let Lila name the estate."

"Like 'The Road to Mandalay'?" Earlene asked. "Like the *road* pictures?"

"I don't think so," Stan said.

"Well, like *Rebecca?* I saw that movie. Like *Manderley?*"

"No, it's Mandelay."

"Do you remember when Mrs. Danvers set the whole house on fire? And the murder? That place was cursed."

"It's not Manderley," Stan said.

"Wouldn't it be funny if she was trying to be pretentious and got it wrong," Earlene said.

"Just cool it."

Actually, as Stan was later to find out, most things made Earlene hostile.

They sat at the long dinner table and Olivia bombarded him with questions about his work. "What happens when you jump off a building?"

"They spread out these large foam-rubber-filled mats, and they stack cardboard boxes under them to help break the fall."

'Well, you knew he didn't hit the ground," Aunt Myra said with her little giggle. "He's still here."

Olivia ignored her. "Do you scream?"

Stan smiled. "You bet. The loudest primal scream you ever heard."

"I don't know why you do it, then," Lila said, disapproving.

"The adrenaline rush," Stan said.

The aunts and uncles looked at each other and at the grandparents nervously, worried what they might make of this. But the grandparents had seen so many amazing things since the 1800s, when they had been born, that they just shrugged.

"What's the scariest trick to do?" Olivia persisted, thrilled to be so close to her strange cousin.

"Gag," Stan said. "They're called gags, not tricks."

"Why?"

"I don't know. Maybe because it's all a joke."

"Some joke," Stan's father, Uncle Eli, grumbled. He had never approved of Julia sending those checks.

"I'd pick . . . probably the explosion and fire gag, where you have to crash a car and then get out of it before it blows up. You have to test to be sure the door will open, and then set off the charge, set yourself on fire and jump out. I'd never do that one with a hangover."

"Hangover!" Aunt Julia gasped. She glanced again at her parents.

"Oh, you'd be surprised," Stan said, and smiled. "Many's the gag that's been done after a hard night out with the guys."

"He's just trying to scare you," Earlene said. She had learned a few things since she'd been going with Stan, and she had a smug little air of authority. "He'd be wearing a protective suit, and there are people with fire extinguishers right there. And there's a little cage inside the car to protect him from the crash. But they won't let him do it yet. He's not ready."

"Good," Lila said.

"How many buildings can you jump off?" Stan said. "Can't make a living on motorcycles. Some years down the road I'm going to be doing everything."

If you're still alive, they all thought; but nobody dared to say it.

Stan and Earlene didn't want the wedding to be at Mandelay; they said they would prefer to have the money. Also, he was converting to her religion, and would be a Christian, for the children they hoped to have. When they decided to elope to Las Vegas and be married by a justice of the peace, the family was greatly relieved. A year later, Earlene gave birth to their first child, a son, Grady—named after some relative of hers—and two years after that their daughter, Taylor.

Every summer Stan and Earlene brought the children to Mandelay for two months, to escape the California heat and visit their grandmother, who still sent checks. After a few days Stan would leave them there and go back to Hollywood to work or look for work. Earlene was restless, disgruntled.

"I don't know why I gave up my career," she would say.

The house was filled with children. Uncle Seymour, the oldest uncle, who had always been independent, had his own estate with Aunt Iris and their children, Charlie and Anna; but the others were there: shy Kenny, Jenny with her dolls, active Melissa, Melissa's brother, confident Nick; Grady and Taylor, and Olivia, who was a teenager now and already dreaming of getting away. Her mother was too possessive and she had no privacy. There were too many aunts to offer unasked-for advice.

Later, when she looked back on it, she realized that all these people living together—doting, intrusive—formed a buffer between Earlene and her children, and that Mandelay was the only place they felt safe.

Grady and Taylor were beautiful children, and Olivia loved them madly. They had perfect little muscles, without even trying, and they were active as monkeys. From the few things she saw, Olivia didn't like the way Earlene treated them. One evening, in the long upstairs corridor, Grady and Taylor got into a squabble, and when Earlene came running to find out what had happened, Taylor said, "He hit me." They were very young. Earlene grabbed Grady, holding him off the floor, and commanded Taylor to hit him. Taylor didn't want to, she was trembling; Olivia suddenly realized it was not her brother but her mother she was afraid of. "Hit him!" Earlene snapped. Taylor took a swing and punched Grady, and then Earlene let him down. He fled sobbing into the bathroom. Taylor ran after him, and Olivia followed.

He was huddled under the sink, crying, and Taylor was huddled beside him, holding him in her little arms, comforting him, and she was crying too.

Earlene and Stan didn't get along, and several times they separated. She had the children alone, and he told his mother things, which Julia told Lila, who told Olivia. One night when Grady was only six, Earlene locked him out of the house. He had been dressed in his swim trunks, watering the lawn, which was one of his chores, and when Earlene demanded he come into the house he dawdled too long. Night falls quickly and cold in Southern California; it is desert country. Earlene locked the door and left him out there, scarcely clothed, shivering, while she went about her business: making Taylor eat supper, putting her to bed, watching a little TV, having a few drinks. Grady walked barefoot for several miles down the road to his father's house, which was how the family found out.

"What do you expect?" Earlene said to Julia. "He leaves me alone with them. I'm the one who has to discipline them. He doesn't do it."

Grady looked like Stan, and Earlene didn't like either of them. She preferred Taylor, who looked like her. Olivia suspected there were other things none of them knew about. Earlene drank too much, and she hit. What the family heard was the tip of the iceberg: perhaps they would never know the rest.

One summer evening, when Grady was about eight and Olivia was home from college, while the family was in the living room watching TV, Olivia was taken by an unexpected depression smashing through her like a black rock. She went to her bedroom and sat on the floor, in the corner, behind the desk, her arms around her knees, thinking about Grady. Then he was beside her. He had a way of creeping around the house without your even knowing until he was there. He crouched beside her, his small body seeking her warmth, and she put her arm around him. Then she started to cry. *There is abuse going on here,* she thought, *and there's nothing I can do about it.* Poor little Grady—what would become of him?

It was the winter when she was seven that Taylor got meningitis. She had a fever so high she almost died, and when she came back to Mandelay that summer the children had been warned she would be different. She was deaf.

To the family it was The Tragedy, but to Earlene it was The Cross I Have to Bear. She acted as if it was she and not Taylor who was inconvenienced by this lonely world of silence. Taylor had started going to a public school for the deaf, to keep her speech and learn to lip-read. She also had to learn to sign so she could communicate with the deaf community, of which she would now be a part. Earlene, Stan and Grady had to learn to sign too, so they could speak to her.

Grady and Taylor swung from tree to tree like Tarzan, they collected cardboard cartons and lashed them together, the air in the boxes acting as an air bag, and jumped into them from the top of the house. Taylor screamed when she fell through the air, a pure, high scream from the most secret part of her being, and so did he.

And then it was the early seventies. Grady and Taylor were fourteen and twelve. Their special bond, which had strengthened through the years, was enhanced by their discovery that their rapid fingers could make fun of people in public and no one else would know. Their grandfather had died, and Earlene had stopped accompanying them on their summer visits to their doting grandmother; she'd had, she said, as much of that boring place as she could take. This, of course, delighted them.

Olivia had gone through her first divorce. She wondered when Stan would finally get around to his, even though he was living with Earlene again. His prophecy about his career had come true: he was allowed to be very versatile in the kinds of stunts he performed. Olivia didn't like action movies, but she went to all of his and tried to figure out which one he was. Afterward she would sit through the list of credits and feel proud when she saw his name.

When he came for his brief visits to Mandelay he still liked to shock the family with macho stories about carousing with the boys. He looked like a weathered old cowboy now, more dashing than ever. He would recount the times he had narrowly escaped death at work, and list his injuries. There were quite a lot of them —he was almost forty.

Late one rainy winter night, his wife and children asleep in the house, Stan got on one of his motorcycles and rode up Mulholland Drive, a dangerous, winding road with a cliff on one side and a sheer drop on the other. It was actually four in the morning, and he took this trip for no reason anyone knew of, or certainly not one he wished to divulge. They knew he had not been sleeping well, and that he often stayed up all night alone watching television, but he had never gone out for a nocturnal ride before, especially in the rain.

Olivia remembered the way she had asked him questions when she was growing up. "When you take a motorcycle off a mountain, how come you don't get killed?"

"I leave it as fast as possible," he had said, and grinned at her.

This time he didn't leave it.

Because he was a stuntman the story was of more than passing interest, and was in the newspapers. The police investigated the accident and ruled it a suicide. The rain was heavy enough to wash away any skid marks, so no one ever really knew. He had not left a note. But motorcycles had been his specialty and he was too good to go off a mountain by mistake; and if he had, he would have jumped away. Grady always believed it was suicide. Taylor insisted it was an accident. The family told his mother it was an accident so she could live with it as best she could.

Earlene decided Grady had to be sent away to an all-boys' boarding school so he wouldn't grow up in a house of women. It was her opinion, one that was common at the time, that putting the teenage boy into a cloistered male world would keep him from becoming gay. Julia agreed, and paid for it. Then Earlene took in a roommate—a woman friend of hers who liked to drink as much as she did—to keep her company, and gave her Grady's room. From then on when Grady came home for holidays, he had to sleep on the living room couch.

Taylor was devastated at the separation from her brother right after her father's death, and it was then she began to compose her face into a little mask. She was relieved, in a way, that Grady would escape the abuse at home, at least for a time, and that she didn't have to watch it anymore, but now she was in that house all alone. At first they wrote to each other, in a kind of code they had invented. Grady was apparently very happy away at school. But Earlene was jealous because her son wrote to his sister far more often than he deigned to write to his mother, and after Earlene went on one of her rampages looking for the letters Taylor had gotten from Grady, Taylor destroyed them to keep her secrets. Then Earlene stopped giving Taylor the pocket money with which she had bought envelopes and stamps, and told her she should spend her spare time doing her homework instead. Taylor got all A's, had friends, became obedient and quiet, and no one but Grady ever knew what she was thinking again.

As soon as Grady graduated from the fancy boarding school he became a stuntman like his father. It was easier for him to break in than it had been for Stan, because Stan had paved the way. Taylor went to a college for the deaf and then became a yoga teacher. Ever since her father's "accident" she had stopped doing anything daring. The day after she graduated from college she married Tim, an artisan who made beautiful furniture, whom she had met at a party in senior year. Tim could sign because his parents were deaf, although he himself could hear perfectly.

Earlene moved to San Diego with a different woman friend. For some strange reason, after Earlene moved away, Taylor and Tim bought a house in Topanga Canyon right near where she and Grady had so many painful childhood memories, and Grady bought one there, too.

For a long time afterward, whenever Olivia got together with her cousin Jenny they talked about Stan's death and tried to figure it out. No one else liked to mention it. What was done was done. When Jenny named her firstborn Sam, Olivia asked her if the *S* was for Stan, to keep his memory in the traditional Jewish way, even though Stan had left his religion and had probably committed suicide. Jenny seemed surprised. She said no, she just liked the name.

He was, after all, just a cousin. It was up to his kids to keep up the tradition; but Grady hadn't married and Taylor had chosen to be childless.

It would be twenty years now since Stan went off Mulholland Drive, but sometimes Olivia still woke up thinking about it.

3

Spring had made its brief appearance and then disappeared, the way it always did in New York, and now summer was going. Olivia wondered why every year time seemed to go a little faster. Her friends had remarked on it too. They said it was because time did that when you got older, and then they laughed nervously because they really didn't want to believe it. She had gotten a postcard from Melissa, who was on vacation in Europe with her husband Bill and the kids, and she had heard from Aunt Myra that Jenny and Paul had taken a weekend house somewhere in Massachusetts on a lake, with their five children, and that Jenny said it was just like camp. She didn't hear from any of the other relatives, but she didn't expect to, nor did they expect to hear from her. Everyone was so busy.

Olivia liked summer weekends in New York with Roger. Everybody who could cleared out and it was easy to get into restaurants and movies. The stores had sales. The family was expected to do their clothes shopping at Julia's, at the employee discount, because it was good public relations for the employees to see the owners there, and Julia's had all the best designer collections, but Olivia liked the little boutiques where she could find the crazy clothes she preferred. Of course the family knew it.

This summer, as usual, it was too hot in New York, and the polluted city air was almost unbreathable, but she and Roger had good air-conditioning. Their four-story townhouse was an oasis.

They had divided their back garden with a picket fence so half was a dog run, carefully kept clean by their assistants—eager young students—and the other half was for the two of them and Wozzle and Buster. There were trees and flowers out there, and vines grew against the brick wall. There was a gas grill on the flagstones, and a table and chairs under a large umbrella. Years ago they had discussed buying a summer place in the country, but all their money was tied up in the house and the clinic, and besides involving traveling and the purchase of a car, and then garage space, a weekend house seemed too much work, and it still did.

Roger had just had his forty-ninth birthday. It was hard to believe that he was only another year away from the dreaded Big Five-O. He had insisted on nothing more festive for his birthday than dinner in a restaurant for the two of them, and when she mentioned that next year she should give him a party, he had said he didn't want to talk about it. They had recently been invited to a fiftieth birthday party given for one of his friends by the man's wife. It was a big, expensive affair.

"Women always give fiftieth birthday parties for their husbands," Olivia said. "But men never give them for their wives. Why do you suppose not?"

"Because women don't want to admit it in public," Roger said.

"*You* don't want to admit it in public. I would."

"Wait till you get there and then we'll see if you say that," he said, and smiled.

He had started going to the gym four times a week, spending an hour on the Stairmaster and then doing weights. He complained that he was fat.

"You look fine," she said. What she really meant was that she was used to him. "I can't stand anorexic men who talk all the time about cholesterol and Pritikin diets. I couldn't stand it if you looked like an anatomy chart and your eyes bulged out."

"What you're saying is you like me fat."

"You're not fat."

Even with all his disciplined exercise he didn't look much different, and she couldn't figure that out, but of course she would never mention it.

They had planned to take ten days off in October and go to

Paris. She had already reserved a room in the charming little Hotel Lenox on the Left Bank, where they had been several times before, and had arranged with a doctor to take over their patients and even let Wozzle and Buster live in his house. In Paris they would do the same things they did in New York: walk, eat, see movies, but it would be in a different place—foreign, exciting—and she was looking forward to it.

In early September, when kids were back from wherever their parents had sent them for the summer and before they had to go back to school, her cousin Kenny was having his son Jason's bar mitzvah in Santa Barbara. Kenny had reserved rooms for the weekend for the entire family at the luxurious Four Seasons Biltmore, which was supposed to be like a resort. As usual, Roger was trying to get out of the whole thing.

"Look, sweetheart," he said, "there's no way I can go to California for a weekend. Two long plane trips, and all that money—you know I won't go steerage—and the hotel. And we're going to take time off in October."

"But Kenny specifically wanted you to come," Olivia said, feeling the disappointment rise up because she already knew he would have it his way. "He put your name on the envelope and the RSVP card. He knows you don't go anywhere—he could have written 'and guest.' "

"Who would you have as a guest?" he asked, teasing.

"Wozzle. She'll go anywhere."

"Because she's got no sense. Besides, someone has to stay here."

"We'll get someone. Other doctors take vacations."

"I don't call that a vacation. You go. You'll get to catch up with your cousins. I'll be fine."

Of course he would be fine, she thought. If he went with her he'd be tired and grouchy, even though to them he would be as charming as he always was. She could understand how he felt about this particular effort, but it was so obvious that Roger didn't have sentiment for any of the important rites of passage in family life that by now it embarrassed her. Everyone else's husband was so good, and her boyfriend—lover? companion?—was so different. Pretty soon the family would stop inviting him to anything.

She hadn't seen Jason since he was four years old, when Kenny and Gloria had still been married and they had taken a trip to New York. She doubted if she would even recognize him. But that wasn't the point. You couldn't let whole lives go by without even trying to look in on them once in a while. They were her blood. She wanted to be there, no matter how much trouble it was, if only for Kenny, and for curiosity.

Kenny was in his first year of medical school when he brought Gloria Weinstein to Mandelay. Olivia already knew he was having an affair with Gloria because he had told her.

"How is it?" she had asked, because Kenny was so shy he'd never even had a real girlfriend before, or at least none she knew about.

"She's not very good," Kenny said, "But neither am I."

He was a young man with a depth of naiveté that was almost childlike, despite having been brought up with money and privilege. Gloria was a plump Bronx blonde with no money, loud and bossy and full of energy, and of course the family didn't approve of her, but Olivia did. She was a secretary with no particular career ambitions, which in that family was fine, but what they didn't like was that she was so open about their sexual relationship, going into Kenny's room and shutting the door and staying there all night, in case they hadn't already gotten the picture from their afternoon "naps"; and this made them afraid she was going to control his life. When he married Gloria his parents changed their wills, putting everything in trust, already planning for what they considered the inevitable divorce.

Actually, Kenny and Gloria seemed to be very happy together. She worked while he went to medical school, and when he decided to move to California and make his practice there she was completely agreeable even though it meant she would have to leave behind all her friends. Kenny had only one close friend, a man he'd known since first grade—Gloria was his best friend, his playmate, his confidante. His parents died quite quickly, one after the other, of heart attacks, and then Gloria became his entire world.

Despite what had been the family's distrust, Gloria settled into the life of the wife of a successful heart surgeon, pillar of the community, patron of the arts, with good grace and a dash of wit. They built a beautiful house overlooking the ocean, with a lot of glass. Gloria became active on various benefit committees. She never complained about Kenny's long hours. She brought the new friends she had made into his life, so that nobody ever noticed anymore how shy he actually was. Twice a year they would take a wonderful vacation; to Europe or South America or Africa or the Middle East; to rain forests or pyramids or historic ruins. They both became good amateur photographers, and the blown-up color photos of what they had seen decorated the walls of their modern house. After a number of years they had a son, Jason, and immediately began taking him along on their trips, even though the family fretted that he was going to catch something. Now big photographs of the three of them began to decorate the modern walls, covering them, until there was nothing left but the bright images of past adventures and the blue limitless ocean beyond.

Then one year, when Jason was six, the three of them went on a trek up the Himalayas. Kenny was still thin then, in good shape, and he and Gloria enjoyed physical activity on their vacations. But when they were ready to start down Gloria said to Kenny, "You go on home with Jason. I'm going to stay here and visit my guru." Apparently she was into Eastern religions at the time, and apparently there was a guru somewhere up there, or maybe not. So Kenny went down the Himalayas with Jason, and Gloria ran off with the Sherpa.

After the "incident" happened no one in the family gossiped about it, as if something like that would go away and be forgotten if it was not mentioned. Gloria and Kenny got divorced, he kept custody of their son, and Gloria married the Sherpa, Tenzing, and moved with him to India, where she embraced his family with much more fervor than she ever had her own. She and Tenzing opened a travel agency and took tourists on treks, where she met several celebrities. On school vacations Jason went to India to stay with her, and since he had been to many exotic places already and was still quite young, he considered this perfectly normal.

As for Kenny, he took it hard. He devoted himself to raising

Jason, and although he was considered a prime catch and dated a variety of women, he did not show the slightest interest in remarrying. He gained weight, even though there was a history of heart disease in his family. He did not know what to do about all those photographs of happier days, and finally just left them where they were—Gloria, after all, was still Jason's mother.

When Olivia first heard the story she thought it was bizarre and something only Gloria would do, but then when she thought about it she began to see it more clearly, even though perhaps only Gloria would do it in exactly that way.

Once she dared to ask Kenny about it. "Why did Gloria run off with Tenzing? What did she want in her life? Was it adventure?"

"Something like that," Kenny mumbled, his eyes darting away, and he looked so embarrassed Olivia knew it was true, and that he still took it personally.

It was over an hour to Kennedy Airport, five and a half hours on the plane, and two hours driving to Santa Barbara in a rented car, but by the time Olivia got to the hotel, because of the time difference it was still daytime, the sun shining brightly. The hotel was an old Spanish-style stucco building surrounded by gardens and palm trees, with the beach and ocean across the street. She unpacked her party clothes and started feeling a little better. Her room was pretty: done in French country-style, with pale colors, nice fabrics and a view of the pool. She thought of collapsing on the king-sized bed for a nap, but the activity below distracted her, so she put on her bathing suit and went to find her cousins at the pool.

Jenny and Melissa waved to her from under an umbrella and she joined them. "Hi, hi, hi," they all said, and kissed.

A pool boy gave her a towel and brought her the iced tea she had ordered. In the near distance were the happy screams of children and the sound of splashing. The sky was deep blue, there was a cool breeze, she had a drink and a book and a lounge to lie on; Roger didn't know what he was missing.

Max and Sam and Abe and Jake, little boys with the names of old men, were playing water polo, their bodies sleek as seals.

"Where are the girls?"

"With their fathers on the beach," Melissa said. "Did Roger come?"

"No." Neither of them seemed surprised or at all condemnatory. Olivia realized it was she they were glad to see, although of course they would have been happy to see Roger too. She would call him later from the room to say goodnight before they went out to dinner.

"Isn't this great?" Jenny said. Olivia noticed that Jenny and Melissa both looked excellent in their swimsuits, even after having all those children. She hoped she looked as good to them.

"It's wonderful."

"What we should do," Jenny said, "is get together like this as a family without having to wait for events like funerals and bar mitzvahs."

"Right."

"At a place like this," Melissa said. "Bill and I were saying that we would like to come here for a vacation sometime. We've reserved a tennis court for tomorrow afternoon after the service."

"We should have a cousins club," Jenny said. "We could get everybody together here, or a nice resort hotel more conveniently located; say, once or twice a year."

"I would do it," Olivia said.

"Like Mandelay," Melissa said. She and Jenny looked at each other and sighed.

"Don't you *miss* Mandelay?" Jenny said to both of them.

"Yes," Olivia said, but she was lying. She had never felt the same way about Mandelay as the other cousins did. They had played happily with their invited friends in that country paradise, but her mother had driven away every friend she ever had, wanting to keep Olivia for herself.

"Nick went to see it this summer," Melissa said. "He drove right up and told them we used to live there, and asked them if he could look around. They were nice about it."

"What did it look like?"

"The same, except they remodeled the kitchen."

"That dark kitchen in the basement," Jenny said. "I liked it. The food . . . Do you remember the wonderful food?"

Olivia did, and the almost ritualistic nature of the elaborate meals, but she also remembered spending her summers dreaming about the enticing, forbidden world outside, where she could have the freedom of her own house, her own life. She supposed she had married as soon as she could not only because it was expected but also to have a buffer against her mother's excessive love and fear.

"You realize we'll never be able to afford anything like that again," Melissa said. "Unless we all get together."

What a fantasy, Olivia thought. I wouldn't do it.

"They should never have sold it," Jenny said. "Nobody asked us."

"We couldn't have afforded it then either," Olivia said reasonably.

"Why did they sell it?" Jenny asked. It was a rhetorical question by now. They all knew the answer. It was too much trouble. Too expensive. People had died. *'The kids will never keep it up.'*

"They should have asked us."

They crunched the last of their ice noisily, the way they had done when they were children, and laughed when they realized they were doing it. "How did you feel being an only child?" Jenny asked Olivia.

"I didn't mind," she said lightly. "I figured there weren't any more kids for my mother to make neurotic."

Neither of them tried to deny this to be nice; they knew how overprotective Lila had been. But Olivia had wondered many times how it would have felt to have a brother or sister, neurotic or not. Somehow she had always fantasized this person as a brother. They would have been the best of friends. Two children, a boy and a girl; a warm and manageable size for a family, in her opinion. Dick and Jane without Spot—oh, well. It had never occurred to her that she might have had a sister.

"I hated being an only child," Jenny said. "Do you remember how I used to sit on the back porch swing with my dolls all day and pretend they were my children?"

Olivia nodded.

"Having children was the most significant thing that happened in my whole life," Jenny said. "You go into a hospital alone and you come out with another person."

"I know," Melissa said. "I felt that way too."

"How many more are you going to have?" Olivia asked.

Jenny looked at her aghast. "No more. I'm not crazy."

A picture flashed into Olivia's mind of Jenny holding one of her children as an infant—was it Sam, the firstborn?—at a family party. Jenny was still overweight from her recent pregnancy, her face round, and the baby was chewing on her cheek. How large her face must have seemed to him, like a planet.

"I was afraid to have kids," she said. "I was sure I'd be a bad mother."

"At least you knew it," Jenny said.

So now I'm everything my mother warned me about, Olivia thought. No parents, no siblings, no children, no husband . . . but I have Roger. He's my husband, my brother, my family. And it may sound crazy, but we have our dogs, and they're our children.

"Where are Grady and Taylor?" she asked, looking around.

"They're going to drive up tomorrow," Jenny said. "There's no point in their spending money on a hotel."

"It's a long trip," Olivia said.

"The way you drive, yes," Melissa said. "The way Grady drives, forty-five minutes."

"Do you think Grady's gay?" Jenny asked. It was a subject the cousins often discussed. It seemed to Olivia that they spent a lot of their time together gossiping about the family, particularly Grady.

"I asked him once," Olivia said. "I told him I wouldn't care, I just wanted him to be happy, but he said he wasn't gay; he couldn't have a relationship or get married because he couldn't trust anybody."

"None of us would care," Jenny said. "It just seems a shame he has to hide it from the family."

"Well," Melissa said, "he's thirty-five and doesn't go out with women, and his men friends are all fifteen years younger than he is—do you remember when he came back from that trip and showed us pictures of that hunk?"

"Aunt Julia used to say they were friends from school," Olivia said. "Grady would have been in prep school when they were six."

"Does Taylor know?"

"She'd have to know, wouldn't she?"

"But he lives with Miranda, or whatever her name is, that actress."

"Used to."

"They broke up?"

"I heard."

"Are we sure it was a romance?"

"Well, they lived together. She was supposed to be his girlfriend."

"Maybe it was a phase."

"Aunt Julia wouldn't have cared if he was gay. Why is he so secretive?"

"Well, stuntmen. That world is so macho. Did you ever hear of a gay stuntman?"

"I've heard rumors."

Grady. They shrugged and sighed. They had wrung the subject dry, until the next time.

"It's hard to be in this family and not be born a Miller," Jenny said.

"It's hard even if you are one," Melissa said.

They all smiled at each other, a little ruefully. "But harder if you're not," Melissa said to Olivia. "Your mother didn't like my mother. She never accepted her."

Olivia was surprised that Melissa knew. Nobody had liked Hedy, the sharp-tongued outsider sister-in-law, but she hadn't thought Hedy noticed. "I guess."

"They didn't like my father either," Jenny said. "He always felt like an outsider, and I identified with him. I always felt like an outsider too."

"Why?"

"I had different values."

"Well, I'm the one they don't approve of now," Olivia said. "I take care of animals instead of people."

"They think you're too independent," Jenny said. "It scares them. But they don't approve of me either. They think I'm too stingy."

Everyone knew Jenny bought her children's clothes at Goodwill and cut their hair herself. She also cut her own hair and was pretty good at it, and proud of it. All her children went to public school, and when dividend checks came in from Julia's they were given to charity or put into the savings bank. Unlike the rest of the family, she and Paul lived completely on what they earned.

"My mother said if I don't spend my money she's not going to leave me any," Jenny said.

"She actually said that?"

"Yes. So don't feel bad."

"Well, I do."

"You have to remember one thing," Jenny said. "No matter what, they will always love you. They will *always* love you."

The little girls came running back from the beach then, all sandy, apparently not jet-lagged, herded by their exhausted fathers. Jenny's three, Didi, Kara and Belinda, flung their arms around Olivia and nuzzled into her, and then threw their heads back to look at her, grinning with joy. Melissa's Yael hung back shyly and glanced away; and Nick's Amber, with an expression of total disinterest, didn't even know her. Well, three out of five isn't bad, Olivia thought.

"Are you sure you really want to go out and get pizza with us?" Jenny asked. "Won't you be bored?"

"No, I'll love it."

When she went up to her room to change there was a message from Roger. "Gone for a bite, will be asleep when you get in, have fun, call you tomorrow." She felt a momentary pang of homesickness for him. She wished he had thought to page her at the pool.

He called in the morning and woke her up. "I woke you, didn't I," he said. "I wanted to be sure to catch you. I'm going out to do some errands."

"My alarm is going to go off any minute," Olivia said. He sounded busy and lively and not very sorry she wasn't there, but of course it was three hours later in New York and almost time for lunch.

"What have you got planned for today?" he asked pleasantly.

"The service and bar mitzvah, then back to the hotel to recover while the kid counts his money, then the big dinner party in the hotel ballroom. The family won't speak to the friends, the kids won't speak to the grownups and everybody will have a wonderful time. What are you going to do?"

"Saturday stuff. Work out. Maybe buy some shirts. Watch the game."

"If you buy shirts, use my charge card at Julia's," Olivia said. "Since you don't use it."

They chuckled at each other, more a shared sound of affection and memories than because it was funny. "I miss you," she said.

"I miss you too, but you'll be back tomorrow."

"Late."

"I'll see you then. I love you."

"I love you."

He hung up and she dialed room service for coffee. Now that she knew he was safe and sound and loved her, she felt liberated, ready to enjoy her day, glad he wasn't there so she didn't have to worry about whether or not he was bored.

At the temple Olivia slid into the seat next to Grady. Sitting between Grady and her husband Tim, Taylor was wearing a long flowered dress that looked like something from "Little House on the Prairie," and she looked about twenty-five even though she was thirty-three. She leaned over to Olivia. "What am I supposed to do?" she asked nervously. Olivia realized it was probably her first bar mitzvah.

"Nothing," Olivia said. She smiled at Grady, who gave her his curly little smile, the one that held secrets and mischief and sweetness; and at Taylor's husband Tim, who smiled back trying to look dignified and nodded, his long hair tied neatly in a ponytail under the yarmulke he had been given.

Taylor pointed at Tim and Grady and smiled too. "My two men," she said.

Kenny was in the front row; Olivia recognized the back of his head. Then, rushed and slightly late, a couple dressed in ethnic clothing came down the aisle looking for their seats. The woman was wearing a sari, which did not disguise the fact that she was a Bronx blonde, and the beaming little man was wearing a black Nehru suit with an embroidered pillbox hat. They were Gloria and Tenzing. Gloria had lost some weight and her skin was radiant; she looked better than Olivia had ever seen her. They disappeared into one of the front rows and the service began.

Olivia had never had a religious education because she had refused to go to Sunday school, and her parents didn't push it, although they would have if she were male. She thought Jason looked like Gloria as a nervous teenage boy. He had been studying and preparing so long for this morning. His hands were shaking but he looked very proud. She didn't know any Hebrew, but still she felt a part of her cousin's rite of passage, of the importance, the tradition. She could sense how alien Grady and Taylor felt to the whole event, and therefore to the family, and it made her a little sad.

Jason had finished his prayers and was making his speech. Now that he was speaking English, Tim began signing for Taylor so she could follow it.

"I have a pen pal my age who is a Russian *refusenik* who recently emigrated to Israel with his parents," Jason said. "We've been writing to each other for a year. My rabbi arranged it as part of our school studies program. Through our relationship we've both learned a lot about other people. Although our lives are very different, in many ways we're alike too. What I am going to do is take one third of the money you have all been so kind to give me as gifts, and donate it to help develop my friend's little town in Israel, where the need is great."

A soft rustle and sigh went through the room: surprise, admiration. What a mature young man, what a nice thing to do. Grady raised an eyebrow at Taylor.

"In conclusion," Jason said, "I want to thank my father, and my mother, and Tenzing, who has been like another father to me."

How sweet, Olivia thought. Another father. Her throat closed up and she tried not to cry. Knowing only the bones of family scandal, it had never occurred to her that they all got along so well.

The bar mitzvah was over and they filed into the next room where a table had been set up with little glasses of wine for the adults, grape juice for the children, and cookies. Everybody was milling around. Kenny was beaming, proud and happy, his arm around Jason's shoulders. Gloria came plowing through the crowd to Olivia.

"Do you remember me? I'm Gloria."

"Of course I do," Olivia said. Does she wear the sari on treks, she thought, or does she wear jeans?

"You're looking very good," Gloria said.

"So are you."

"It's been a long time."

"Yes."

"Nobody ever understood my relationship with Kenny," Gloria said. "I thought somehow that you did."

"Maybe I did," Olivia said.

"Kenny and I were always best friends," Gloria said. "We still are. Kenny can't do anything without consulting me. He's always on the phone—what should I do about this, about that. That's why he never remarried. He's too dependent on me."

Maybe if he remarried he wouldn't have to be, Olivia thought, but she nodded agreeably.

"I know no one ever forgave me for running away," Gloria said.

"Kenny and Jason did," Olivia said. "That's all that matters."

"You're right," Gloria said, pleased. "I knew you would understand."

They stood there looking at each other. There wasn't that much to say.

"Well, it was nice seeing you," Gloria said.

"You, too." And she was gone, back into the crowd again.

"Was that Gloria?" Grady asked. He had Taylor in tow and was translating for her. Olivia could see Tim in the corner talking to Uncle Seymour.

"Yes," Olivia said.

"We were saying," Grady said, "that you should come visit us sometime. Now that we've got you to come this far."

"I'll try. You know I'd like to."

"I'd love you to see my new house," he said. "It's right up in the trees. You can stay in the guest room. I'll take you for a ride on my motorcycle."

"I don't know about that," Olivia said. "I can't ride a motorcycle."

"You just hold on to me."

"He has a beautiful house," Taylor said. "Or you could stay with us."

"Do you ride motorcycles too?"

"No."

"Good."

"I ride horses. Are you scared of them?"

"I only deal with small animals," Olivia said.

"Remember you're invited," Grady said. "Thrills and spills." He gave her a wicked grin and she thought how sometimes, just for an instant, he did remind her of his father.

"Do you guys ever see Kenny?" Olivia asked.

"No."

"But he lives so close."

"We just don't."

"Nobody in the family has ever seen my house," Taylor said.

"They haven't seen mine either," Olivia said. "It isn't even new anymore."

"I never hear from anybody," Taylor said. "Nobody cares about the half-breed in California."

Poor Taylor, Olivia thought. She hoped Taylor was only kidding, but she knew she wasn't. "They do care about you," Olivia said. "Nobody calls you because they don't have a TTY, but the other cousins almost never call or write to each other either. And you don't write them. It's nothing personal." She remembered what Jenny had said: *They will always love you.* "That's why we have to come to these family events, to keep up."

"Well, that's why I come."

"I'll visit you when I get some time. I promise," Olivia said. "And now we have the rest of the day together and tonight's the party. Let's have fun."

Taylor and Grady both gave her the same quizzical look. It was amazing how alike they were. "Fun," Grady said.

"Try," Olivia said. She thought of Roger. He would have said the same thing. Suddenly she missed him very much, and the festivities ahead without him stretched long. It had made perfect sense for him not to want to make the trip, and she couldn't fault him, but all the same she wished he were with her, instead of in New York.

4

It was a perfect September Saturday in New York. The sky was blue, the leaves in the park were beginning to turn, the air was crisp and cool with an overlay of sunshine that made it comfortable walking weather. There are very few such days in New York, and they are precious. Everyone seemed to be out—tourists with their cameras, families shopping, lovers holding hands, divorced fathers taking their kids to the zoo on custody weekend. On this bright and lovely early afternoon Roger Hawkwood entered an almost empty movie theater, and after a moment of looking around chose a seat on the center aisle.

The lights had not yet been dimmed. Background music played. The movie quiz was on the screen, over and over, with the scrambled names of stars. He noticed some elderly couples and some people alone . . . mostly women. The women who were alone were all reading something, usually the newspaper, and they had carefully chosen seats that had several empty seats around them so no one would intrude on their space. But he knew they were lonely. He could always tell. He opened the newspaper he had brought and pretended to read it, glancing at the young woman three seats to his right.

She was about thirty, and beautiful, with a classic profile. When she moved her head her hair swung across her face like a sheet of butterscotch-colored silk, and then she ran her fingers through it, pushing it back with the nervous gesture of a teenager. She was wearing jeans and a sweater. She was tall and slim and full-breasted, like a model. You would wonder why someone who looked like her didn't have anyone to go to the movies with or, indeed, anything better to do this afternoon in the first place. She finished reading her newspaper and put it into her tote bag, and then she sensed he was looking at her and turned to look at him. Her eyes were an amazing bright clear blue.

Roger smiled at her. She appraised him for a second and then smiled back. He knew he didn't, after all, look dangerous. A kind, merry face, pressed jeans and Gap T-shirt and Armani jacket, his expensively cut hair still thick and dark auburn, with a little help from his barber—they were called hairdressers now and he still couldn't get used to it—he seemed as out of place here in the Lonely Matinee as she did.

"Would you like my newspaper?" he asked, holding it out to her. "I'm finished."

"Thank you," she said, and took it, her slim hand reaching across the empty seats between them. She wore no wedding ring. Of course, neither did he. "Oh," she said, and smiled at him again. "I already read this one."

They should be having lunch together at an outdoor cafe, enjoying the early autumn day. He thought of Olivia. They had met in a movie line so long ago, but they had both gone there to see the picture. He hadn't come here today to see this picture, he had come to indulge his fantasy. A beautiful stranger, interest at first sight, let's run away together, I have the whole weekend. Tell me why you chose me. Turn me on.

"I've seen you," she said. "In the neighborhood. You have a golden retriever."

"Yes," he said. "Buster." His heart began to pound.

"You're sweet with him."

"I'm a sweet guy."

She pondered this for a minute. "You should have an Irish setter," she said.

"Why?"

"To match your hair." *She's flirting. I'm going to get this one. Yes!*

"Then I guess you have to have my retriever," Roger said lightly. "To go with yours."

"Can I really trust a man who would give away his dog?"

"It would give me an excuse to visit him."

She fastened her gaze to his and chewed down on her lip, as if she was asking herself what kind of man tried to pick up women in movie theaters. But he thought men probably tried to pick up a woman who looked like her wherever she went. Besides, she was picking him up, more than the other way around.

"Isn't this silly," he said, indicating the space between them. "I can't hear you."

"You're not waiting for anybody?" she asked.

"No." *I'm waiting for you.*

"Well, then," she said lightly, and ran her fingers through her hair. Then she got up and moved to the seat next to his.

"I'm Roger," he said. He held out his hand and smiled.

"I'm Wendy."

They shook hands. Hers was cool and delicate. He felt his getting damp and he could hardly catch his breath. He hoped his voice didn't sound odd. "We've made a terrible mistake," he said.

"Oh?"

"Coming here to this stuffy place on such a beautiful day. There may never be a day like this ever again."

The lights went out and there was a drawing of a soft-drink cup and a container of popcorn on the screen. "Refreshments are on sale in the lobby," a deep voice said from the sound system.

"Wouldn't you rather have champagne?" Roger whispered.

A pause. "Yes."

"Outdoors. At a sidewalk cafe."

"I like that."

Work fast, he thought. When the picture starts she'll get caught up in it and you'll have to wait till it's over. By then she'll be a different person.

The drawing changed to one of pursed lips with a finger on them. "Please, no talking in the theater," the voice admonished.

"Talking," Roger whispered, "is a vanishing art."

"But are you good at it?"

"I pretend to be."

She smiled.

"Shush!" the elderly woman in front said, turning around to glare at them, and turned away again.

A bright ray of light touched a drawing of a trash can with a ping. "Please deposit all trash in receptacles," the deep voice said. Roger held up his ticket stub.

"Such as this?" he whispered. Wendy smiled again. "Come on," he said, and held out his hand. She gave him a long and careful look, while he felt the thumping of his heart rock his body with the combination of the fear of rejection and the anticipation of the relief of success. Then she took his hand. They ran up the aisle together and out into the sunlight on the street.

He took her to a restaurant on Madison Avenue with little tables set out on the sidewalk, with white tablecloths and tiny bunches of flowers on them. Everyone there looked European and was smoking cigarettes. They ordered champagne, which came in delicate flutes.

"What do you think of fantasies?" he asked.

"Nothing wrong with fantasies as long as they don't hurt anybody."

He thought for an instant of Olivia and then shut her out of his mind. She was in California and she would never know. "You're so pretty," he said. "You don't have an angle in which you're not beautiful."

"Thank you."

"Why did you pick me?" Roger asked.

"You picked me."

"But you let me."

"I love your face," she said slowly. "I love your eyes. And your hands. They're very sensitive."

"I'm a doctor," he said.

"I'm not surprised."

"A veterinarian."

"Then you *are* kind."

"I am," he said.

"Kindness," she said, "is more of a lost art than conversation."

"Who could ever be unkind to you?"

"Oh . . ." she said, and let it trail off. She sipped her champagne.

"I would protect you forever," he said, and just for that instant he meant it. He wondered what it would be like to have her in bed for a week. In this fantasy there was no AIDS, no danger.

And besides, in the reality world he had a package of condoms in his pocket.

"Say that again," she murmured.

"I would protect you forever."

"You're turning me on."

"Am I?"

"You have no idea. Do you do this often? Strange women in movie theaters?"

"Never," he said.

"Public places?"

"No. Do you?"

"No," she said. "I'm a stockbroker. I'm extremely straight and proper. I work very hard and I like to be alone. It helps me unwind. It's just that you . . . you brought out something in me, I don't know. I really never act like this."

"I never did but I always wanted to," Roger said. "Just once in my life."

"Can we take a walk now?" she said.

They walked hand in hand up Madison Avenue, and when they reached the corner where there was a red light they kissed and held each other. He knew she could tell he was aroused, but she didn't move away until the light changed. "Where are we walking to?" he asked.

"My apartment."

He felt the throbbing in his groin and thought how crazy it was, and hoped they didn't run into anyone he knew. "Do you really want to do this?" he asked.

"Yes. Don't you?"

"You have no idea."

She lived in a big old white building with a formal lobby and a doorman. They walked in, out of the autumn sunshine, into the soft golden glow of artificial light.

"Miss Wilton," the doorman said, nodding. "Dr. Hawkwood."

"Hello, Victor," they both answered pleasantly.

As soon as they got into her apartment they tore off their clothes and Roger entered her without foreplay. He did not use the condom in his pocket. She began to come almost immediately, and after what he considered a decent interval of self-restraint he did too.

He had been having an affair with Wendy for six months now—his first affair since he had met Olivia eleven years ago. He had met her at the gym. The Stairmaster, the nineties equivalent of the singles bar. She was seductive and playful and he was surprised that she liked him. He had bought her a juice. Before they finished it they had sensed a kind of complicity in each other.

The next time they met at the gym he took her to lunch. She was so wise, so knowing, reaching into a part of him he had been too serious—or perhaps too afraid—to see. After a brief period, when they realized they were sexual conspirators, he stopped working out three times a week and worked out only twice, telling Olivia he was going to the gym four times, and therefore leaving two days a week when he could sneak away to have sex with Wendy.

His fantasy, he realized, was that he was still young and irresistible to women, that it was the seventies, and life was still a candy box of sexual opportunities. Wendy's fantasy was that he was going to nurture, protect and take care of her. She was neurotic enough to have so far avoided finding a man who actually would, even though Roger was sure that with her looks and brains it would have been easy. He loved Olivia and intended to continue to make his life with her. He never wanted to do anything to cause her pain. But she was reality, and she was now. He sometimes had difficulty believing, even after these six months, that someone as young and beautiful as Wendy wanted him and enjoyed playing out their dangerous games.

As long as fantasies don't hurt anybody, he thought.

5

THANKSGIVING WAS OLIVIA'S favorite holiday. There were no religious overtones of guilt that she wasn't doing things properly, or not at all, and there was no need to pretend to be happy the way she felt she had to on Christmas or her birthday. On Thanksgiving all you had to do was eat too much and rejoice that you had survived another year. The other thing she loved about Thanksgiving was that she gave her wonderful feast for all their friends who had nowhere else to go—her waifs and strays—in the home she shared with Roger and their dogs, surrounded by people she cared about: a grownup now. Thanksgiving was the only holiday she felt she was really good at.

Because of work she couldn't prepare everything, so some of her friends brought part of the meal; pies, salad, a specialty if they liked to cook. She made the turkey, the stuffing, the too-sweet sweet potato pudding with marshmallows on top, the cranberry sauce, the winter vegetables, the corn pudding and the hominy—another starchy thing she had added over the years. It took her the entire day, helped by Peggy, their cleaning woman, and by the time the preparations were nearly finished their guests would already be gathered in her large kitchen sipping champagne, talking, helping or just watching her as if she were putting on a show. The table would be set in the dining room she and Roger seldom used, with flowers, candles, the good dishes and silver inherited from her mother and cloth napkins tied with yarn for napkin rings. Wozzle and Buster, freshly groomed for the occasion, would be basking in attention and looking for handouts, knowing they were clean and cute and that everybody liked them.

Aunt Myra, who served as sort of the family secretary, called to say she was going to Cambridge to spend Thanksgiving with Jenny and Paul. Jenny had her in-laws with their three children and Aunt Myra visiting for the week, in addition to her own five children, and claimed she was having a nervous breakdown, although Aunt Myra, giggling, said she sounded so cheerful it wasn't true. Aunt Myra also reported that Melissa was going with her husband Bill and their three children to spend Thanksgiving in Florida with her father, Uncle David, and that Nick, with his wife and child, would be there too.

Olivia knew that Uncle David had been seeing a woman in Florida for a long time, but wouldn't let her get too close. She was described as "a good friend." Melissa always said he was still grieving for Aunt Hedy after all these years and would never get over her, but Olivia's father had told Olivia that Uncle David didn't want anyone but his children to inherit his money. Apparently Uncle David's good friend was not spending Thanksgiving with him and his children and grandchildren because she had children and grandchildren of her own.

Nobody could call Taylor, but Aunt Myra said she had spoken to Grady, who was going to be on location in Canada in a movie, and that Taylor and Tim were going to fly there to join him for the holiday. And Kenny called from California to wish Olivia a happy Thanksgiving and to say he was going to some island she'd never heard of with the woman he was dating at the moment. His son Jason was spending the holidays skiing with a friend from prep school and the friend's parents; whether he was finally branching out on his own because he was older now or because he didn't like his father's new girlfriend, Olivia couldn't tell.

She remembered the old Thanksgivings at Uncle Seymour and Aunt Iris's before they all became such a mob and went their separate ways; the large Fifth Avenue apartment packed with relatives, everything flawless—the food, the flowers, the table settings, the sweet little uniformed maids coming around the long table barely able to carry the giant silver platters laden with sliced turkey and its accompaniments. After the death of their grandparents Uncle Seymour had quite naturally taken over as patriarch of the family. Aunt Julia had been older, but she didn't have the slightest interest in running anything. In the early days Olivia had been seated between her parents, and when she got married she sat next to her husband. In between husbands, and afterwards, before Roger, she was seated between her parents again, as if only marriage prevented her from being an eternal child.

And then there were the two years after her second divorce, when she didn't come to the family Thanksgiving. Her mother called one morning. "Uncle Seymour and I are coming over to talk to you about Thanksgiving," Lila said in the stern, tense voice Olivia knew so well.

"What about it?" Olivia asked.

"Never mind. He'll tell you. He has a bone to pick with you. We're coming over Wednesday night." It was typical of Lila and Uncle Seymour to set up anxiety for a certain period of time before coming to the point.

Uncle Seymour arrived without Aunt Iris, who liked to distance herself from anything unpleasant of a family nature, since she was a sister-in-law and knew exactly how to handle the protocol. Grady had been in New York visiting his grandmother and had come to Olivia's apartment to help her put together the new stereo components she had finally gotten around to buying, her ex-husband having taken the good ones. Her parents arrived with Uncle Seymour, but her mother might as well have left her father at home—he sat on the most distant chair and fell into his usual half doze. Her father hated unpleasantness more than any of them. Grady was looking as if he had sneaked into an interesting movie, a look he usually had when he was around Olivia.

Her mother and Uncle Seymour sat down facing her as if they were at a business meeting. Olivia offered them something to drink and they refused. Uncle Seymour was so upset and angry that his voice cracked. "You don't come to Thanksgiving anymore," he said. "I heard you don't come because you said it's too damned *boring*."

"I never said that," Olivia said, genuinely amazed. Had Lila told him that? Had she ever said that to Lila? Her stomach immediately tied up into a knot of fear. There was a long silence while the two of them looked at her sternly. She remembered that awful last time she had come to his apartment for Thanksgiving. "I stopped coming because of what Hedy said," she said.

Their expressions seemed to soften slightly. They didn't like Hedy.

"Don't you remember?" Olivia said. She could feel the pain again. "I had just left Stuart. Marriage number two, smasheroo. And Hedy said to me, 'When are you ever going to do something I'm not ashamed of?' Anna got up and left the room. I ran out too and Anna said to me, 'That was so totally unfair. I'm not going to stay in the same room with that woman.' Anna said that to Aunt Iris too. Ask her."

She could see Uncle Seymour's face relax. Invoking the name of Anna the Perfect as her comrade-in-arms had made her distress totally valid.

"Well," he said, "you should have told us."

"I told my mother," Olivia said, glaring at Lila.

"Nobody cares what Hedy says," Lila said. "Everybody knows she's impossible."

"Next time you don't have to sit near her," Uncle Seymour said. "Problems have solutions. Now, will you start coming to Thanksgiving again?"

"Yes," Olivia said, although the thought made her nervous.

"It's important for the family to stay together," Uncle Seymour said. "We have to keep up the traditions of the holidays. Thanksgiving, Passover . . ."

Olivia remembered Passovers of her youth when she had always been there, but Charlie the Perfect and Anna the Perfect had not because their parents had let them go to their school's spring dance. No social event had ever been allowed to take precedence over The Family in her home. Yet now Charlie and Anna were more devoted to their parents than she was to hers.

"These events are for the family to be together," Uncle Seymour said. "It's too easy to become estranged. We have to make an effort not to drift away. You should come to these occasions."

"Okay," Olivia said. "I will."

Lila was rocking her body back and forth in the wing chair,

rubbing her hands together with smug glee. Olivia realized her mother looked just like a witch. "From now on the family comes first," Lila announced.

"It doesn't have to come first," Uncle Seymour said mildly.

Olivia felt as if someone had tied a rope around her and then let it go. Lila cast him a desperate glance as if she had been betrayed.

"Tell her about the lawyer," Lila said.

"Ah, yes," Uncle Seymour said. "Did you explain to her?"

"When do I ever get to talk to her?" Lila said.

"The whole family is going to use the same lawyer to make out their wills," Uncle Seymour said pleasantly. "He's someone we've worked with in business. I don't know who you used before, Olivia, but he'll get in touch with you and you'll redo yours with him."

"Then everybody's will be the same," Lila said.

"We want someone we know," Uncle Seymour said.

"You don't know how to take care of yourself," Lila said to Olivia. "Do you remember when you wanted to leave some money to your cleaning woman and I talked you out of it?"

"She died already," Olivia said.

"And animals," Lila said to Uncle Seymour. "She gives to those animal causes. And charities all over the place."

"You're a Jew," Uncle Seymour said. "Never forget that. You have to give to UJA Federation. Now, while you're alive, not just later. They cover most of the other charities you like under their umbrella. If you give to them, you don't have to worry about giving to anybody else."

"I give to UJA," Olivia said.

"That should be your main contribution," Uncle Seymour went on. "The family has given to UJA very generously all through the years because we know who we are. We have to take care of our people. Who else is going to do it? Everybody takes care of their own. Do you think anybody else cares about you? It's very important for you to remember always that you're part of the Jewish community, that we are Jews."

"Okay," Olivia said.

"That's settled," Lila said. She got up. "Wake up!" she said to Olivia's father. "We're leaving. You can sleep at home."

Uncle Seymour stood too. He smiled beatifically at Olivia as she handed him his coat. "Good night, Olivia darling," he said. "Good night, Grady."

When they left, Grady turned to Olivia and made a little face. "That speech," he murmured.

"What about it?"

"How do you think it made me feel?"

It was the first time Olivia had realized that Grady felt like an outsider. When she looked back on it she couldn't ever remember him and Taylor at any of their family Thanksgiving dinners, even though their grandmother lived in New York, but she had simply thought it was because they lived so far away and had lives of their own.

"How do you think this whole thing makes *me* feel?" she said, to cheer him up. "Now they have someone to report to them what I do in my will. No secrets anymore. Complete control even beyond the grave."

Grady smiled.

The following Thanksgivings she had gone again to Uncle Seymour's, where there were so many people that they took up the entire dining room and spilled out into the gallery, and Aunt Iris thoughtfully placed Hedy and Olivia in separate rooms so they never had to say anything to each other besides hello. Then she met Roger, and the first year they were together they went to the family to prove they were a couple, to be welcomed, and so she could show him off. After that they bought the house, and he had wanted them to have their own Thanksgiving in it, with their friends. The first time Olivia felt guilty and nervous, as if she and Roger were being unfriendly, but her mother, without even being told she wasn't invited, rejected her first by saying "Of course you know I have to go to the family"—as if *she* weren't family. It was actually a great relief.

The year her mother died, Olivia brought her father to her Thanksgiving dinner, and the year after that he was remarried and traveling around the world with Grace. Olivia's Thanksgivings with Roger eventually became established as a tradition, albeit a strange one, and Aunt Iris didn't bother asking her anymore, although Olivia knew the door was always open.

* * *

Thanksgiving Day was bright and clear. Roger had bought dried corn, and Olivia put it with the flowers on the dining room table, giving the centerpiece a wild but comfortable look. She was wearing a black bodysuit under one of her little boutique finds: a crocheted dress in autumn colors—thin and see-through and sexy—ballet slippers, and big crazy earrings. The kitchen smelled wonderful. Roger was pouring champagne. They had twenty people this year, some of whom they saw only every few months because everyone was so busy. Their friends were all getting along with each other, and everyone was saying how starved they were, how they hadn't eaten all day, how they had been saving themselves for this feast. Because of the conversation and laughter you could hardly hear the CDs she and Roger had so carefully selected and put on the changer, but they were a cheerful background anyway.

Her friend Alys—the spelling her own—whom Olivia had known since high school, which was probably why she put up with her, was there alone, having recently broken up with her latest bad choice, and she was already slightly drunk. It was a shame, Olivia thought, that she didn't know any nice available man to fix her up with. She looked around the room fondly at her friends. Alys came to stand beside her.

"What a politically correct party," Alys said. "The homosexual couple; the turkey-baster single mother; the black couple; the black homosexual—that's even better; the man whose pregnant wife could pass for his daughter; the woman whose boy toy could pass for her son; the psychic; four people in AA drinking San Pellegrino; one stray Oriental; assorted children—where are the lesbians?"

"She is not a turkey-baster single mother," Olivia said. "Her child's adopted."

"Where did you get these people anyway, Central Casting?"

"Only you," Olivia said.

"What are they, patients?"

"Clients," Olivia corrected her. "The patients are animals."

"Sounds like the men I meet."

"Some are clients and others are people Roger and I have met through the years."

"Did you ever dream back in high school that you would know so many different kinds of people? Is this New York in the nineties or what?"

"I never really thought about it," Olivia said truthfully.

"You never really thought about anything," Alys said. "You just did it."

"I don't know about that."

Alys sighed. "You're so lucky to have Roger," she said. "He's adorable."

"I think so too," Olivia said.

Roger was showing around the photographs he had taken of their trip to Paris. Alys's eyes unexpectedly filled with tears. "Oh, God," she said. "People showing pictures of their trip just breaks my heart."

"It does?"

"It's so square and corny and family and wonderful. And romantic. All the things I sometimes think I'm never going to have. Remember that guy I was seeing for a year? The married one? The only compliment he ever gave me was: 'I like the way your comb is always so clean.' He meant so it was nice for him when he straightened himself up to go home to his wife. Can you believe I stayed with him just because he was great-looking and the sex was good?"

"People have stayed around for less," Olivia said.

Alys wiped her eyes. "You know what? I wouldn't have wanted him even if he was available. He thinks a woman is a life-support system for a vagina. And still I was actually proud of myself for dumping him! It wasn't easy. You have no idea how vile it is to be single and terminally lonely out there. You're just so lucky to have Roger and a relationship and this house and your work together."

"I know," Olivia said gently. "Thank you." She hugged Alys. "You'll find somebody. It just takes time. My single years were so unhappy I've practically blocked them out of my mind. You'll be all right—you'll see. I have to take the turkey out now." But she wasn't so sure Alys would ever find anybody. She moved away to the oven.

Peggy helped her take the large, heavy turkey out of the oven and put it on the counter to cool a bit before they would transfer it to her mother's silver platter and take it to the table to be carved. The skin was crisply brown and shiny, and she could already tell that the inside would be juicy and moist. She concentrated on the tangible things: the food, her friends, the party, her home, Roger looking so solid and good. Alys's life was from some bad world that she would never have to enter again. She was so grateful for that.

She went over to Roger and kissed him. "What can I do to help?" he asked her.

"Just be sure everybody's happy."

"They are. And I am."

"Me too."

Her Thanksgiving party was a success, as it always was. Roger stood up and made a toast, thanking her, and they all applauded while she beamed. Everyone got along with everyone else, ate and drank too much, and afterwards there were just enough leftovers to prove she hadn't been skimpy but not enough so she would have to eat them for a week. She sent what was left of the desserts home with Peggy to get them out of the house. The dogs were exhausted from all the attention, already dozing on their mats on the bedroom floor.

She and Roger blew out the candles, locked the door and went upstairs to bed.

They lay on their bed and cuddled, in a state of such serenity it was almost a stupor. Olivia ran her fingers along his familiar skin. She loved the way his skin smelled, musky and toasty.

"I love you," he said.

"I love you too," she said. She was so relaxed she almost didn't notice the cat scratch on his thigh. Then she did. She touched it lightly. "What's this?"

"What?"

"This scratch."

"I don't know," he said. He sounded annoyed.

"It's a cat scratch," Olivia said.

"Don't be silly."

"I know a cat scratch when I see one."

"Well, probably one of the little bastards didn't like getting his shots and attacked me."

"Don't you remember?"

"This is ridiculous," Roger said. He pulled the sheet up over himself and turned his back. "I'm going to sleep now."

She felt the ache of rejection beginning and she wanted desperately to go back to the calm and peaceful, almost infantile bliss she had felt in his arms just moments before. "No," Olivia said. "Hold me."

He turned around and looked at her. Then he smiled. "Okay." He put his arms around her and she nestled against his chest. He kissed her hair lightly. "Go to sleep," he whispered. His heart was thumping very hard.

She listened to the wildly leaping beats, counting them. She hoped he hadn't eaten and drunk so much that he was going to have a heart attack. That was her greatest fear, that she would lose him someday to death. But his heartbeats finally settled down, and after a while she heard his breathing grow deeper and then he began to sigh his way into sleep.

At least it didn't look infected, she thought.

She slept.

6

"YOU'LL HAVE TO LOCK your cat up the next time I come over," Roger said to Wendy. He was on the phone in his office while Olivia was in surgery. "She saw where he scratched me."

"Oh, I'm so sorry," Wendy breathed. "Gregory is really a nice cat. He's just jealous."

"I'm not interested in his motivations. She almost caught me." Actually, Olivia had never mentioned the cat scratch again, but that didn't mean she wasn't thinking about it. All he needed was another mistake and he would be in real trouble. Unaccountably the tension only made him more excited.

"Oh, God," Wendy said.

"Meet me at Julia's tomorrow," Roger said.

"Julia's?" she said, sounding pleased. "That's risky."

"In Couture. You'll be the house model."

"Far out."

There was a childish eagerness to her that sometimes made him feel vulnerable and afraid he was going to get too fond of her. She crackled through his blood like electricity. He had to keep reminding himself that all these Wendys didn't really exist, that she had created them for him. But that ruined the fantasy that it *was* real. He thought of the old Meat Loaf song: *I want you, I need you, there ain't no way I'm ever gonna love you . . .* He just had to remember that, no matter what he told her. His being in love with Wendy was *her* fantasy, her part of the game.

Julia's was a very elegant store, quiet and airy, with an atrium, high-speed escalators overlooking a small courtyard with plants in it, which were changed seasonally, soft music and soothing colors. There was a restaurant which served popovers and cheese sticks instead of health food, and none of the clothes were bizarre or cheap or too trendy, even in the junior department. It was never mobbed with bargain hunters tearing things off the racks, but it did very well. It catered to the kind of clientele that rarely returned anything.

When Roger, carrying his gym bag, entered the couture section he noticed it was mercifully empty of customers, except for a toothpick-skinny woman who was having a fitting and complaining that her stomach was sticking out because today she had done something she never did—had lunch. A chic middle-aged saleswoman approached him.

"Can I help you?"

"I'm just going to look a little."

"Call me if you need anything."

"Thank you."

She moved away out of earshot. Wendy was standing next to a rack of evening gowns. She was wearing a little black mini-dress with the price tag hanging down, and her gleaming butterscotch-colored hair was up in a neat French twist. "Hello," she said to him in a pleasant, neutral voice, and smiled.

"Hello."

"Are you looking for something in particular?"

You, he thought. You're gorgeous. "A very sexy black evening gown," Roger said. "Floor-length."

"For a lucky woman," she said. Her voice was warmer.

He smiled back at her. He touched one of the dresses in the rack. "Would she be lucky to have this?"

She took it out and held it up against her. It was long, black, simple, tight, low-cut and had a price tag that looked like a phone number.

"She'd be lucky to have you."

He flicked the price tag. "I suppose so."

"No, because you have the kindest face I've ever seen. And beautiful topaz eyes. Doesn't she tell you that?"

"No."

"She should. You're an amazing-looking man."

"Thank you," Roger said.

"Would you like me to try it on for you?" she asked.

The saleswoman glanced over. She had seen these couples before—a younger woman with an older man, angling for something outrageously expensive, the man showing off, definitely going to buy her something—so she bided her time and went back to the skinny woman who had eaten lunch.

"Yes," Roger said. "I would."

"Wait here."

Wendy disappeared into the dressing room, and came out a short time later wearing the long black dress, gliding and sensuous. "It's not fair," Roger said.

"What isn't?"

"No one could look as wonderful in that dress as you do. It would only be a disappointment to see it on someone else."

"That's my job," she said lightly.

"What's your name?"

"Nicole," she said, without missing a beat.

"I'm Roger."

"Hello."

"Hello." Their eyes locked.

"Maybe I should look at something else," Roger said.

"Of course." She took another dress off the rack. It was thin and filmy with tiny black beads sewn on it. "This is very nice."

"Yes . . ."

"Would you like to come into the dressing room?"

He nodded and followed her in. The dressing room was large, with a three-way mirror in front of a small raised platform where alterations could be pinned. There were shiny straight pins scattered on the thick peach carpet. There was a loveseat in flowered fabric, and a side chair with a small round table next to it. The door was made of heavy louvers, and it could be locked. Roger locked it.

Wendy hung up the beaded dress. "Sit down," she said, indicating the chair. He sat, and watched as the long, simple dress fell to the floor. She was wearing tiny black lacy lingerie that he had never seen before. She bent gracefully and picked up the dress and hung it up. Then she put on the other one. It fit her like a strange and otherworldly skin. She looked distant, exquisite.

"Do you like it?" Her voice was soft, almost hypnotic.

"Yes. It looks very fragile." He was having difficulty breathing, and the tone of his voice matched hers. They were beginning their dance, the steps of which they each knew separately, and which would have to bring them together.

"It is."

"I'd be afraid something would happen to it."

"You'd have to be careful."

"Always."

"Are you a careful man?" she asked.

"Very. I never destroy. I only protect."

"Why don't you stand there?" she said, pointing to the platform in front of the three-way mirror. He got up and stood on the platform, knowing he was ready for her. She knelt on the platform in front of him, unzipped his pants and took him into her mouth. He looked at the reflection of the two of them, repeated and repeated: of himself on his pedestal, exalted, her avid tongue; and then he looked down at her moving, servile head; and then he didn't look at anything at all. His orgasm was so forceful it was all he could do not to cry out.

She swallowed, very neatly, and then she lay back on the loveseat and as neatly folded back the delicate dress that did not belong to them and removed her underpants, and this time he knelt before her and buried his face between her legs. Her body shuddered and she made the tiniest sound in her throat when she came.

We could get arrested for this, Roger thought.

They stood and rearranged their clothes. Wendy turned in front of the mirror, inspecting the dress to be sure they had not done anything to it. "You leave first," she said.

"I love you," he said. He opened the dressing-room door, looked around and quickly stepped outside.

The saleswoman had a new customer. When he walked past them the woman turned around: head of thick, dyed gold curls, too-cute little upturned 1940s nose job, inquisitive bright eyes, and looked at him as if she couldn't quite place him, and indeed,

Roger almost didn't recognize her either—and then he did. It was Olivia's aunt Myra.

"Is that *Roger?*" Aunt Myra said. His legs turned to rubber. For once he was grateful for her piercing voice. He hoped she hadn't seen him come out of the dressing room, he hoped Wendy would stay the hell inside.

"Myra," he said with forced cordiality.

"What are you doing here?" she asked.

"I thought I'd buy a surprise for Olivia," he said. He felt dizzy and his head was beginning to hurt. "For the wonderful Thanksgiving dinner she made."

"Oh, well, you had a good time?"

"It was superb."

"Are you buying her a dress?"

What else, you moron, he thought with unaccustomed rage, this is a dress department. Why did she have to be here? What horrible luck.

"Yes."

"I'm glad," Myra said. "She wears those weird clothes—I'd call them *shmatas* but I don't want to be rude—you should get her something presentable. And don't forget to use the family's employee discount; designer clothes cost an arm and a leg these days."

He glanced around surreptitiously. Wendy came sneaking out of the dressing room wearing her own clothes. She put the two dresses back on the rack.

"I'll be with you in a minute," the saleswoman said.

"So which one are you getting?" Myra asked. He glanced warningly at Wendy. Wendy kept her face completely blank and moved away to another rack.

Roger took down the dress Wendy had been wearing when they had sex in the dressing room. "This one."

Aunt Myra seemed to think Wendy was a salesgirl and ignored her, concentrating on the dress. "Very pretty. Awfully formal, though. Do you think Olivia will wear it?"

"I hope so."

"I guess you two go to black tie affairs."

"Sometimes."

"Well, it was nice seeing you."

"Nice seeing you too, Myra."

Myra disappeared into her dressing room and the saleswoman turned to Roger, who was standing there with the dress in his hand and his shirt wet with perspiration. "Will that be a house account?" she asked.

"No, I'll write a check."

They went to the front desk where Wendy was standing with a beatific look on her face. "That will be thirty-five hundred dollars," the saleswoman said. "Plus, of course, the tax." She glanced at Wendy, trying to decide whether she was Olivia, and then decided she had to be. "Enjoy your dress," she said.

Thirty-five hundred dollars, Roger thought, feeling ill.

"It's not mine," Wendy said sweetly. "I'm just helping. Men have no taste. Don't say anything to Myra. Roger wants to pretend he picked it out all by himself."

"Of course," the saleswoman said. She put the dress into a box and Roger handed her the check. "Here's my card." She gave it to both of them, Roger grabbed the box, and he and Wendy fled to the escalators.

"Why did you say that?" he hissed.

"Say what?"

"That you weren't Olivia?"

"Would you rather she tell dear Myra how adorable I am?"

"I guess not," he said.

"I'm better at these things than you are."

"I know."

"Sometimes I think you have a death wish," Wendy said.

"No."

"Yes, where we're concerned."

"Wrong."

"Sometimes I worry."

"Don't ever worry. Just be careful." They were safely down at the lobby level and he felt warmth flood through him. "I love you so much. I wish we could have lunch together."

"Me too." They looked at one another and sighed.

"We will soon," Roger said. He handed her the box. "This is for you."

"Oh, Roger . . ." She glowed. "That's so sweet."

"Whenever you wear it you'll think of today and of me."

"I'll get hot."

"Don't get hot with anyone else."

"No. I'll just miss you. I'll be hot for you. You're the only one."

"I can't believe how lucky I am to have you," he said, as they hailed two different cabs.

When he got home he dumped his unused gym clothes into the washing machine so no one would see them. The next day he was obliged to go to the gym in order to stay in some kind of shape—twice a week was maintenance—but afterward he rushed frantically to one of Olivia's favorite funky boutiques and bought her the wildest, sexiest, most far-out thing he could find. The saleswoman, who had a shaved head and who knew Olivia, assured him she would be thrilled with it.

He presented the dress to Olivia over their takeout Chinese dinner and opened a bottle of wine. "This is to thank you for Thanksgiving," he said, "and just for being you."

"Oh, Roger! Thank you. I love it! It's perfect."

"I bought you a dress at Julia's the other day," he said. "But it was so conventional I had second thoughts and returned it. I ran into Aunt Myra in the couture department and she liked it, so I knew that was the kiss of death."

Olivia laughed.

He realized it had been two weeks since they'd had sex, so after dinner when she tried to initiate it he responded. Lately he was always afraid he wouldn't be able to get a hard-on, but he somehow managed even though it took longer than it used to; and whenever he succeeded in making love to Olivia he remembered again how beautiful she was, and how warm, and how safe he felt with her. She was there for him all the time, any time he wanted her. There was nothing about Olivia he could possibly complain about or want to be different. Except for one thing. . . .

He wanted their affair to be fresh and new, as if they had just met.

And even as he yearned for that, he remembered how nervous and uncomfortable he had been with her at the beginning, how afraid of exposing his vulnerability and being destroyed, and how relieved he had been when that anxiety finally went away. He had traded fear for happiness. But somewhere along the way he had also traded in excitement.

Why did peace cost such a terrible price?

7

Once a month, usually on a Sunday, Olivia accompanied Roger when he went to visit his mother in the old-age home. He had been forced to put her there when she accidentally set her apartment on fire for the third time because she forgot to turn off the oven. He had already removed the toaster-oven and the coffeemaker, but he couldn't take out the oven so he took out his mother. He felt very guilty about it.

His parents were not young when he was born, so his mother was now eighty. His father had been dead for ten years. He had one sibling, an older brother who lived in New York with his wife and two children, but the two brothers disliked each other and had always fought about anything and everything. They took turns going to visit their mother, ostensibly to spell one another but actually because then they didn't have to meet.

Olivia thought it was sad that people who could afford to send their old parents away hardly ever took them in to live with them anymore, in a familiar house, with a large, close family to share the burden, but she was also relieved that Roger's mother was not living with them, and she had been relieved when her own father had remarried after her mother's death. Men, she thought, had it easier than women: if their first wife wasn't there to take care of them they could fade away with a young second or third wife by their side.

The old-age home was on the Upper East Side, with a view of

the river. There was always a long waiting list to get in because it was a relatively pleasant place, conveniently located for visiting. Roger and Olivia went in the early afternoon, bringing a plant and his mother's favorite chocolate chip cookies, the kind his mother used to bake and now they bought at Mrs. Field's.

Roger's mother was small and sweet-faced, with thin white hair and heavily veined hands that had done a lifetime of work tending her family. She was a simple woman who had never gone anywhere or done anything, partly because she had an unadventurous husband and not much money. Whatever she and her husband could put aside had gone to educate their two sons, the doctor and the lawyer, of whom they were very proud.

The family's one luxury had been that they owned a little cabin on Candlewood Lake, and every summer they went there for two weeks and for weekends while the boys were growing up, until the boys grew up and grew apart, and made excuses not to come there anymore. Then she and her husband went alone. When he died, everyone was surprised that the cabin was worth so much more than they had paid for it.

It was gone now, and so was her apartment. She lived in this neat little room, with a roommate. There were two twin beds made up with chenille bedspreads, a shared night table on which was a small framed photograph of each of the respective dead husbands, a round table with a vinyl tablecloth and a live plant on it, and two chairs. In the corner there was a television set which Roger had bought her. There was no space for anything else.

She was sitting on the edge of her bed with her hands in her lap, doing nothing, when Roger and Olivia walked in. She looked up. They never knew in advance whether she would recognize them.

"Roger!" his mother said happily. Maybe it would be a good day.

"Hi, Mom." He hugged his mother and handed her the cookies.

"Hello," Olivia said. She put the new plant on the windowsill. She didn't want to call his mother Mrs. Hawkwood after all these years, but she felt uncomfortable calling her Mom since she and Roger weren't married, and it somehow seemed disrespectful calling such an elderly woman by her first name, although she knew that was her own problem, so most of the time she didn't call her anything.

"Hello," his mother said to her, with a friendly smile and eyes that showed no recognition at all. Well, maybe it wouldn't be such a good day.

"We brought your favorite cookies," Roger said.

'That's nice. Sit down." Olivia sat on one of the two chairs and Roger sat next to his mother on the bed. "Do you want a milkshake?" his mother asked. "They bring you anything you want."

"No thanks, we just had lunch."

"The food here is good," his mother said. "Where's Virginia?"

"She's not here."

"Why not?"

"We're divorced, Mom," Roger said. "Long ago."

She looked stricken. "Divorced?"

"You knew that."

"Why did you get divorced?"

"We didn't get along."

"When did this happen?"

"Years ago."

She nodded, thinking about it. "What's over is over. Don't be upset."

"I'm not."

"Good." She patted his hand.

"This is Olivia, Mom."

"Hello," his mother said, still as if she had never seen Olivia before.

"Hi," Olivia said, and smiled at her.

"Do you like your room?" Roger's mother asked him.

Where are we now? Olivia wondered. Sometimes his mother thought this was a hotel.

"I'm not staying here."

"If you don't like your room you can sleep here in mine," his mother said, concerned. "See, there's another bed."

"It's okay."

"Look at the ocean," his mother said. She stood up and went to the window, where you could see the East River glittering below in the afternoon light. "Isn't it beautiful? This is a very nice ship."

Roger nodded. "Why don't we have some television?" he asked, and got up and switched it on. There was a news program with a story about children. His mother looked at it for a moment and then turned to him, confused.

"Those children," she said. "Are they here?"

"No."

"Yes they are," she said, nodding. "There's a nursery on the ship for the children and they play there." She ignored the set until the picture changed to a story about rioting and then she looked alarmed. "Oh!" she said. "Oh!"

Roger turned off the set.

His mother looked relieved. She sat down on the bed again. "Maybe we should have some tea," she said. "The people who work here are very sweet. You can have anything you ask for. It's wonderful to be able to afford a trip like this."

"Yes," Roger said quietly. He sighed.

"Did you see the water?"

"Yes."

"Where are we now?"

"Where?" he asked.

"Where is the ship? You know sometimes I forget things."

There was a pause. "Venice," Roger said.

"Venice!" his mother breathed happily. "Ahh . . ."

They sat there for a while in silence, each with their own thoughts. Olivia watched them, moved. It was this way more and more often lately: Roger's mother steeped in her fantasy, Roger trying to bring her back to reality and finally joining her in her world because it brought her contentment. Sometimes he even seemed to enjoy it, and led the game. It didn't matter to either of them that what she thought was a ship was not a vaporetto, and that Venice had canals.

"Where's Daddy?" his mother asked.

"On deck."

"Where's Mike?" Michael was Roger's older brother. "I don't want him to fall in the water."

"He's with Daddy," Roger said.

"That's good. When are we going to get off?"

"Well . . ."

"When we get closer we'll get off and look around," she said.

"Tomorrow." She smiled at Olivia. "And ask your friend to come."

"Okay," he said. "And the next day, guess where we're going then."

"You tell me," his mother said.

"We're going on to Rome. You always wanted to go to Italy."

His mother nodded politely, her eyes bright, not sure where she had wanted to go but glad to be where she thought she was. "You'll be there too?"

"Yes."

"It's wonderful that we can all be here together." She took his hand in her gnarled little one and held it tightly. Then, in a sweet, high voice, she began to sing.

"Oh, the hills and the hollows
and the bales of hay,
Where the road goes I'll follow
till the end of the day . . .
of the day . . ."

"Of the day . . ." Roger joined in softly. Olivia fought back tears.

"I used to be pretty once," his mother said.

"You still are."

"Oh," she said, and winked at Olivia. "Little boys just *love* their mothers."

8

It was the season between Thanksgiving and Christmas. The leaves had fallen off the tree in Olivia's backyard, and without them and the flowers that were long gone the area she liked to think of as the garden looked pathetic. The metal furniture that had seemed so charming in summer now trembled in the wind like old bones. She hadn't even gotten around to buying any Christmas presents yet, and every morning when she opened the New York *Times* the Bloomingdale's ad with the big calendar of the days remaining to shop jumped out at her like a reproach. She would go to Julia's of course. If she had to give something away she liked having the discount—she wasn't as completely rebellious and crazy as the family thought.

Grady called. He was in New York, staying at his grandmother's apartment. Because of the recession he hadn't been able to sell it for nearly a year now, not even a nibble. He had decided to fix it up to look more modern, have it painted white, take off the faded old wallpaper in the kitchen and bathrooms and replace it with "something cheap, just to make it look good." He and Taylor were paying maintenance every month, annoyed about it because they didn't intend to live there. Olivia invited him to come over for Sunday lunch and spend the afternoon.

Hearing his voice on the phone, she was reminded of Mandelay, when she thought she knew him. He was an adorable, bright and active child, and there hadn't seemed much more to have to know. How intensely she had loved him! Life had seemed so much simpler then, but of course it had never been simple, it was only that she had been young and didn't understand.

"I'm going to leave you two alone to discuss all your family stuff," Roger said.

"Oh, you don't have to," Olivia said. "Grady would love to see you."

"I'll go to the gym. Maybe I'll start on my Christmas shopping."

"Are you sure?"

"Yes." It occurred to her, as it sometimes did, that Roger hardly ever had any time away from her, that they were always in the same building, at work and at home. This space would be good for both of them.

"Okay," she said. "I think I'll make pasta and a big salad. He'd better not want red meat."

"He's from California," Roger said. "I'm sure he doesn't."

Grady arrived at twelve-thirty. The dogs nosed their way through the front door, barking and protective, and then decided he was a friend and bumped against him in greeting. He scratched their heads.

"Down," Olivia said. "Enough."

"It's okay." He had cut his hair in an unbecoming crew cut, and he looked tired and tense. When she hugged him he seemed bigger, more muscular than she remembered, hard as wood. He was so remote and formal she might as well be embracing a statue for all the warmth he gave her. Olivia held on to him for a moment, pouring her affection into him, and then he relaxed and smiled his curly little smile and became Grady again.

"Hello," he said. "Where's Roger?"

"Buying me a present, I hope. Come in." She took his sheepskin coat. "Can I get you something to drink?"

"Bloody Mary," Grady said. "Do you want me to make it?"

"Please."

"One for you too?"

"Not right now. I'll have champagne with lunch. It's not supposed to go with spaghetti, but as far as I'm concerned champagne goes with everything."

"I like it too," Grady said.

They settled down in the kitchen. "How long have you been in New York?" Olivia asked.

"Two weeks." He noticed her look of surprise and hurt. "I've been really busy. There's a lot to do on Grandma's apartment. And I saw Uncle Seymour. I think someone should watch how they're running the store."

"You do?"

"They can do anything they want. None of us care. We just get our checks."

"But they're big checks," Olivia said. She wished he wouldn't make trouble. She didn't even want to think about it.

"I'm going to watch them from now on," Grady said. "I'm going to look at the books. I'm going to come here more often, ask questions."

She was surprised at the bitterness in his tone. He finished his Bloody Mary and poured another from the pitcherful he had made. "Will you have time?" she asked.

"Oh, yeah. Work has been really slow. I haven't had a job in a year. That picture in Canada? I lied. Taylor and Tim and I just took a vacation."

"But I thought you were Harry Hubbard's stunt double," Olivia said. Harry Hubbard was a macho, middle-aged star whose action movies Olivia would never have gone to see if it weren't to watch Grady—or Grady's body, which was really all she saw, usually hurtling through the air.

"Well," Grady said, "he hasn't had a job in a year either."

"Why not?"

"People don't like him as much as they used to. You know how that is. His last two movies bombed."

"I never could figure out how you could do his stunts when you don't even look like him."

"Yes, I do," Grady said. "Same body type. Same coloring. Same shape face. And I can move like him. I'm just younger, which I have to be to do what I do, but I don't feel it anymore. I'm getting real beat up. I'm thirty-five years old and I've already had a hip replacement."

"That's terrible," Olivia said, shocked. "Maybe you should quit and do something else."

There was a pause. Grady finished his Bloody Mary and poured himself another. "I don't think so," he said.

"I bet you're starving. I'll start lunch." She put a pot of water on to boil for the thick spaghetti she liked and hoped he wouldn't get drunk. She had never thought of him as a heavy drinker, but then she knew so little about him these days, and in fact hadn't for years except for the news from Aunt Julia. She put some feta cheese and a bowl of kalamata olives and a fresh baguette on the kitchen counter. "Nibble on this. Do you want to eat in the dining room or the kitchen?"

"Whatever you want." He took an olive.

"I would think that having been Harry Hubbard's stunt double and being so good you would be hired to do other work," Olivia said.

"Oh, I would," Grady said. "It's just that you have to eat crow to work, and it's not worth it to me. There's not what *I'd* consider real money, and with the income I'm getting from the family it would put me into a higher tax bracket so I'd end up getting less than if I didn't work at all."

"But you want to work . . . ?"

"Sure," he said. "So the stunt coordinator called and asked if I wanted to do a full body burn on a fan descender—that's a device with an air brake on it on a spool. I would fall seventy-five feet through the air, and crash through a plate-glass window . . ."

"On fire?" Olivia said.

"Of course; it's a fire gag. So he offers me four thousand dollars. I give him a bid of seven thousand because that's what it's worth to me. He says no, that's too much, it's not fair to the company, and he gets somebody else. So then there's another picture, and I'd get eighteen hundred for the week, and roll a car at the end of the week. You get an adjustment for the stunt, and since this one involves a car rollover I say okay but I want three thousand more. He laughs at me. He gives the job to a friend of mine who I know did it for just an extra twelve hundred. A lot of guys are working cheap just to worm their way in. I could get hurt and my career could be over tomorrow; I want to make a lot of money. Now the word is out that Grady Silverstone is difficult. They say I have a big ego, that I'm pricing myself out."

"Well, it's very dangerous," Olivia said. "They couldn't pay me enough to do something like that, ever."

"I love it, it's what I do, but I'm not going to kiss butt to do it," Grady said. "Especially since it ends up that I'd be paying the government for the privilege."

It's the family money, Olivia thought. It's taken the edge off his ambition. If he loves being a stuntman so much, why does he care about his tax bracket? But the thought nagged at the back of her mind that there was something more, and she didn't know what it was. "That's awful," she said.

"And that's why I haven't worked for a year."

"You should try to be a stunt coordinator."

"Not if they don't like me," Grady said. "In this business it's all whether they like you or not."

"In any business," Olivia said. "Mine too."

"Besides," Grady said, "if you're a stunt coordinator you're never home. I'm tired of packing bags and living in hotels and eating movie food."

"Well, today you're going to eat my food." She put the spaghetti into the boiling water and took the salad out of the refrigerator. "So what do you do all day when you're not working?"

"I have plenty of things to do. I work out. Clean my motorcycles. I do work on my new house."

"We're going to eat soon."

"Where's the bathroom?" Grady asked.

She showed him where it was and decided to set the table in the dining room because it would be more festive. She used the good silver and china because she wanted to make him feel special. She had two bottles of champagne chilling in the refrigerator, so Roger could have some with them when he came home, and she took two of the beautiful old cut crystal champagne glasses from the set of glasses her mother had bought long ago to use at Mandelay for family parties and put them at the places she had set for herself and Grady.

"Can I help you?" Grady called from the kitchen.

"It's okay."

"I'll take the spaghetti out," he called. "It's ready."

She wanted to say *be careful,* but she didn't. And suddenly there was a loud, horrendous scream from the kitchen and Grady came running out with his sleeve on fire. "Owwwww . . ." he yelled, weaving around in pain. He ran to the window as if he were going to set the drapes on fire in his panic, and then he came running full tilt toward her as if he were going to set fire to her. He was drunk and frightened and she was terrified.

"Come to the sink!" she cried and tried to take hold of him, but he was too fast for her and went back to the kitchen screaming. The dogs were barking hysterically, getting underfoot. "Grady!"

She heard water running. Then he walked calmly out of the kitchen with his eyes gleaming in mischief, and the sweetest little smile, holding a wet towel to his blackened shirtsleeve, and then lifted the towel like a chef taking the silver cover off a special dish, revealing his completely normal, unburned arm.

"Gotcha," he said.

"Grady! You shit!" She almost fainted from relief.

"I tested the spaghetti before I lit the match," Grady said. "It should be ready about now."

"How did you *do* that?"

"Zel Gel. I took some home from the set on my last job. It's a fire-retardant gel. I coated my arm and hand with the gel in the bathroom, put on my shirt, put rubber cement on my sleeve, and set fire to that. Were you scared?"

He was her little cousin Grady again, and she didn't know whether to hug him or shake him, so she did both, although he was too big and too solid to shake and she ended up rocking against his chest. "Yes, I was scared. Don't do anything like that to me again."

He grinned and moved away, and helped her prepare the rest of the lunch. They sat in the dining room and ate, and drank the first bottle of champagne while soft jazz played on the stereo. His playful mood faded.

"My father committed suicide," he said quietly. "No one in my family would ever admit it. They called it an accident. Big Earl said he lost his nerve and went out to test himself. Taylor made up some fanciful scenario that he got a phone call in the middle of the night and had to go save somebody. She had to make him a tragic hero. I agree with the cops."

It was the first time he had ever mentioned Stan's suicide to her. She was touched and saddened. "Do you have any idea why he did it?" she asked.

"No. We were so young. He was away a lot on location. But he was a wonderful father when he was with us. Whatever was bothering him had to be the most important thing in the world to him to make him leave us."

She remembered them again as children, and her throat closed with the threat of tears. "It always is," she said.

Grady's eyes filled for an instant and he looked away, and then he sniffed. "My sinuses are still bothering me," he said. Now he didn't look sad anymore but only angry. "I had my nose fixed after you saw me last, because I got hurt and my sinus collapsed, but I don't think it's going to work."

"Your hip, your nose . . . these jobs . . ."

"It didn't happen on a job. Big Earl got drunk and knocked me down one night when I was seventeen, and she kicked me in the face and broke my nose. It never healed properly."

"Your mother?" she said in horror.

"Yep."

"Knocked you down? Kicked you in the face? Oh, my God, I never knew it was that bad."

"Oh, yeah."

Oh God, poor Grady. Poor Taylor. She remembered Earlene, big and drunk and frightening, but at seventeen Grady had been as large and strong as she was. He was an athlete. He could do a back flip over a bar. But that was then, and the back flips were now and the fights were faked. Still, he could have protected himself, he could even have hit her in return and made her think twice about abusing him.

"Why didn't you stop her?"

He looked at her and didn't answer.

Because she was too fast for him? Maybe. "How could you have let her do that?"

He just shrugged.

Because she was his mother, Olivia thought.

"Do you ever see your mother anymore?" she asked.

"Yes." He looked disgusted. "From time to time she insists on visiting. She pretends to be the devoted mother and acts like she can't remember anything from the past. I won't let her stay with me. She has to stay with Taylor. I won't let her in my house."

"How does Taylor get along with her?"

"She can't stand her either, but she does the best she can."

"What's Earlene doing anyway?"

"Still living in Santa Fe. She's got her widow's pension. Is there any more champagne?"

"A whole bottle," Olivia said. "And how about coffee?"

"Sure. I'll help you."

He cleared the table and started drinking the second bottle of champagne while Olivia made the coffee. She wasn't even high because he had done most of the consumption. She wondered whether he was drinking so much because stuntmen did, which she had heard; or because he had inherited the tendency from his mother, which was likely; or because he was obviously so unhappy. His depression was palpable, a presence in the room.

She brought grapes and a plate of biscotti back to the table for dessert, and Grady pulled some photographs out of his wallet. "You still haven't seen my new house," he said. "It's near the one I used to have, which you also didn't see, but bigger." He laid the pictures out on the table.

The house looked like it belonged in an architectural magazine, with high beamed ceilings, fireplaces, a rustic motif and a look of tasteful if slightly fussy luxury, set in a thickly treed area. "It's beautiful," Olivia said.

"There are a few things from Grandma," he said. "See?"

"I never understood why you and Taylor wanted to go back to live in Topanga after your horrible childhood," Olivia said.

"It's our home. We like it there." He dipped his biscotto into his champagne. "You know, it hurt me a lot when Earlene gave my room away."

"I guess it was because she needed the money, and you were at boarding school. That's how she'd think."

"Mm. But this house is giving me a lot of trouble. I'm suing the people who sold it to me because they lied and said I could get a variance to build my deck out over the side of the mountain and it turned out I can't. The deck was half finished and then I found out. I'm not allowed to complete it and I refuse to tear it down so it sits there like an eyesore and every time I look at it I feel sick.

I've spent a fortune in legal fees already." To her surprise he was shaking with emotion. Olivia remembered how Aunt Julia used to say that Grady was a perfectionist where his living quarters were concerned.

"These things take time."

"I won't give up." He put the photos back into his wallet carefully, as if they were of his loved ones. The sun was going down and the room was getting dark. She wondered where Roger was. "I took a camping trip to Yosemite last month," Grady said. "It's very beautiful there."

"By yourself?"

His eyes glittered. "I always find someone to amuse me." He smiled. "I met this young guy and we were hanging out, and we went to the bar to drink. We ordered drinks and all of a sudden it turns out he's under twenty-one, which is drinking age in California, and they wouldn't serve him. It had never occurred to me. So I had to keep ordering the drinks and sneaking them to him. It was pretty funny."

What's so funny about it? Olivia thought. Why are you telling me this story?

"So we finally had to go back to my tent to drink."

Oh sure, back to your tent to drink. Is this a drinking story or a gay story, she wondered, but she was sure it was both. She didn't want to ask him again if he was gay because he had already denied it, but she also felt he was trying to tell her something else in this afternoon of confessions, so she would know him better. Except for his brief prank with the burning sleeve, there was such a heavy sadness about him, such an air of isolation. She thought back over the things he'd said all afternoon and not one of them was optimistic. They were filled with anger and grief. A wave of tenderness washed over her for him.

He held up his empty glass. "I remember these glasses," he said. "Mandelay."

"Yes," Olivia said.

"The big family parties. Kenny used to hide in the kitchen he was so shy, and we had to drag him out."

"I remember," Olivia said, and smiled.

"We had fun then," Grady said. "I loved Mandelay."

"You all did."

"Didn't you?"

"I was unhappy a great deal of the time, but there are things about it I realize I miss," Olivia said.

"Grandma took the dishes when they sold the place and divided everything up," Grady said. "Now Taylor and I have them. They mean a lot to me. I actually use them."

"I'm glad." Still filled with that tenderness, she wanted to reach out and connect him somehow with herself. "I'll give you something of my mother's," she said. "Do you have any idea what you'd want?"

"I'd like something from Mandelay."

Suddenly unexpectedly proprietary about her dead family, she thought about what she could bear to part with. Everything had a memory attached to it, and not all were bad. Some were unexpectedly poignant. She remembered the happy faces around the long table when there was a birthday to celebrate. She would share some of the glasses.

"Would you like to have a pair of champagne glasses?" she asked.

His face lit up. "Don't you need them?"

"I have the rest."

"Thank you. I'd like to have something of Aunt Lila's," Grady said. "She was good to me."

She went to the cabinet where she kept the cut crystal glasses and took out two. They sparkled in the kitchen light. A rush of memories poured through her of those beautiful dinners. She imagined Lila, still young, buying the glasses, looking forward to the summers with almost the whole family at Mandelay, maybe even looking forward to her life. There were so few things that had made Lila happy.

"They're your early Christmas present," Olivia said, and wrapped them gently in a kitchen towel and put them into a shopping bag and gave them to him.

Roger came home then, and dumped his gym bag and packages in the bedroom. It was six o'clock. "Hi, Grady," he said cheerfully, coming into the dining room. "Are you two still having lunch?"

"Yes," Grady said. "It's become the cocktail hour."

"We saved one glass of champagne for you, Roger," Olivia

said. When he leaned down to kiss her cheek she could smell that he'd already had a drink. He took an ordinary champagne flute from the kitchen and poured himself the rest of the champagne. "How was your day?" she asked.

"Good. And yours?"

"Good."

"I didn't know it was so late," Grady said, glancing at his watch. "I have to meet a friend."

"Things going okay, Grady?" Roger asked.

"Fine, thanks."

Olivia brought Grady his coat and hugged him goodbye. "You should call when you're in New York," she said. "I want to see more of you."

"I will." She wondered if he would. "Thanks for lunch."

Grady left, carrying the shopping bag with Lila's two glasses in it. Olivia was so glad she had given them to him. "What are you and I going to do about dinner?" Roger asked.

"What? Oh. Let's just go out. I've been in all day."

She cleared the table and put the place mats into the washing machine. "Give me your gym clothes," she said. "I'll have Peggy do this load in the morning."

"Oh," he said. There was the barest pause. "I didn't work out today. When I got to the gym it was too crowded, so I left."

"That's too bad. So what did you do?"

"A little shopping."

"Did you have lunch with anybody?"

"With myself."

She thought of the wine on his breath. Well, Roger had always been self-sufficient, and it was the holiday season and a Sunday: why shouldn't he have a decent lunch? She didn't want to ask too many questions and be like her mother. He seemed in such a good mood that having been alone all afternoon to wander around obviously agreed with him. That was all that mattered.

"When we have dinner I'll tell you about my lunch with Grady," Olivia said. "It was really very disturbing."

9

From time to time, and especially around the holidays, Olivia thought about Jenny and Melissa, and missed them. They were somehow mysterious to her, living their distant lives, and she wondered what they were doing. She thought how their children were growing older, and how she was not there to see it. Her little cousins were like her nieces and nephews, since she didn't have any, but their mothers never called her because they were so busy, and out of consideration for this, and because she was so busy herself, she didn't call them either. She thought of Jenny and Paul and their kids most often, because it was Jenny whose baby picture she had carried in her wallet when she was young, as if Jenny were her child or her baby sister, and it was she who Jenny had come to with her teenage complaints so long ago. So a week before Christmas Olivia made one of her infrequent calls to Jenny in Cambridge.

"We're all leaving tomorrow to go skiing," Jenny said.

"I'm glad I caught you. How is everything?"

"Crazy. You know sometimes when I come home from work I sneak upstairs and get into my bathtub and just stay there for half an hour before anybody knows I'm home, and then I can face them."

"I don't wonder, with five kids," Olivia said. "And that job of yours." She thought how as a domestic relations lawyer Jenny dealt all day with battered women, deadbeat husbands, and damaged children, but never seemed to bring her day home with her and never talked about it. Jenny had a helpful husband and a good baby-sitter, but Olivia had still always been amazed at how she could manage to juggle her job and her family so well. She was successful in her career, and her children were thriving.

"Do you know how much money ski lift tickets *cost* for seven people?" Jenny said.

Actually, Olivia had never thought about it, because she had never had any interest in skiing in her entire life. To her—and to her mother, of course, who was afraid of everything—it had seemed like a sport in which you were sure to be seriously hurt. Her token sports had been tennis and swimming (but she didn't dive), and now she just went to the gym. "They all ski?"

"Sure. Kara and Belinda are still beginners, but they've all been on the slopes since they could walk. It's a good thing for the family to do together."

"I envy you."

"You and Roger could do it. Or you could ice-skate. They have that at those places too."

"Maybe." But what she meant she envied was the happy family, not the winter sports. She and Roger had always preferred to go to the movies on winter afternoons.

"I love everything about skiing," Jenny said. "The ritual of putting on the clothes, the air, coming back for lunch . . ."

"Being able to eat as much as you want because you've burned up so many calories," Olivia said.

"That too."

"What else is new?"

"Didi wants singing lessons. But I don't know. She had piano and violin and guitar, and none of them worked out. I don't want to throw good money after bad."

"Maybe she hasn't found herself."

"She looked up singing teachers in the Yellow Pages," Jenny said admiringly. "Can you imagine a nine-year-old doing that?"

"I think you should let her have them."

"We'll see."

"I hope to see you all sometime," Olivia said.

"You will. Don't forget Sam's bar mitzah in the spring. Can you believe we're going to be parents of a teenager?"

"No," Olivia said. She still thought of Sam as a little boy.

"I have to go," Jenny said. "There's yelling and crashing around in the other room. I'd better see what they're up to. Have a nice holiday."

"You too. Love to everybody."

"Same."

While she was still in the mood Olivia called Melissa in Houston.

"Hiii!" Melissa said. Olivia had forgotten how sweet her voice was, and how glad Melissa always sounded to hear her.

"Hi. I called to wish you Merry Christmas, or whatever."

"I hate Christmas," Melissa said. "It's not *my* holiday. I wish they'd stop playing Christmas carols all the time in public places."

"Freedom of speech," Olivia said. She hadn't been aware that Melissa had become so religious, or perhaps Melissa always had but she hadn't noticed.

"Why do *I* have to listen to them?"

"Are you going anywhere for the holidays?" she asked to change the subject before they got into an argument. She had always liked Christmas carols.

"Yes, Hawaii. We've never been, and it'll be nice for the kids."

"I've never been there either," Olivia said.

"Have Roger take you. Or you take him."

"It's one of the places on my list."

"Don't make lists—do it. Life goes by too fast. You see that when you have children. One day they can't bear to be away from mommy, and the next they want to go away on their own, and you cry and miss them so much, but you know you have to let them go."

"Yours are still young."

"Abe and Jake have been going to sleep-away camp."

"That's hardly college."

"Don't even say college," Melissa said with a nervous little laugh.

It reassured Olivia somehow to hear Jenny and Melissa talk about their busy, ordinary lives. But she wished they could all be together more. Nobody had mentioned the idea of a cousins club since Santa Barbara.

She thought about Grady. He hadn't called her again since she had seen him, nor had she called him. She imagined him showing up at Uncle Seymour's office and asking questions about business and wondered how he had the nerve. Grady had probably been charming, and Uncle Seymour had doubtlessly enjoyed explaining things to him, but on the other hand, if Grady had done anything to upset Uncle Seymour's sense of absolute control it would have gone badly for him.

The memory rose up before her of the dinner Uncle Seymour and Aunt Iris had given to celebrate her father's engagement to Grace. Actually, it hadn't been an engagement party but their polite way of acknowledging Grace's arrival in their lives. Her father, after all, had been married to Uncle Seymour's recently dead sister.

It had been at a very expensive, very cholesterol-laden French restaurant, where none of the patrons looked to be under sixty-five. The only other guests were herself and Roger. Grace was wearing a beautiful designer dress Olivia's father had bought her to look nice for the family, and she and Olivia's father were glowing. Olivia was seated next to Uncle Seymour, who was not glowing. He morosely spooned the last of his vichyssoise into his mouth and then he turned to Olivia.

"I have a bone to pick with you," he said quietly, so the others wouldn't hear him. "I'm not going to discuss it here, but I want to talk to you later."

"What about?" Olivia asked. She was already cold with anxiety. He always managed to do this to her, and knowing he did it on purpose didn't make it any less frightening.

"I'm upset about what you did," Uncle Seymour said. "I'll discuss it later."

"I think you should tell me now."

"No."

"Please?" She knew she would not be able to eat a bite and wished this dinner were over so she could flee.

"Later."

"You're making me too nervous," Olivia said. She glanced across the table at Aunt Iris chatting graciously with the betrothed couple and knew that even though she was staying out of it as usual, Aunt Iris was aware of everything that was going on. She cast a desperate glance at Roger, who was oblivious.

Uncle Seymour took a sip of his water and patted his lips with the damask napkin. "I understand you used your own lawyer for your new will," he said.

She nodded. How did he find out these things anyway?

"We all used Barney Pashkin and then you went and got someone else to redo yours. Who is this guy anyway? I never heard of him."

"He's good," Olivia said. She was beginning to get a tension headache, but at least she now knew what he disapproved of.

"You don't know anything about business," Uncle Seymour said. "Why do you always do everything on your own? Why can't you be a member of the family?"

"I am one."

"That other lawyer you used before I got you to use Barney Pashkin—Price English," Uncle Seymour said, his voice rich with contempt. "I knew Price English when we were all growing up in Brooklyn. His family changed their name. Of course he was a good deal older than I was. But he was always an idiot."

If he was older than you were he'd be retired, Olivia thought. The idiot part she ignored. "I'm sure he wasn't older," she said. "He's in his sixties."

"That's what he says. So now you have this new one you found by yourself."

She didn't say anything.

"Who is your executor?"

"Charlie," she said. She and Roger at that time didn't know if their relationship would last long enough to get involved in each other's wills. At the mention of his son, Charlie the Perfect, Uncle Seymour nodded. "Does he know that?" he asked sternly.

"I'll tell him."

"You'd better."

"Okay."

He turned then and dismissed her, focusing on his roast lamb and his guests, leaving her shaken and gulping down her wine.

Afterward she tried to figure out what was bothering him. The only thing she could think of was that Uncle Seymour, the eldest son of a powerful man, was still trying to run all their lives the way his father, her grandfather, had run his children's. The fact that her elderly father, always something of an outsider because he had only been married to a Miller, had brought in a new wife, definitely an outsider, might have set Uncle Seymour off. Perhaps he was afraid that Olivia, who had not done so well with men, would leave her shares of stock in Julia's to some stranger they might have problems with. Maybe even to Roger. But she couldn't, not the way her grandfather had set Julia's up.

Many, many years ago, old Abe Miller, who wasn't old when he did it, had created the family business with the legal stipulation that no one could give or leave a piece of it to anyone outside the Miller family, which of course included their spouses and children. They couldn't even leave their stock in Julia's to charity, because nonprofit institutions were run by people they didn't know, who might butt in. If she married Roger she could leave him her share, but if they continued to live together until they were very old and she died first, she could leave him no part of Julia's, only what money she had made herself and of course what income had come to her from Julia's in her lifetime. She could specify one of her cousins as the recipient, or else it would all go back and be divided among the family, making the rich richer. It made no difference whom she used to draw up her will —no one could change that.

She remembered her mother, years ago, telling her: "Stay close to the family; we're all tied together in business." At the time it had seemed heartless. Surely a family stayed together because they loved each other. What did she know about those other things? She was a veterinarian.

Uncle Seymour gathered them into the fold when they were loving and good, and pushed them away when they misbehaved. She remembered how pleased he was when Kenny, the bon vivant good catch of Santa Barbara, had started flying in to New York more often, and coming to see him. "I think Kenny wants to get closer to the family," Uncle Seymour had announced, and suddenly they all felt sorry for orphaned, divorced Kenny and tried to be nice to him.

As for herself, she had apparently misbehaved. A year later, at Passover at Uncle Seymour's apartment, he had drawn her aside almost immediately and said, "I understand you want to sell your piece of Julia's."

"Where did you ever get that idea?" she had asked, astonished.

"Your accountant called me and wanted to know some figures."

"Because he's doing my income taxes," Olivia said.

"If you want to sell your piece," Uncle Seymour went on, "we'll buy it from you."

"I don't want to sell it."

"I thought you did."

"I don't."

"We'll be glad to buy it."

"I don't want to sell it. It's a good investment. I'd only have to look for another."

"Let me know if you want to sell it back to us. Any time."

She had walked away. She felt as if he was trying to get rid of her, and it hurt.

"Why am I so afraid of him?" she had asked Roger later.

"I don't know. You shouldn't be."

"I'm afraid he won't love me."

"He's probably afraid you don't love him," Roger said.

On Christmas Eve she and Roger lit a fire in the fireplace, opened a bottle of champagne and gave each other presents. She bought him a very expensive Ralph Lauren bathrobe and he gave her an even more expensive gold bracelet from Cartier. It was indulgent, but they didn't have anyone else in their immediate family to give nice things to, except his mother and the dogs, the former unaware two minutes later, the latter satisfied with anything they could chew. She and Roger had written loving cards to each other, and she put the one from him into a scrapbook she kept with everything he had ever written to her.

On Christmas Day they stood on line to see a movie, with what seemed like the rest of the world, and then they went to a friend's party. On New Year's Eve they stayed at home, as they always preferred to do, with smoked salmon and champagne by the fire, and watched the ball fall down the tower on television from their bed. Roger was asleep five minutes later. Olivia was a little disappointed, because she was aroused from his closeness and the champagne, and watching him snoring was not what she'd had in mind. But she was also glad she didn't ever have to go to another New Year's Eve party again with its frantic pretense of joy. She decided that her New Year's resolution would be to get Roger to be interested in sex more often.

After the holidays were over, winter pulled its bleak and dismal curtain over the city. The wind cut, and dark came early. Aunt Myra called to say she was going to Florida to spend February with her brother, Uncle David. Aunt Myra and Uncle David had both married late, and before they settled down to have families of their own they had often taken trips together and were very close. Uncle David had been much more sweet-natured and fun-loving than his older brother, Uncle Seymour, with whom he worked side by side, and who always wanted to make all the business decisions himself. After decades of arguing and trying unsuccessfully to be listened to, Uncle David had decided to abdicate to a more congenial climate and have a pleasant old age.

Aunt Myra also reported that Grady had had an unusual stroke of luck in finding a buyer for Aunt Julia's apartment, although, she added, he had been forced to accept less than he and Taylor had hoped for. It was the recession; real estate was so bad everywhere. But he said they were both relieved to have that responsibility off their minds. He was apparently still trying to get permission to finish building his deck, and was very upset about the situation. Olivia wished he would get a job so he would have something else to think about.

One day she walked past Aunt Julia's apartment and looked up at the windows. The new owners had put up what looked like a mirrored wall and new window treatments. Did they ever wonder about who had lived there before, about that long and vivid and finally tragic life, or did they just feel pleased that they were starting a new chapter of their own? She supposed the latter. It had been only a year since Aunt Julia died, and already she was fading away with her blue grasscloth walls.

Her New Year's resolution about more sex with Roger had not gotten her anywhere. He was as affectionate and cuddly as ever, but when it came to passion he treated her like an afterthought. She wondered if she should say something about it, and if so, what she should say. She was afraid that making an issue about it would only make things worse. He seemed so vulnerable. At night he had bad dreams, and tossed and turned and mumbled, but in the morning he claimed not to remember. It was the season, she thought. It was trying for everybody. Even the dogs, reluctant to play long outside in the cold, were restless, and twitched in their sleep with dreams of their own.

It was only she, apparently, who slept well; hiding, awakening from time to time to notice Roger's distress and then hiding again —her way of escape, biding her time.

It was a Sunday afternoon. She was blow-drying her hair, getting ready to go to a movie with Roger, when the phone rang. It was Taylor's husband Tim, from California.

"I have bad news," he said.

She froze. *Something's happened to Taylor.* "What is it?"

"Grady killed himself."

10

GRADY KILLED HIMSELF. Olivia felt numb. At the same time, the thought came into her mind that she wasn't entirely surprised. He was the unhappiest person she knew—but she would never have thought that he would do something like this so soon, so young. His life was ahead of him; he was practically a child!

Not any more.

How angry he must have been, and none of them had suspected.

"When?" she asked. "How?"

"This morning. He was supposed to be in a motorcycle race with some friends, but he called one of them and said he didn't feel like going. He was very drunk. And then he said: 'Goodbye.' His friend got scared from the tone of his voice and drove over to Grady's house, but Grady was gone. There was a suicide note. He took his motorcycle off the top of Mulholland Drive."

The way Stan did, she thought.

"The police found him," Tim said. His slow voice was grave and calm. Thank God for Tim, Olivia thought; he's Taylor's rock.

"How is Taylor?"

"She's full of tranquilizers. She's also in shock, but functioning. She's sorry she couldn't call any of the family herself."

"I'm sorry I can't talk to her. What did the note say?"

"Well, the police have it, but Taylor and I read it. He said he was going to kill himself because he couldn't build his deck. He said his house meant everything to him, that it was his home and his peaceful refuge. Yes, those were the words he used: *peaceful refuge.*"

"I can't believe he killed himself over a deck," Olivia said.

"Well, there were a couple of pages of recriminations against the people who sold him the house, and he wanted them to be sued."

"Even in our family, nobody's crazy enough to kill themselves over a deck. It had to be the last straw."

"Well," Tim said, "the deck was what the whole note was about. Except at the end he added that if his mother wondered why he cut her out of his will she could ponder about it while she remembered how she had treated him as a child."

"Oh, poor Grady," Olivia said.

"The funeral is Wednesday morning, at the church. He's going to be cremated, that's what he and Taylor both wanted for themselves. She's got to scatter his ashes in Mexico. Some little place, apparently very pretty, on the Sea of Cortez. He did a movie there once, and he liked to go back there by himself. But she'll do that when she feels up to it, maybe in the spring. Are you coming to the funeral?"

"Of course," Olivia said. "Please tell Taylor how terrible I feel for her."

"I will."

She had to ask him what she had on her mind, even though it was difficult for her. "Tell me, Tim . . . do you think he had AIDS?"

"We don't know. It's something we wondered too. They're doing an autopsy. I'll see you at the funeral. I've got to call some more people now."

He hung up and she tried to cry. But all she felt was a strange pain somewhere in the area of her heart, as if it had been scraped. She had cried at Aunt Julia's funeral, and even at Jason's bar mitzvah, she choked up when very sick, old animals had to be put to sleep, but not today, not now. She caught a glimpse in the mirror of her white and distorted face and looked away. She felt sad and in pain and horribly angry. What had Grady expected, if not this feeling of rage? Didn't he know how angry everyone who had loved him would be that he had left without ever giving any of them a chance? He must have been so terribly lonely, but except for that one long drunken lunch with her, he had presented them only with the pleasant, rigid facade he wanted them to see.

Why hadn't he let any of them know what he was really like? All those years he hadn't even trusted them enough to let them know he was gay. He had denied it, and after that she hadn't asked again, waiting for him to tell her. She and the cousins wouldn't have cared. Aunt Julia wouldn't have cared. On some level Aunt Julia probably knew. All her excuses, her friends-from-school myth—she had been an intelligent woman, not a fool. They had been Grady's excuses to her, and she had gone along with them because that was what he wanted. Grady and Taylor were all Aunt Julia had.

The picture rose in her mind of Grady when he had been very young, just discovering the miracle of words. They had been at Mandelay, and he was being held up high in his father's arms, trying to touch the leaves on a tree. His little face was stubbornly intense. "Dat?" he had asked, again and again, pointing at each new object, as Earlene and Julia and Olivia and Lila stood there admiringly.

"Dat?"

"A leaf," Stan said.

"Dat?"

"A tree."

"Dat?"

"The house."

"Dat?"

"Daddy's shirt. And who is that?"

Grady had grinned. "Olivia."

He had been such a bright, eager little kid, doing what little kids did at that age, discovering the world. It had seemed at that moment he could become anything, anybody. But it was not even possible that he could be what should have been his most basic of rights: happy.

She went into the living room where Roger was watching some financial program on television. He took one look at her and was alarmed. "What happened?"

"Grady's dead," Olivia said. She sat close to him and he encircled her with his arms. After a while she told him all about it.

Uncle Seymour called then to tell her that his travel agency would order the plane tickets to California, and that they were all to go together on Tuesday afternoon and stay overnight. "It's too late to get a Super Saver," Olivia said, "but I want to go Coach."

"We're going First Class," Uncle Seymour said. "Don't be silly. This is no time for you to scrimp on money." Thousands, she thought. Now she was angry at Grady again for killing himself, and annoyed about how much the plane tickets would cost for them to arrive with their solidarity and respect to his ashes that he had not let them give to his person.

Roger had decided not to go. She didn't try to persuade him. She thought about Kenny in Santa Barbara, and suddenly felt the need to be closer to him, the way they used to be when they were young. She called him, and luckily he was in and already knew all about what had happened.

"Kenny, I don't want to stay in a hotel at a time like this," Olivia said. "I'm too depressed. Could I stay with you?"

"Sure," he said. "You can sleep in Jason's room. He's away at school."

Aunt Myra called. "I guess you heard about Grady?"

"Yes. Why do you think he did it?"

"He was upset about his deck."

"You can't believe that."

"That's what he said," Aunt Myra said. "Now, how are you getting to the airport? Do you want to pick me up on the way, or should I go to Seymour and Iris's and you pick us up there?"

"I'll meet you at the airport."

"How can we find you?" Aunt Myra said, sounding panicked.

"We're on the same plane."

"No, I think we should all take a cab there together. We'll get a big one. I don't suppose Roger's coming. That's all right; he's busy. Maybe we'll use Seymour's car service. I'll call you back."

As it turned out, none of them even spoke to one another on the long plane trip. They read and ate and slept, and when they were awake they looked grim.

Good-natured Kenny picked them up at the airport and drove the others to their hotel; then he took Olivia home with him.

"Awful thing," he said.

"Yes."

After that they didn't talk about Grady at all. When she got to Kenny's he made her a sandwich and showed her his view of the ocean, all silver in the moonlight. The house was full of things he had collected on his various trips, but it was too neat and looked as if no one lived there. She supposed that was what a house started to look like when the children—or the child, in his case—had gone. Jason was in his first year of prep school, and then he would be off to college and after that would probably get an apartment of his own.

Kenny took her to look at the new home gym he'd had installed in what had been the guest room. He was very proud of each piece of equipment and insisted on showing her how it worked. His round face was beaming proudly.

"I use it every day," he said.

"Good for you; it's about time," she said, not unkindly.

"I know."

"Roger would love this," she said.

"You could have one in your house."

They sat in matching big chairs in front of the fireplace in his bedroom and talked. "I've met a woman," Kenny said.

"You always do."

"No, this one is different. The others always had something wrong with them. But this one is very spiritual. She's not college-educated or intellectual, but she has such a strong sense of what's real and what isn't. She's one of the most perceptive people I've ever known. She's bright on a really *deep* level. I think she's the one."

"Where did you meet her?"

"At a singles party for Jewish professional people."

"You went to a singles party?"

"Everybody was there. All the women were chasing me and I was chasing her." He smiled. "Her husband died six months ago. He had Huntington's chorea—a horrible disease. She nursed him for years. She was very devoted. They had no children. She's a responsible, good person. I just had a sense she was the woman for me right away. And guess what? She's my age."

"That's new."

"Her name is Pam," Kenny said. "I think I could marry her."

"Really!"

"Yes."

Olivia thought how strange it was that at this moment of grieving for a life lost, another one was about to renew.

"What does she look like?"

"She's cute."

Kenny had devoted himself to raising Jason, and Pam had taken care of her invalid husband. Now they were both free, or at least Kenny was freer than he had been. Pam would never desert him on top of the Himalayas as Gloria had done. He was her adventure. She would take care of him.

"I'm looking forward to meeting her," Olivia said.

She slept that night in Jason's room, on his water bed. Or rather she lay on it, rocking uncomfortably, muscles cramped and aching from the icy cold, shivering under blankets. She had never slept on one of those things before but she was sure they were highly overrated. She wondered if you could get hypothermia from a water bed. That would be a bizarre death to add to the family history. However, she was not afraid enough to sleep on the uninviting, uncarpeted floor. The room seemed singularly uninhabited and deserted.

"I nearly froze last night," she told Kenny at breakfast.

"Oh, I forgot to turn the heat on in the water bed," he said casually.

She was sure he never had guests.

The Church of the Spirit, where Grady and his family had worshipped, was in the Pacific Palisades, high on a bluff overlooking the ocean. It was a simple building, set among old trees, reached on foot by a gravel path. At first Olivia thought with a flicker of surprise that it was an Eastern hideaway for meditation, a compromise Stan and Earlene had reached when he decided to change his religion, but then she saw the cross on the roof.

The simple chapel where the funeral was to be held was very peaceful. It had pews and a stained-glass window, and a plain cross on the white painted wall above where an altar would be if there was one. Instead there was a small table on top of which was an urn. It was completely surreal to see what had so recently been a large and powerful man transformed into something that would fit into that little metal urn. Olivia almost expected to see Grady jump out like a genie. Beside it was a floral arrangement from Taylor, and that was all. Some soft classical music which she didn't recognize was playing from the loudspeakers.

In the pews on one side of the room were Grady's friends, ten or twelve of them, mostly couples, and on the other side was the family. You could certainly tell which was which. The men on his side looked like cowboys or ex-football players, with muscles and mustaches and outdoor skin. They wore suits, out of respect, with cowboy boots under them. Their wives were tough-looking and pretty, with none of that soft, polished Eastern look.

Grady must have met many people in his career, but the funeral was very small—whether he'd had only a few close friends, or whether Taylor hadn't wanted to draw a lot of attention to his suicide by having a large funeral, Olivia couldn't tell. Whoever these friends were, they were probably fellow stuntmen. None of them were "friends from school."

Jenny and Paul were there, as were Melissa and Bill. Nick and his wife were not there, nor were Uncle Seymour's middle-aged children. There were Olivia and Kenny, Uncle Seymour, Aunt Iris, Aunt Myra and Uncle David from Florida, looking sad and bewildered at this topsy-turvy event in the life cycle. Earlene was sitting in the front row, on the friend side, dabbing at her eyes with a damp handkerchief. Taylor was wandering around looking stoned, wearing a dark dress with tiny flowers on it, greeting Grady's friends with the hand sign for "I love you" that Olivia had learned as a child.

Index finger and pinky up, two middle fingers down, thumb sticking out; remember to use the thumb, without the thumb it's the sign for the Devil. "I love you" was just a finger away from "You are the devil," Olivia thought, taking liberties with the image, and wondered whether Taylor blamed these macho men and the world they lived in for Grady's forced secrecy about his private life.

Tim came and got Taylor then, and brought her to her seat on the side with the friends. The music stopped. One of Grady's friends got up and went to the front of the room to speak.

He spoke of a Grady she had hardly known, of pranks and fun and good times, of a Grady who was a leader, full of life. To hear Grady described this way he seemed such a happy, vital person it was hard for her to imagine him even thinking of killing himself. Then who had been that miserable, vulnerable and beaten creature she had known? The same Grady, different view. The friend sat down and a young woman came to the front of the room.

"Miranda," Aunt Myra whispered to Olivia. Grady's ex-girlfriend.

She looked like an actress, ingenue-type. She had a pretty face, thick, sun-streaked hair and a body in great shape. Her eyelashes were so long Olivia could see them defined even from where she sat, and her large dark eyes were brimming with tears.

"Grady changed my life," Miranda said. Her voice broke, but she composed herself and continued. "He gave me the gift of joy and spontaneity. He introduced me to my friends. He showed me how exciting and magical the world could be. I will . . . always . . . miss him." She was sobbing now, and sat down.

This was Miranda the girlfriend? The "phase"? The cover-up? Whatever she had been, she certainly seemed to love him. They all seemed to have loved him. It had obviously not been enough.

Another friend of Grady's was eulogizing now. Olivia looked across the aisle at the group of close-knit mourners. There was a young man sitting all alone, in the last row. He was rather slight and frail, dressed more formally than the others, and nobody seemed to know him. He was watching and listening with a sad intensity, but he also looked as if he were ready to break and run away if he had to. In a way he looked as if he had wandered into the wrong funeral. She wondered who he was.

The friend who had been speaking went back to his seat. The soft music began again. The funeral was over. They all left the chapel and stood for a while in the hall outside, murmuring to each other.

"We're going to Taylor's house," Aunt Myra said. "Does everybody have the directions?"

"Oh," Big Earl said to Olivia, to anyone, "it's so terrible to lose a son. It's unnatural. A mother shouldn't have to outlive her child."

You should have thought of that when you were trying to kill him, Olivia thought. She noticed that Taylor kept herself as far away from her mother as possible, and that no one could bring themselves to offer Earlene condolences. She stood there, the puffy-eyed pariah, waiting for someone to tell her how tragic she was, but no one did, and finally she left.

The young man whom no one knew went over to Taylor. She didn't seem to know him either. "Taylor?" he said.

"Yes?"

"Can I speak to you?"

Tim, who had not left Taylor's side, began to translate. The young man led them over to the side, where no one could hear him, and very quietly began to talk.

They all went to Taylor's house, which was large and open, with a view of trees and brush. The dining table was covered with platters of food for the mourners, and there was a well-stocked bar. Earlene was drinking scotch. Again, Grady's friends kept to themselves, and the family to themselves, since the two worlds had never met and now it was too late because their link was gone; but from time to time they glanced at each other with polite sympathy.

It was strange to see Taylor without Grady, and harder to imagine her living the rest of her life without him. She seemed terribly lost and vulnerable. She kept going up to Miranda and hugging her, and saying, "We have to stay in touch. We both loved him. I don't want to lose you." She was so drugged from the tranquilizers and grief that she was mumbling.

How could Grady have deserted Taylor? All their lives they had taken care of each other whenever they could. It was hard to imagine two siblings any closer. They had protected each other, and they had both needed special protecting. Perhaps, at the end, even Taylor couldn't give him enough.

Olivia went to the buffet and picked at some coleslaw, and then she went to sit with Jenny and Melissa. On the way she passed Paul and Bill, who were, she was not surprised to notice, talking about business.

"Why do you think he did it?" Jenny asked her.

"I don't know."

"Sometimes I worry that depression runs in our family," Jenny said. "We don't know why Stan killed himself either."

"Suicide is most common among fathers and sons," Melissa said. "The first one breaks the taboo."

"How do you know that?"

"I read it."

"My mother told me that Earlene went to visit Grady the week before he died," Jenny said. "You know he would never let her stay with him, but Taylor was sick and couldn't deal with having Earlene over, and Earlene wouldn't postpone her visit, so he agreed to have her. I wonder if she upset him."

"Big Earl always upset him," Olivia said.

"But more, I mean."

"I don't know."

"Too many funerals," Jenny said. "I hope the next time we meet it's when everybody's happy."

"Sam's bar mitzvah in the spring," Melissa said. "You must be very busy."

"Oh, yes. You're all coming, I hope."

"Of course."

"Kenny told me he's getting married again," Olivia announced.

The two cousins turned in delight to look across the room at Kenny. "No! To who?"

"Someone named Pam. She's his age."

"Do you think he'll invite us to the wedding?"

"I hope so."

Jenny looked at her watch. "Paul!" she said. "We have to start moving along."

"We do too," Melissa said.

The family was leaving to catch their planes. They were kissing and hugging each other, saying how it was a shame they hadn't had more time to talk, but next time it would be better. "How are you?" they asked, almost in the same breath as "Goodbye," and they all answered "Fine," because there wasn't time to be anything but fine, and if they weren't fine this wasn't the time or place to start complaining about it. It was a funeral a continent away from home, in the middle of the week, and they all had families and jobs and lives to attend to.

"Thank you for coming," Taylor said politely.

When they left, most of Grady's friends were still there to console her, and of course there was Tim, to comfort her and run interference between her and Earlene. On the way to the airport Olivia remembered that the young man who had gone over to talk privately with Taylor after the funeral had not come afterwards to her house with the other friends, but then she forgot about him. He probably wasn't anybody she needed to know about anyway.

11

ROGER HAD FIGURED out a way to keep Olivia from giving him a fiftieth birthday party. His birthday wasn't until summer, but she kept saying it would be impossible to make plans if he left everything to the last minute, and finally he figured out what he really wanted. He wanted to go to Paris again, just the two of them, for five days, stay at the Plaza Athénée and fly back on the Concorde. He wanted to drink champagne and dine at expensive restaurants and tell himself that he wasn't older, just richer.

When he told her, she loved the idea. She said it was glamorous and romantic, and insisted on paying for the whole thing. After all, she had been planning to pay for the party he wasn't having.

"I'm richer, too," she said. And she was. Their practice was going as well as they had hoped it would when they pooled everything they had to buy the house, set up the clinic and merge their medical destinies.

He told himself he had everything he needed for a happy life—success in a career he cared about, comfort, health, decent looks, a loving life's companion, a sexy girlfriend, a wonderful dog and just the right amount of illicit excitement to keep him virile. Why, then, did he have disturbing dreams that made him awaken tired in the morning, unable to remember them but knowing they had been there to disturb his sleep?

He remembered only one of these dreams. He was at a Mardi

Gras, or some costume party like that, and everyone was wearing masks. He had been enjoying himself, dancing to loud music among a swirling crowd. A woman he knew was Olivia came to claim him as her partner, and then just as they were smiling at one another she pulled off her mask, and it was not Olivia at all but Wendy. Somehow he felt . . . abandoned. Where was Olivia? How could Wendy have fooled him so completely with just a party mask?

But didn't they always pretend she did? Wasn't that the point? His throat felt icy-cold, and then he woke up and Olivia told him he had been moaning in his sleep again. He wondered what the dream meant. He hoped it wasn't a prophecy of bad things to come. He didn't want to have to lose either of them.

And then one afternoon he was walking past one of the examining rooms, where Olivia was talking to a new client who had brought her little brown Abyssinian cat, and he realized in horror that the woman was Wendy.

Olivia looked up and her face glowed with pleasure the way it always did when she saw him, and Wendy gazed at him as if he were a total stranger. Gregory, however, reacted with his usual hostility—when the little bastard saw him he arched his back and twitched his tail. Roger gave Olivia a little wave hello and backed away as fast as he could.

His heart was pounding. What was Wendy up to, anyway? She had her own vet, and had always purported to like him. If Wendy had wanted to act out an office sex fantasy she would have made the appointment with him, not Olivia. No, this was obviously a visit to check out her rival, and when Roger thought of Wendy intruding on his territory—his own home was upstairs!—he wanted to pull her bodily out the front door. He was not intrigued or aroused; he was nervous and angry.

When Wendy went up front to pay her bill he hid in the back so she wouldn't get it into her head to approach him. He thought that when Olivia had been in California for Grady's funeral it would have been exciting to have sex with Wendy in the operating room, for example, but he had been too busy doing double duty and hadn't thought of it, and now with Olivia in the building it was unthinkable. There was a fine line between fantasy and true folly, and he hoped Wendy was still aware of what it was.

He waited until all the patients were gone, and then when Olivia went upstairs he pretended he had some paperwork to finish and called Wendy.

"What were you doing here?" he demanded.

"Don't you even say hello?"

"Hello. Why were you here?"

To his surprise she burst into tears.

"What is it?" he asked, concerned.

"You never yelled at me before," Wendy said. "I hate it."

"But you never did anything like this."

"What did I do?"

"You went to see Olivia."

"I wanted to see what she was like."

"Why?"

"*Why?*" She sounded incredulous. "Don't you think I was curious?"

"But she has nothing to do with you."

"Try telling her that."

"What did you two talk about?" he demanded, thinking that perhaps he had made a mistake, that Wendy wasn't perfect after all, that she might even be dangerous.

"My cat. What did you think?"

"I didn't know."

"Don't you think I have feelings?" Wendy asked.

"You can't come to my office and check out my wife."

"She's not your wife."

"She might as well be. You could have caused serious trouble."

"And I suppose nothing you and I ever did before was risky."

"It isn't the same," Roger said.

She had stopped crying. "This is exciting and you know it," Wendy said.

Was it exciting? Why wasn't it? "If Olivia finds out about us, I'll have to stop seeing you," Roger said.

"Well, that makes me feel like I'm nothing."

"You know what I mean. She'll insist on it. She can't find out."

"She won't."

"She'd better not." Was this exciting? Was he exaggerating the danger of Olivia finding out? After all, Wendy hadn't done anything.

"I'm not expendable, you know," Wendy said.

"I just meant . . ."

"I'm a human being. I don't think you want to know me at all."

"I can't stay on the phone to discuss this now," Roger said. "She could pick it up at any moment."

"Does she make a habit of listening to your calls?"

"Accidentally. She could."

"What about me?" Wendy said. "You're supposed to protect me. Not only her. You make me feel like shit. You're just like all the rest of them."

"I'm not."

"You are," she said, and burst into tears again and hung up on him.

He pounded the desk and hurt his hand. He sat there inspecting it, thinking how it was his instrument, and was relieved that it was unharmed. He shouldn't have been so unkind to her. She had made up so many different lives and identities for him that he realized he had lost sight of who the real Wendy was—if he had ever known. Their understanding had always been that he would be kind to her, take care of her. She was like a needy child. He had never heard her cry before. Suddenly he felt like a villain. Maybe he should call her back and make up with her.

He stared at the phone. Had he actually made her feel worthless? What kind of person did that make him? She should never have come here to meet Olivia, not really because it was so risky, but because seeing the two of them together was more than he could handle. Although he had told Wendy he would have to stop seeing her if Olivia found out, he had no idea what he would do. He didn't even want to have to think about it.

He dialed Wendy's number. It rang four times and then her recording began to play. "You have almost reached Wendy Wilton. If you leave a message after the beep, maybe you will."

Beep. "Wendy?" Roger said. "Are you screening? It's me. Pick up the phone."

Nothing.

"Wendy?" Maybe she had gone out, stormed out, rather, furious at him. Or maybe she had left the apartment because she knew he would call her back and she wanted to punish him. "Wendy, I'm sorry," he said into the machine.

"Roger," she said at last. Her voice sounded weak and slurred.

"Are you all right?"

"No."

"What is it?" he asked, alarmed.

"I took . . . pills."

"How many? What kind?"

"A lot."

"Wendy, what did you take?"

"We had . . . fun, didn't we," she said. Her voice trailed off.

It hadn't been that long. She must have swallowed a whole bottle to sound this bad. "Wendy," he said urgently, "stay awake!"

He heard her labored breathing, and then she dropped the receiver into the cradle with such dazed difficulty that he heard it rattling and clicking before it finally fell home.

God! He dialed Olivia upstairs on their private line. "Honey, I'm going to go out for a little bit, to get some air."

"What do you want to do about dinner?" she asked. "Should I just make something?"

"Sure. That's fine."

"Pasta?"

My mistress is dying and we're talking about what to eat for dinner, he thought. "Great," he said. He threw on his coat and rushed out into the street and found a cab, cursing the traffic, rubbing Wendy's keys in his pocket like a talisman. He remembered when she had first offered them to him and he had refused them, and finally had agreed. Now he was so lucky that he had them.

"Dr. Hawkwood," Wendy's doorman greeted him pleasantly. Roger nodded as pleasantly, forced a smile, and went upstairs.

He let himself into the apartment. It was dimly lit. He waited for the hated Gregory to spring out at him, but the cat was nowhere to be seen. Wendy was in the bedroom, lying on the floor, on her thick, white carpet, dressed in a white satin bathrobe, her silken hair spread out around her pale face. There was an empty bottle beside her that had held sleeping pills. It looked like a tableau of tragic death.

He rushed to her and saw that she was breathing. He knelt to take her pulse. Her pulse was still strong and even. But how could he be sure how many pills had been in the bottle when she had taken them, and how she would be an hour from now? When he tried to pick her up her body was dead weight.

He was terrified, sweating. Maybe he should take her into the bathroom and make her throw up. But even if he did, he was still afraid to leave her. The intelligent thing would be to call the nearest hospital and admit her into Emergency, but if he did that he would have to explain why the hell he was here in the first place. What could he say, that she had called his office because it was the last place she had been before she went home and got suicidally depressed? That he had answered the phone? Bribe the doorman to pretend he had never seen him before? Pretend he didn't have her keys and that the doorman had let him, despite the fact that he was a total stranger, into her apartment because she claimed she was not feeling well? He supposed it would work—it had to. He didn't know what else to do.

If he could only rouse her enough to tell him what she had swallowed. "Wake up!" he said, and shook her. Nothing. He picked her up and started walking her around the room like a large rag doll, trying to bring her back, even though it was wasting precious time. She leaned on him heavily, unconscious, but her heartbeat was still strong and even. If only he knew that she could sleep it off, that he wasn't going to let her die . . . He could hardly think rationally.

He put her down. He would have to call 911. They took forever to come; maybe he should just carry her to a cab and . . . no, that would be worse.

He picked up the receiver and dialed.

The number was busy, of course, just when he needed help. He dialed again, and it rang through. "Hello," Roger said. "I want to report an overdose of sleeping pills."

Behind him, Wendy moaned.

He turned around, and saw that she was moving. "Wait a minute," he said into the phone, and went to look at her.

She was moving, just a little, but just enough so he knew none of this was what he had originally thought. "Never mind," he said to the operator, and hung up.

He knew her so well, but she had caught him off guard and

had actually fooled him. She might have taken one sleeping pill, at the most two, but probably none. He began to tremble with relief, and then with rage.

She had never gone this far.

He tried to figure out what she wanted. It was obvious that she wanted him to save her. But he was in no mood to enter this ill-timed fantasy, and it did not arouse him at all. He cradled her in his arms and kissed her face and her hair and wished the hell she would decide it was appropriate to come back to life again so he could rush home before Olivia got suspicious.

"Darling," he murmured. "Live, please live. I'm sorry. I love you." Crazy bitch, he thought.

Wendy's eyelids fluttered open. She looked at him and sighed. "You saved me," she said softly.

"Yes."

She sat up and put her arms around his neck. "Thank you."

He moved away from her embrace. "Suicide is out of bounds," he said. "It's serious. Olivia's cousin just killed himself. This hits too close to home."

"But still you were here for me."

"It doesn't do it, if that's what you have in your head. The last thing on my mind right now is sex."

"That's all right."

Suddenly the softness of her flesh was frightening, almost alien. "Then what was this all about?" he asked.

"You don't get it, do you?"

"No, I don't."

"I just wanted something for myself," Wendy said. "Today all you cared about was you. So this was just for me."

"For you."

"Yes. For me. For *me!* You can go home now if you like. I have to let poor Gregory out of the kitchen and then I'm going to have a nice bath and go to sleep." She sounded so calm, the victor.

"I'll call you," he said lamely, backing out.

Did he want to call her? Did he even want to speak to her again?

"And when you do, I'll be there," she said, and smiled.

She's crazy, he thought. She was too reckless, too selfish. She had endangered his entire happiness because of her need to be reassured. He had hurt her, and so she had used him. It was not in the rules of their game.

But on the way home in the cab he wanted her anyway.

12

IN THE SPRING, to Olivia's amazement, Roger agreed to go with her to Jenny and Paul's son Sam's bar mitzvah. Perhaps it was because Cambridge was not that far away; the shuttle to Boston was less than an hour, and even with the long ride to and from both airports, it could almost be considered commuting. It was a far cry from the trips to California he had declined. She wondered if he finally felt it was appropriate to show some kind of family solidarity, not only with her but with her kin. Whatever his motivation, she was delighted to have him with her.

Cambridge was old and historic and pretty. Houses had gardens in front of them, there were cobblestoned streets, and little patches of ice still lurked in the grass, reminding her that they had had a harder winter than the New Yorkers. The cab passed Harvard, ringed with old red brick buildings, and Harvard Square, filled with college students rushing around. Paul taught there, and Olivia wondered what it must be like to spend your life in a place where fresh young faces came and went, on their way to their unknown future lives, while you just stayed there, getting older.

There were some very good hotels to choose from in the area, but Jenny had put the family into a no-frills hotel none of them had heard of, because she wanted to save them money. The lobby was dark, with a big aquarium for decoration, and even the fish looked dispirited. The halls smelled like an omelette, which was either age or the shampoo that had been used to clean the carpet. The rooms had thin towels and tiny pieces of deodorant soap in the bathrooms. Olivia and Roger's room was dark too, and had no view.

They had passed some of the other cousins in the lobby, checking in or going upstairs, and none of them had been pleased.

"Motel Six," Nick said, and laughed. He was there with his wife Lynne and their young daughter Amber. "Don't you miss the Biltmore in Santa Barbara?"

They were a handsome family; Nick the successful New York ad man, Lynne the vivacious beauty, Amber in her crinolines and little ruffled socks.

"Amber's never been in a hotel like this before," Lynne said. "When we got to the room she said, 'Where's the fruit? Where are the flowers?' " She chuckled proudly at her daughter's consternation. "She's used to the Four Seasons. 'Where's the fruit? Where are the flowers?' "

"It's only for two nights," Olivia said, feeling sorry for Jenny that her good intentions had been off the mark, and hoping Roger didn't dislike it that much.

They unpacked in their ugly room. "The bed's good," Roger said.

"And the room is really clean," Olivia said.

"I found a shower cap in the bathroom," he said, "so we know it's not Motel Six."

"It's fine. Don't say anything to Jenny tomorrow. I know they'll all complain and upset her."

He ordered a bottle of inferior red wine from room service—their best—and put a porno movie on the hotel's pay TV channel. "Let's pretend we don't know each other," Roger said. "This is our first date."

"Some first date," Olivia said, laughing. "What am I, a hooker?"

"Call girl," he said. "You're much too classy to be a hooker."

"Okay," she said, but she couldn't take it seriously. The movie was more silly than sexy, and the wine, she could tell right away, was going to give her a headache in the morning. They were lying in the big bed. She was wearing the white satin nightgown she wore when she traveled, and Roger was wearing the pajama bottoms he wore when he traveled. Impishly, she poured a little of the wine on Roger's chest and licked it off. It tasted better on him than it did in the glass, but then she had always liked the way he tasted. He immediately undressed.

Ah, she thought hopefully, and undressed too. As she was about to kiss him he pulled away and said, "Wait." With an expression of very serious concentration he poured some wine on each of her breasts and began to lick it off. It felt quite pleasurable, but it was also peculiar. The wine was cold and wet, and even though Roger had been careful, it was running down her sides onto the sheets. They were going to have to sleep in that. She didn't even want to imagine what previous guests had dumped on this same mattress.

"What did you think when you saw me?" he asked.

"When?"

"Tonight."

"Tonight?"

"When you came to the room," he said.

"Oh," she said. "Right. I'm the call girl. Well, I was thrilled. You're just my type. You are, you know."

He had dribbled the wine onto her belly now and was licking it off, and she wished he would stop. It tickled. Over his shoulder she could see the actors on the TV screen—three of them, a man and two women—doing things to each other and making appreciative noises. She was sure Jenny would never have dreamed that any of the relatives would be using their hotel room this way the night before the momentous rite of passage, and in spite of herself she started to laugh. Once she started to laugh she couldn't stop.

There are moments, she thought, and there aren't. This just isn't one of them. There was nothing about the porno movie that could turn her on, and right now Roger didn't either. She felt they were more like two kids playing than lovers. He was so sweet she wanted to hug him. He was her best friend, he was funny. . . .

He looked up and gave her a glance: not amused, as she was, but almost pensive. Oh, sweetheart, she thought, I hope I haven't hurt your feelings.

"I'm sorry," she said.

"For what?"

"For laughing."

"Well," Roger said cheerfully, "this room's atmosphere isn't conducive to passion."

"I know. That was the point, wasn't it?" Olivia said.

"Of course it was." He clicked off the movie. "I'd better get a towel for these sheets."

"Then we won't have enough to take a shower tomorrow," Olivia said. "Avoiding the wet spots will force us to cuddle."

"I don't need anything to force me to cuddle with you."

"I love you," Olivia said. She curled into Roger's embrace.

"I love you, too," he said. He turned off the light, and after a while they fell asleep.

In the morning they went downstairs to the hotel dining room to have breakfast, which was included in the price of the room. Nick, Lynne and Amber were already seated in a booth and Lynne waved them over.

"It's so nice to see you," Olivia said. "It's been too long."

"I know," Lynne said. "We all live in New York and we never see each other. We should make a date."

"Absolutely," Nick said.

The waitress came over and took their orders.

"Try the yogurt," Nick said. "They can't ruin it."

"What do you think of the hotel?" Roger asked.

"We're moving to the Ritz this afternoon."

"Should we do that, Olivia?"

"Why bother?" Olivia said. "The Ritz is in Boston, it's too far away. It's not worth the trouble; we're here."

"Olivia has acute separation anxiety," Roger said. "Even from bad hotels." They all laughed.

"Who else is here?" Lynne asked, looking around.

"Taylor and Tim, Uncle Seymour, Aunt Iris, Aunt Myra, Kenny probably," Olivia said. "I wonder if he'll bring his girlfriend. Melissa and Bill are coming with their kids, aren't they?"

"Of course," Nick said. "And my father. He's been staying with them."

Anna the Perfect was not coming, because years before when she had given her son's bar mitzvah she had not allowed Jenny to bring her children. At the time Jenny had only two, and she was insulted. Bar mitzvahs, she had told Olivia, were for family, and cousins should get to know each other. So Jenny and Paul had refused to go, and now, of course, Anna and her family had declined the invitation to come here. They were probably relieved. They, like Charlie the Perfect, had their own busy lives and hardly knew the other cousins; and their children (and Charlie's grandchild) didn't know them at all.

The waitress brought their food. "So how is life?" Nick asked.

"The clinic is thriving, we're fine and we're going to Paris for a long weekend this summer for Roger's birthday," Olivia said. "And your life?"

"Haven't lost any clients," Nick said. "The renovation on our new apartment is finally finished. And the next time you see our bank commercial, look carefully at the guy at the end of the line—it's me. I put myself in for a kick."

"You wanted to be an actor when you were a kid," Olivia said.

"I don't remember that."

"I do."

"And I've taken up helicopter skiing in Colorado," Nick said. "It's what I did last winter whenever I could get away."

"What is it?"

"A helicopter takes you to the top of a mountain where it's completely newly fallen snow. Four feet of virgin powder. No one else has been there. It's so quiet and peaceful and beautiful you can't imagine. Then you ski down."

"I'd prefer he had a different hobby," Lynne said mildly, smiling; but Olivia could see the apprehension hidden behind her smile.

"Oh, it's completely safe," Nick said. "I'm an expert skier. I'm even getting bored with the double black-diamond trails."

"What are those?" Olivia asked.

"The steep ones that go straight down with the trees sticking out of the snow. You know, it's just as dangerous on the bottom. The other skiers bump into you."

"And on top," Lynne said lightly, "there are only avalanches and holes you don't know about." She shrugged. "Nick doesn't want to go with a partner."

As if that would be any help in an avalanche, Olivia thought, but she didn't say anything because little Amber was there, picking off tiny pieces of her cold croissant and carefully arranging them around the rim of her plate.

"A partner would destroy my solitude," Nick said. "And besides, I don't need one. I have a ski suit with two signaling devices sewn in that alert the helicopters in case anything happens to me. They're on one arm and one leg, on opposite sides for whichever way you fall. Then the helicopters send in rescue parties."

"Rescue parties?" Amber said, looking up and brightening. "What kind of parties are they?"

"Oh," Nick said, improvising, "they make a bonfire and roast marshmallows. Balloons. The usual."

"Amber, don't you want some jam on that?" Lynne asked, changing the subject.

Rescue parties so they can find the body, Olivia thought. She glanced sympathetically at Lynne, who was fussing over her child's breakfast. What is it about people, she wondered, that makes them think risking their lives is fun? If you're poor, and just your daily subsistence is a frightening struggle, you dream of security, but as soon as the rent's taken care of you start bungee-jumping.

Stan and Grady had been at one extreme, but the others, each in their own way, looked for excitement. There was careful Jenny, who loved the "ritual" of skiing, and then there was carefree Nick, who wanted to ski in uncharted places. Even Charlie the Perfect, who could fly First Class anywhere in the world, insisted on flying his own small plane around America every chance he got. He simply considered it a sport, like tennis, but more interesting. Once Olivia had asked Taylor—who had given up risks herself but understood and sympathized with the motivation of people who hadn't—why people wanted to do dangerous things, and Taylor had looked at her as if she were simpleminded. "It makes life worth living," Taylor had said.

After breakfast they all went back to their rooms to dress up. The temple was conveniently within walking distance of the hotel. She and Roger were half a block behind Nick and Lynne and Amber. Amber had on a perfectly coordinated Little Victorian Girl outfit, and was holding each of her parents' hands, walking fast to keep up with these taller people, her gait cheerful, obviously looking forward to seeing the cousins of her generation and playing with them, and to going to this happy event.

Olivia imagined Lynne and Amber carefully shopping for that outfit, and thought how strange it was that after all these years she still could not identify with a mother as much as she could with the child. She had no interest in choosing children's clothes. But even if she'd had to do it, most kids today were strong-willed enough to insist on having what they wanted anyway.

She thought of her own childhood trips to the store. They were battles she always lost. "You're my little doll," her mother had told her, even in high school, buying her a ruffly pink party dress when Olivia begged for black. "I always dressed you like a doll." She remembered the mother-daughter dresses, which Olivia had hated, that Lila had insisted they wear. *I don't want to be you,* she had thought. And she wasn't, nor was she what Lila had wanted her to be. She was nobody's doll. But what a struggle it had been. . . .

The temple was large and beautiful, with sunlight streaming in through stained glass. She and Roger sat behind a row of whispering, giggly girls who were probably Sam's classmates. "I'm glad you're here," she said to Roger. He patted her hand.

Sam's brother and sister, Max and Didi, were sitting in the front row with their parents, trying to look grown up, but his younger sisters, Kara and Belinda, lasted about five minutes into the service and then left to go to the room outside that was for the little kids. Olivia looked with admiration at the three girls' intricate hairdos and thought about the chaos and excitement that must have reigned in their household that morning.

After the service, the rabbi, who seemed young and zippy, got up to say that he let each bar mitzvah choose his own part of the Bible to discuss. Sam came up, wearing a suit and tie. He was pale but self-possessed, thirteen, at that transition age when he looked a little like each of his parents and not really like what he would when he grew up, an unfinished puppy, today about to become a man in the eyes of his religion, if not anywhere else.

"I have chosen this section because I have three sisters and a brother," Sam said, "and I know about sibling rivalry. Today I am going to discuss the story of Cain and Abel."

Olivia grinned at Roger. "That's my cousin," she said proudly. Around her she could see the other relatives smiling too, at the outrageously forthright young man cheerfully discussing the betrayal and murder of one's own family member.

The lunch party afterwards was held in an old mansion known as the Haunted House, which was used for children's parties and was both picturesque and childproof. It wasn't a very large party —all the girls and boys from Sam's class, the family, the proud in-laws, and a few of Jenny's old friends. There were separate tables for the adults and the kids, and different menus, since Jenny was serving fish, which most kids hated. On one side of the room was a small, lively band, and on the other a table which had been set up as an ice-cream bar. The boys and girls were dancing, and their enjoyment was infectious.

Kenny was there, from Santa Barbara, with his son Jason but not yet with the woman he had said was the One. Olivia went around the room kissing everybody in the family, and then sat at the large round cousins' table between Roger and Taylor. She had not seen Taylor since Grady's funeral, and she looked a lot better. She wondered if Taylor was still on tranquilizers.

Jenny, in a silk print dress, which Olivia knew she had not bought at Julia's, went from table to table accepting congratulations and apologizing. "I know you don't like the hotel," she kept saying. "I'm sorry. I just wanted to save everyone money, and it's close."

"It's fine," Olivia said.

"I picked the Haunted House because I wanted this party to be really for the kids," Jenny said, "and not an expensive status thing for the adults."

"They love it," Olivia said.

"I think so, too. And don't forget, everyone's coming back to our house this evening. I'm having a buffet supper."

"We'll be there. Did you ever decide to give Didi singing lessons?"

"We haven't decided yet. But she's in her room practicing all the time with her tapes. She's very persistent. We'll see."

"How are you?" Olivia asked Taylor.

"I'm coming along. I'm going to a therapist. I'm going to be on Prozac for a while."

"It's supposed to be good."

"I got the result of the autopsy. Grady didn't have AIDS, but his blood alcohol was six times higher than a sober person's."

Olivia nodded.

"He knew he had a drinking problem," Taylor said. "He was going to get help. Soon, he said."

But obviously not soon enough, Olivia thought, and sighed.

"Do you remember the young man who was at the funeral who nobody knew?" Taylor asked. "Sitting in the back?"

"Yes."

"He came over to see me. It turns out he was Grady's lover. Grady told him he would never acknowledge him. Never. Their two worlds would have to be separate. We got friendly. He's very nice, very spiritual. He's interested in reincarnation. He gave me some books to read. He comes to my house and we have long talks."

"That's good," Olivia said.

"I have to have something to believe in," Taylor said. "The thought that people come back, that helps."

"Yes, it would."

"I never knew Grady was gay," Taylor said. "You have to believe me. I never knew."

"How is that possible? You were so close."

Taylor shrugged. For someone who had not known anything about Grady's secret life, she seemed to be taking the new revelation with great equanimity.

"I told Grady's friend he could have something of Grady's to remember him by." Taylor said. "I hope you don't mind—I gave him the two glasses you gave Grady from Aunt Lila. Grady's friend asked for them. He said they drank a champagne toast last New Year's Eve out of the glasses and they meant a lot to him."

"I don't mind," Olivia said. So this is a new step in the journey of inheritance, she thought. My mother's crystal glasses to me, then to my cousin, and then to his gay lover. The links of family go everywhere. She was touched that Grady's "friend" loved him.

The music had stopped. "We have a surprise for Sam," the

piano player said into the microphone. Everyone looked over to the band area. "Didi is going to sing."

Ten-year-old Didi was standing at the microphone; straight as a soldier, in her velvet dress, her braided hair like a crown, looking proud and excited and not nervous at all. "I want to sing this song for you, my beloved brother Sam," she said with a twinkle. "Even though you want to kill me."

A little ripple of laughter went around the room as the relatives remembered the story of Cain and Abel. Olivia glanced at Jenny and Paul. They were looking apprehensive. It had been one thing for Didi to beg for lessons, but another for her to get up to sing in front of so many people. They were probably hoping she wouldn't disgrace herself. The band started to play. Didi began to sing one of the pop songs she had been listening to on tape, which Olivia had heard before and knew vaguely was a hit. Her voice was surprisingly deep and rich and resonant for such a young girl: she sounded like a juvenile cross between Bette Midler and Ethel Merman.

"She's good," Roger whispered, surprised.

"I know."

Jenny and Paul's tense faces relaxed. They began to smile, and then to beam. Olivia thought how wonderful it would be to have a celebrity in the family someday, and thought: I'm worse than a mother. When the song was over everyone applauded, not just politely, but with real enthusiasm. Didi and Sam hugged each other.

"I guess you'll get lessons," Jenny said.

Didi sat down, grinning, and Paul got up and went to the microphone, his arm around Sam's shoulders. Paul was kind and gentle and professorial-looking. "Sam," he said, "all these years when you were growing up, everybody always said: 'What a great kid.' From now on they're going to say: 'What a great young man.' "

That was the speech. That was it. How could you ask for more? Paul and Sam hugged and kissed, holding on to each other with pride and love. Olivia's throat closed up and she started to cry. She remembered when Sam was just old enough to sit at a table, still the only child of young parents, Jenny pregnant with Max. They were at some family event at Uncle Seymour's and Aunt

Iris's, and Sam had accidentally knocked over a stemmed water goblet. As the ice water spread into the linen tablecloth he had started to cry. Paul had scooped him up into his lap.

"It's all right," Paul had murmured soothingly. "You think we're mad at you for spilling the water, but we're not. It was an accident. We love you."

Who had ever said that to her? She only remembered being screamed at when she made a mess—wasn't that what parents always did? Harsh words and unkindness left her sick inside and stony on the outside; goodness melted her and made her fall apart. She had grown up to be a woman who always cried hardest at happy endings.

Roger handed her a tissue, but she already had one.

Aunt Myra came over to their table, making the rounds. "Isn't this a nice party?" she said. "Nobody's too full except me. I ate too much. And we have to eat again later at their house. Did you see Melissa? She ate nothing."

"Melissa doesn't eat," Olivia said.

"Well, I guess that's why she keeps so thin," Aunt Myra said with her little giggle. She looked at Olivia's dress, trying to hide her distaste. It was black and French and very expensive—it also had white stitching that looked like basting, and safety pins on it. "That's something new," Aunt Myra said.

"Yes."

"It looks like it isn't finished yet."

"Thanks."

"Oh, you."

After lunch they all had three hours to do what they wanted. Nick and Lynne changed their hotel; Uncle Seymour and Aunt Iris, with their age as an excuse, went back to New York; Melissa and Bill left their children with Uncle David and went running with Taylor and Tim along the banks of the Charles River; Kenny took Jason to look at Harvard Yard in case he decided he wanted to go to Harvard someday; and Olivia and Roger found a revival of the old silent movie *Metropolis* with a new rock score and went to see it.

Jenny and Paul's house was large and very old, with a picket fence in front, big trees, and a basketball hoop on the garage door.

"The kids cleaned their rooms," Jenny said by way of greeting. "Be sure you compliment them on it. They worked hard."

Obviously everyone had worked hard; the house was very orderly. Only the worn look of the serviceable furniture, which Jenny and Paul had bought when they were first married, revealed that this was a house where five children lived.

"What a wonderful room! So neat!" Olivia and Roger said, taking the tour, pretending surprise, while Sam looked nonchalant and the younger kids beamed.

A buffet table in the dining room was covered with platters of heaped-up cold cuts, bread, potato salad, coleslaw and paper plates. The eight youngest cousins were playing; Sam and Jason, who now considered themselves adults, were with the men; and Aunt Myra, Uncle David, and Paul's parents were with their generation. After a moment Roger went over to talk with the men—he was being such a good sport, Olivia thought; she hoped he wasn't bored, she hoped he might even be having a good time—and she joined the women cousins in a corner of the living room.

There were Jenny, Melissa, Lynne—the cousin by marriage who had missed their childhood—and Taylor, with Tim to translate. Olivia looked at his long, thin, aesthetic face, his straight, clean shoulder-length hair. He was a very quiet man, and she didn't know if it was his nature or a habit he had gotten into with the family. He's always right there with her, Olivia thought, until he becomes like another part of her body. She lip-reads, but it's not that accurate or easy—for a real dialogue the family can't talk to her without him. Her mother can, but they have little to say to each other. Taylor must feel so lonely with us, Olivia thought, compared to the way she feels with her deaf friends . . . and with Grady. With them she could be one on one, face to face, intimate and private.

Taylor's expressive hands lay still in her lap when she spoke to her cousins, because they could hear, and when the cousins spoke to her Tim's hands became a kind of telephone. But he was a man, and there were things the women didn't want to say. It was too bad none of them liked to write letters, it was too bad nobody had bothered to get a TTY, it was too bad they had never learned anything but the most rudimentary ways of signing. They loved

Taylor, and she them, but out of laziness and self-involvement they could hardly communicate.

But what about Grady?

Olivia still found it hard to believe that Taylor hadn't known Grady was gay. He would have told her, even though he told nobody else. Wouldn't he? And how could she not have noticed? The others had.

From the other room they could hear the laughing and screeching and banging around of the little cousins playing.

"I always wanted lots of children and now I have them," Jenny said contentedly. "I have exactly the life I fantasized about when I was an only child all alone."

"You weren't so alone," Melissa said. "You had us."

"Just in the summer, and it wasn't the same."

"Did you have a happy childhood otherwise?" Olivia asked.

"I'd say so."

"So did we," Melissa said. "We went on such wonderful trips as a family. The skiing . . ."

"Melissa is a much better skier than I am," Jenny said. "I didn't learn until I had kids and needed something to do with them."

"I had a very happy childhood," Lynne said. "Nick and I want to have at least one more child. For Amber, and for ourselves."

"Taylor and Grady used to swing on trees and jump off roofs," Olivia reminisced.

"I don't remember my childhood," Taylor said.

"But you must remember Mandelay?" Jenny said, surprised.

"Yes. I felt safe there."

"Then what don't you remember?"

"The rest of it. California. It's called repressing." Taylor shrugged, her face stubborn and vulnerable.

The others looked at each other, their concerned glances saying Poor thing, no wonder, it was so terrible.

I wonder what else she's chosen to forget, Olivia thought.

13

It was in the sixties, in New York, that Roger had met Virginia, the young woman who was to become his wife, and then his ex-wife. For women, who were still called girls, it was the time of miniskirts and little white boots, of aggressive hairpieces and thick false eyelashes and white lipstick, of trying to look like a malnourished child from outer space. The birth control pill had been invented, discos were newly popular and many people were not yet as politically involved and aware as they would be soon. The party was still going on.

Fittingly, he met Virginia at a party. She was very attractive; vivacious and thin in her simple black dress, her short, thick black hair like a shiny helmet with bangs, her large dark eyes circled and extended with black eyeliner and fringed with upper and lower false eyelashes, her face like a pale mask. She told him she was a part-time model for Rudi Gernreich, a designer so outrageous that he had created a bathing suit which completely exposed a woman's breasts. But best of all, she was funny. Her conversation was peppered with a kind of slang he had never heard before and only partly understood; he thought perhaps she dated gangsters.

They stayed up almost all night, talking and dancing and drinking and smoking, and the next day he called to ask her out.

"Why don't you come over tonight," she said. "I have a color TV, and I like to watch 'Bonanza.' I'll give you a Mexican TV dinner, which, since I don't cook, I serve right out of the tray it comes in. Could you bear it?"

"Of course," Roger said. "I'll bring the wine."

She gave him the address, one of those large prewar buildings on Central Park West, overlooking the park. "And when you see me," she added, "you won't recognize me."

He found that intriguing, but he was in no way prepared for how startled he would be. The girl who opened the door in a baggy sweater and narrow jeans had a scrubbed face, long light brown hair pulled back into a ponytail and smallish but pretty eyes. She looked about ten years younger than the Virginia he had met the night before. When she saw the expression on his face she smiled.

"It does shock people," she said. "This is the other me."

"You were right," Roger said. "I almost didn't know you." But he was not at all disappointed, and he could tell she knew that, too. He thought she looked a little like Audrey Hepburn, who was his favorite actress.

"Paint is such fun," Virginia said.

She showed him around the apartment, which had large leather furniture and a spectacular view. They watched "Bonanza" and ate their TV dinners out of the foil trays, and she drank very little and did not use any offbeat slang at all. He still didn't know her well enough to know which was the fantasy, the girl he had met last night or this one, but they both fascinated him. He was very turned on, and spent the night. After that they saw each other all the time.

Sometimes she took him to all-night after-hours clubs, or to the kind of parties he had never known existed. She took him to the Factory and introduced him to Andy Warhol. At home she gave him peanut butter and jelly sandwiches and taught him how to play dominoes. What he liked most about Virginia, even more than her looks and irreverent humor, was that she was two different women, and that he never knew which one would be waiting for him. When he was with one he always knew the other was there, too, hiding. In a time of outrageous masklike makeup, wigs and artifice, she was like a kind of geisha, or even a transvestite. He was simply a veterinarian.

He fell confusedly, besottedly, in love.

One June day they had a nice little wedding, attended by only their immediate families. His parents liked Virginia. His brother, who never agreed with him on anything, didn't; probably, Roger thought, because he was jealous. What none of them knew was how much Virginia loved her little red and black pills. Seconals and blackbirds. . . .

Roger married her in awe, lived with her in growing disillusionment, frustration and acrimony, and divorced her in sad resignation. They had fought until neither of them cared enough to fight anymore. They had been married for four years, and the day he finally left she was too stoned even to say goodbye. He supposed he should have noticed from the outset that she was addicted, and that probably neither of the two people he was living with were the real Virginia, but he was used to the uncomplication of small domestic animals whose secrets were pure.

After his divorce from Virginia, Roger went out with many women, most of whom were easy conquests enjoying their new freedom. It was as if they and he were like loaves of bread lined up on a grocery shelf, dated for quick consumption. He didn't know if he liked this or not. The part of him that had been hurt and made wary by his marriage preferred it to making another mistake. The part of him that thought longingly of stability was lonely. And the part of him that needed fantasy and newness, the part Virginia had tapped into, was taken care of by all this romantic turnover, and so Roger was hardly aware it existed at all.

It was ironic that he met Olivia in a line to see an Audrey Hepburn movie, but that was a long time after Virginia had stopped looking like his favorite actress anyway. Olivia was tall and beautiful, with long wavy auburn hair with gold glints in it and topaz eyes; and, he thought, quite sensual—but there was also something about her that seemed grounded and intelligent, as if those qualities could not often be found all at the same time. She was wearing an odd-looking, shaggy brown sweater.

He saw these things in an instant, with a kind of déjà vu. She looked unique but familiar somehow, as if he had been waiting for her all his life, and when he saw her he was so afraid of losing her that he didn't have the courage to speak to her. But she smiled at him. Not just a polite smile, but a big, delighted child's grin. Her life force and her joy poured out, warming and moving him.

"Where did you get that coffee?" he asked, as if he didn't have eyes to see to the corner.

"Over there."

"Will you save my place?"

"Absolutely."

Luckily it was one of those little theaters that let you bring food and drinks inside because they didn't sell any. When he raced back from the coffee shop the line was just beginning to move. He managed to sit next to Olivia, and since they were both alone and liked what they saw they made small talk while they were waiting for the picture to begin. They had both seen it before.

"That's an interesting sweater," Roger said. "What's it made of?"

"Yak."

It was obviously not; it was some kind of fabric. He laughed. "I don't think so," he said.

"Are you a furrier?"

"No. I'm a veterinarian."

"Do you take care of yaks?" Olivia asked.

"Dogs and cats mostly. One spider monkey."

"Do you know the chances of two veterinarians sitting next to each other in a movie theater?"

They bantered some more and exchanged cards, and his life began.

But now it was over a decade later, and he was afraid of getting older, which was inevitable anyway; afraid of death, which was equally inevitable; and afraid of his ambivalence in the dangerous tightwalk between Wendy and Olivia. He didn't know why it had taken him so long to realize that Wendy, with her sleeping pills and faked suicide, had reminded him uncomfortably of Virginia. Virginia had never tried to kill herself, but she had seemed headed toward doing it accidentally and had refused to do anything about it. She was now so far gone from his life that after she remarried and he could stop sending her alimony payments he didn't even know where she was and had no reason to care. But something remained; it had to. He hadn't thought about her in years, and Wendy had brought it back.

Was he attracted to crazy women who lived on the edge? And if so, what miracle had brought him to Olivia, who wanted serenity and sanity? Why couldn't he just let Olivia be who and what she was and be content and grateful for it? Was *he* self-destructive? No, he was just a man who needed adventure once in a while to feel alive. What was so unusual about that?

He called Wendy. It was one of those early spring days in New York that gives a seductive hint of the softness to come and then the next day disappears.

"Can I come over at six o'clock?" he asked.

"Yes."

"Surprise me."

He rang the bell to her apartment instead of using his key, because he knew she was going to be a stranger. Wendy opened the door and smiled at him like a little mouse. She had her hair tucked neatly behind her ears and was wearing small round horn-rimmed eyeglasses.

"You're here to see the apartment," she said.

"Yes."

"Mr. Hawkwood."

"Dr. Hawkwood."

"Oh, I'm sorry."

"Call me Roger."

"I'm Caroline," Wendy said. "Come in."

There were cardboard cartons on the living room floor and it looked as if she were in the midst of packing her books. She was wearing a prim suit and blouse, corporate image, just back from the office. "You see the living room is quite large," she said. Her voice was soft and sweet, her manner tentative and shy. She glanced at him and then looked away.

"Yes."

"I hope the mess of packing doesn't distract you from the really nice space."

"Not at all," Roger said. "Are you leaving New York?"

"No. Just moving downtown. To be closer to work."

"Ah."

"Let me show you the kitchen," she said. She led him there. "It's very well-organized for a small New York kitchen," she said. "Do you or your wife like to cook?"

"I have no wife."

"Oh." She blushed, as if she had been fishing to see if he were available. "And this is the bedroom. King-sized bed, as you see, fits in easily, and two large closets." She opened the doors to show him. The clothing hanging inside was all hers. He noticed the cat carrier next to the dresser. Two familiar hostile eyes glared out at him. "And the bathroom," she said, moving on.

She had obviously straightened out the bathroom for his inspection; it had that look of being on display. She had even put paper guest towels on the side of the sink. The entire apartment, except for the packing, was very neat. "Did I show you the dining area?" she asked, sounding flustered.

"No."

"Well, here it is. Right off the living room. You could make an office out of it if you wanted to, and eat in the living room. But . . . I guess you . . . don't have dinner at home very often."

"Not very often," he said.

"Oh," she said. "Well." A little smile slid across her face and she looked at him wistfully. "Let me show you the sunset."

She led him to the window. Between the buildings there was a red streak against the sky. Roger looked at her. She was doing the perfect impersonation of a demure young woman with hidden fire and longing inside. But he would have to woo her. He moved closer to her at the window and she shivered.

"It's great," he said. Actually, you couldn't really see much.

"Would you . . . like a drink?" she asked.

"For the sunset?"

"Yes."

"All right," he said. "Thank you."

She poured each of them a glass of white wine and they sat on the couch. "It's a romantic apartment, don't you think?" she said softly. "Especially for a bachelor."

"I'm surprised you're giving it up," Roger said.

"Oh . . . I have some memories that aren't so good. Time to move on."

"A woman like you shouldn't have painful memories."

"What is a woman like me?"

"Beautiful. Intelligent. Sensitive."

"I'm not beautiful," she said.

"Caroline, believe me, you are."

She looked down, embarrassed and pleased. "Thank you for saying that. Even though I don't feel it."

"Someone must have hurt you very badly to shake you that much."

"It was a long time ago."

"Apparently not long enough."

"These painful things linger. Not the person. Just the bad feelings he gave me about myself," she said in a matter-of-fact and very vulnerable voice. She sipped her wine.

He felt a warm and wistful feeling, and then the stirrings of desire. He wanted to take off her conservative clothes and feel her body—even under that suit it was apparent how tempting it was. He laid his hand on hers, and when she didn't pull away he enveloped it comfortingly. He touched her pulse with his thumb and felt it was jumping.

"No one has a right to hurt you," he said.

"No one has the right to hurt anyone."

"If you were my woman I would never hurt you."

He heard the intake of her breath.

"I would cherish you. You deserve that."

"You have such wonderful hands," she whispered.

Roger ran his finger gently across the back of Wendy's hand and she trembled. He took a few of the soft blonde hairs on her forearm between his thumb and forefinger and lifted them. She gave a desperate sigh, almost a moan. "Who are you?" she whispered, "Coming into my life like this . . ." Her head was back, exposing her long, lovely throat.

"I'm your destiny," Roger said. *Destiny! What idiotic things I say to her in these sex games,* he thought, glad no one else could hear him. *But it turns me on.* He slowly began unbuttoning her corporate blouse, and where each button had been he laid his lips.

He had never before been so leisurely and caring when he had sex with her. He undressed her deliberately, kissing and caressing every part of her, holding himself back, fending off his intolerable pleasure, enjoying how out of control he made her. When he slipped inside her and she came for the last time, she screamed, and then he heard another voice, deeper, more primitive, crying out; and he realized it was himself.

They lay on the couch for a while, dazed and exhausted. Then Wendy got up and brought back two glasses of water, and they drank thirstily.

"This was the best we ever did," he said. "It's always been hot and fantastic between us, but this was unbelievable."

"We're good together," Wendy said.

"Yes. And I love you." He kissed her lightly and stood.

"Where are you going?"

"To take a shower. If I lie here a minute longer I'll fall asleep."

"What's wrong with that?"

"I have to go home."

"Oh," she said flatly.

"I'm expected for dinner," Roger said. He didn't like the tone of her voice or the look she was giving him. She had never done this before. "Honey, you know how it is," he said mildly, hoping she wouldn't make him feel guilty. She knew the rules. She always had.

"Yes. I know how it is." She went into the bedroom. He hurried into the bathroom, as much to escape her criticism as to wash away all signs of what had just transpired so he could return to his ordered life.

When he came out to dress Wendy was sitting on the couch hunched in a terrycloth robe, moodily drinking her wine. She didn't look like a contented, relaxed woman who had just had four orgasms—she looked like a neglected waif.

"We need to talk," she said. The sky was black outside the window.

Roger looked at his watch. It was, he noted nervously, after eight. "I have to go. Can we talk later?"

"When is later?"

"Tomorrow. I'll call you from outside."

"I need to talk face to face."

"Next time."

"Not next time. This time."

"What is the matter with you?" he asked. He picked up his glass of wine and took a quick gulp. The wine had gotten warm. He began to feel the tension creep into the back of his neck.

"Take some fresh from the cooler," she said, gesturing.

He wavered. "I have to go."

"Hear me out."

"All right," Roger said. He took a glass from the bar and poured himself another.

"This isn't enough," Wendy said. "I need more of the real you. I need time for us together just doing the things normal people do."

"We do that—"

"When she's away. I don't want to be second best."

The tension squeezed the back of his neck and his jaws until his head began to hurt. "You're not second best," he protested. "You have the part of me no one else knows."

"I appreciate that. I would also like to wake up with you on Sunday mornings."

"No, you wouldn't. It's no pleasure."

"I want to cuddle with you. I want to take a walk with you, go to a play, a party, show you off. I want to have a goddamn whole meal in a restaurant with you."

"Oh, Wendy. Why are you doing this now?"

"Because I'm in love with you," she said.

All the times she had told him that, he had enjoyed believing her because it was a necessary part of their affair. Now, suddenly, when she said it, it was ominous. He wished he didn't have to believe it.

"I don't want to hurt you," he said. "I never meant to."

"You tell me you'll protect and cherish me and then you don't."

"But . . . it's part of the *game,*" he blurted out.

Wendy's eyes filled with tears, and then they overflowed. "I know," she said quietly.

"Oh, Wendy." He put his arms around her and held her. He was awash with tenderness for her, this wounded creature, and at the same time he felt choked and trapped. This was never the way it was supposed to be. "Please don't," he said, smoothing her hair off her forehead, letting her cry against his shoulder. His skin was crawling. She was so unpredictable. She could do anything. As soon as she stopped crying he stood up.

"Now I really have to go," he said with authority, and this time she didn't stop him.

When he got home the assistant was finishing up before closing the clinic for the night. He went upstairs to Olivia, who was in the living room watching television. "Oh, there you are," Olivia said. "You're so late." He patted the dogs, who were overjoyed to see him.

"Buster, Buster," he said. "Wozzle, Wozzle." Now he could face her. "I needed to unwind," he said, "so after I worked out I ran some laps around the track."

"How was it?"

"Good. You should try it sometime."

"Maybe I will."

She had set two places on the coffee table in front of the television and opened a bottle of wine. He put down his gym bag and poured himself a glass of wine to disguise the scent of Wendy's wine on his breath.

"I'm making plain steamed vegetables tonight," Olivia said. "I'm tired of everything else."

"You mean I need to go on a diet."

"Will you stop?" she said.

"I know you."

"Well, I know you too."

They smiled at each other, best friends. He kissed her on top of the head. While the vegetables steamed they watched the news on CNN for a few minutes. Later they would discuss their day. He looked at her and thought how happy and contented she made him, not by any one thing in particular that she did, but just by being there, by helping to weave this cozy fabric of their life together. And she was still so beautiful. If he weren't so exhausted, later he would have tried to . . .

"Dinner is ready," Olivia said, as the timer went off in the kitchen. He helped her carry the food to the living room and they settled down.

"This is good," he said.

"Because it's fresh."

"I could eat this more often."

"We always say that and then we forget."

"No, because we crave spareribs and fried rice."

"I don't crave spareribs," Olivia said. "I crave chocolate."

The phone rang. They both looked at it.

"Ignore it," Roger said.

"No, it's the clinic line."

"It's my turn," he said reluctantly.

It was the assistant, Terry. "Mrs. Adler's here with her Great Dane," Terry said. "I don't know how she managed to get him here. He's as big as a truck and he's having some kind of a fit."

"I'll be right down," Roger said. Olivia looked at him questioningly. "Adler's Great Dane."

"Do you want me to help you?"

"No, it's all right. I'll be back soon. Terry's there."

The huge old dog, it turned out, had been having a series of little strokes, just like a person, and was crazed with fear. By the time Roger got him stabilized and it looked like he was going to live, it was midnight. The dog would spend the next few days at the clinic for observation. Mrs. Adler, who was as big as her dog, insisted on staying with him; so since it was late and Roger was too tired to move, much less argue, he let her sleep on the couch in the waiting room.

"What people do for love," he told Olivia later.

"Of course," she said.

He crawled into bed beside her, inhaling her scent, feeling her warmth. Just as he fell into sleep, as if he were floating into a deep, soft well, a thought scratched at the edge of his mind. The gym bag. Where was the gym bag? Was it still in the living room? He hadn't even looked.

But if Olivia had gone to put his workout clothes into the washing machine, and discovered they were unused, she would certainly have said something to him. She wouldn't have just left the subject of his lie alone.

No, it was fine. He'd take care of it tomorrow. She had acted the same as ever when he came back upstairs. And if there was one thing he knew about Olivia it was that unlike him, she never kept secrets.

14

WHEN ROGER WENT DOWNSTAIRS to the clinic to take care of Mrs. Adler's dog, Olivia cleared away the dishes. She put the rest of the steamed vegetables into the refrigerator and made a fast fat-free dip so he could eat them cold in case he was hungry later. As she corked the wine and put it into the fridge she thought that perhaps they should stop drinking every night. Wine had a lot of calories. She never kept any fattening treats in the house anymore, not even frozen yogurt, but Roger, despite his strict regimen at the gym, didn't look much different from when he had started. Sometimes that happened when people got older; their metabolism slowed. Poor Roger. Working out so hard just to maintain.

She noticed his gym bag lying on the living room floor where he had left it, and she opened it to put his used gym clothes into the washing machine the way he always did. That was another thing she liked about Roger: that he was so fastidious—he wouldn't leave those smelly, sweaty things in the bag any longer than he had to.

But when she reached in and took his gym clothes out she realized with shock that they had obviously not been used. There was his gray sweatshirt, fluffy and folded and still smelling faintly of fabric softener; there were his fresh, unironed shorts; there were his pristine white socks; still folded in half the way Peggy, the cleaning woman, liked to do it.

For an instant it didn't quite register. Then she felt a chill stab of fear. *He said he was late because he had worked out longer.* He was very tired, but he hadn't been to the gym at all. Her stomach turned over.

He had lied to her. Why?

Maybe he had washed and dried his clothes at the gym. Impossible. Bought new ones? Not these.

She always worried that he would die because they were so happy, and you never knew when your luck would run out. Had he been to the doctor and was he hiding it from her—having secret tests? Cancer? Heart problems? But not so late in the evening, and his hair had been damp. He had taken a shower. You didn't take a shower at the doctor's office or after a few hours at the hospital, even if you'd had a stress test, and his hair had been damp from a shampooing, not from perspiration.

Why were you lying to me, Roger?

Standing there with Roger's clean workout clothes in her hands, she was suddenly repelled by them, as if they were the instrument of her betrayal, and she put them down. A part of her already sensed—no, knew. He was having an affair. And at the same time that she knew, the rest of her kept pleading that it not be true. She was numb with pain and loss.

She wondered if it was her fault. What had she done wrong, what lapse, what disappointing things to make him feel something was missing from their relationship, even to hurt him? She remembered with an ache how she had laughed in the hotel room in Cambridge when he was trying to initiate imaginative sex. Had his affair started then, or before that? Was he just tired of her?

She tried to think back to see if there had been other suspicious times she had not noticed when Roger had lied to her, incidents she had dismissed. She was too shaken to remember, and she realized she was in a kind of shock. She felt as if her mind was walking under water. But she had to remember . . . try, try. . . .

All those times she had gone alone to see her family and Roger had refused to go, he could easily have started an affair then. It was unlikely he had been seeing a woman all these years without her suspecting something, but anything was possible. Who was he anyway, this man she loved so much and had thought she knew so well? In one horrible moment he had become a stranger.

His fascination with exercise had begun about a year ago. Maybe longer. She couldn't even remember exactly when. When had things started to be different? He had kept his trail so hidden, or maybe she had refused to see.

Grady had come to lunch and Roger had returned home with wine on his breath, saying the gym had been too crowded so he had gone out to lunch alone instead. Maybe that had been true—now she didn't know.

He could have met the woman at the gym. Or when he was home all by himself he could have met her in a movie line, the way he had met *her*. He could have met the woman anywhere; she could even be a client.

A client . . . the cat scratch. Last Thanksgiving when Olivia had noticed the cat scratch on Roger's thigh. He'd said it happened at the clinic, and at the time it had never occurred to her to wonder how a cat could have scratched him so deeply on the thigh right through his clothes.

But now she knew: *because he hadn't been wearing them.* The thought made her sick with rage. Roger making love to someone else. The pain rose inside her then with full force and she started to sob. How could she survive this?

Finally, cried out, drained, she wandered into the den. They kept their personal appointment books there, and she looked through Roger's. There was very little they had not done together—they even saw their accountant together—and his other appointments were equally innocuous: checkup, dentist, haircut. He was so precise he had even written down each time he went to the gym.

Or, as she now knew, even the times he had not gone to the gym.

She looked through his phone book. There were no names there she didn't know. Why would there be? The next time he went to "exercise" she would look through his client's phone book downstairs and see if she could remember every woman who had a cat; if, in fact, his girlfriend was a client at all.

What was she supposed to do now—put up with it and spy and nail him? Tell him, as soon as he came upstairs, that she knew? Leave or throw him out, and tear up the life they had made together, now that he had started the mortal rip? Swallow her devastation and humiliation and fight to keep him? He didn't seem to be going anywhere; he liked things just the way they were. That thought more enraged than comforted her. How could she even sleep in the same bed with him tonight?

How could she sleep in that bed alone, without Roger, for the rest of her nights?

She went into the living room and put Roger's unused workout clothes back into the bag and zipped it up. She would survive, but she had to figure out how. Whatever she did, it would have to be according to her own timetable. She would watch, and she would wait. She wouldn't confront him tonight. She wasn't ready. She couldn't bear to think how she would handle it if he admitted everything before she was ready to hear it.

When he came back a little after midnight she had herself under control. Oblivious that anything had changed, he told her the story of big Mrs. Adler insisting on sleeping all night on the reception-room couch to be near her dog.

"What people do for love," he said.

"Of course," Olivia answered. He had no idea that she was talking about herself.

15

OLIVIA WOULD NEVER have believed that she had so much stealth in her, or that she could dissemble so well. Looking at Roger doing his ordinary things, saying his usual pleasant words, she composed her face and wondered if he suspected anything. When he came out of the shower into the bedroom she looked at his body with the eyes of another woman seeing it for the first time, and then glanced down to his penis which she now shared with some stranger, and wondered if her anger showed. Sometimes she remained numb and bewildered, and other times her feelings swirled around inside her and made her feel ill.

What was perhaps even worse, she thought, was having to look at his lips. He had lied with them, and probably spoken love with them, and he had kissed another woman in places she didn't want to think about, and somehow that seemed even more intimate than fucking.

"What are you looking at?" he asked once, and she answered innocuously, "You," as if that were normal; and there had been a time it was. *You* was so ambiguous. *You,* the cheat. *You,* my love. *You,* my lost love, the betrayer.

They continued to use the Jacuzzi together as usual, but now she too pretended to be too tired to do anything there but unwind. He massaged her shoulders as he always did. "You're so tense," he said. She merely sighed, and he took it as assent and relief at his ministrations.

I'm tense because you're someone I don't know anymore, she thought. Because you've ruined what we had and I hate you. And because I want you to keep touching me and I love you.

She knew she needed time.

When he returned from the gym, or wherever he really went, he always put his gym clothes into the washing machine for Peggy, and Olivia waited until he was otherwise occupied and then took them out to inspect them. He had a pattern. He went to the gym twice a week, and lied to her the other two times. He was having a regular affair, not just an occasional thing, and that made it more terrible. She wondered if he was planning to leave her.

Wouldn't it be ironic if all the time she was gathering up her courage to confront him, perhaps leave him, he was intending to do it to her first?

She wanted to catch him making a phone call to the woman. So far she had been unable to—the office was too busy, there were too many people around to wonder what she was up to. Then, one day at lunchtime, when the assistants were out and the phones had been turned over to voice mail, Olivia saw the little red light go on indicating Roger's office extension. That watchful little red eye, the alarm to her brain. Slowly, carefully, she picked up the receiver in her own office and listened, her hand over the receiver so he would not hear her breathe, if, indeed, she was breathing at all.

"Roosevelt Island Tramway," she heard him saying, in a voice she was not used to.

"Cool," a soft female voice answered; the word drawn out, a prurient whisper.

"Is someone on this line?" Roger asked sharply. "Hello? Olivia?"

"Oh, sorry," Olivia said briskly, as if it had been a simple mistake, and hung up. Her heart was pounding. Sorry? Sorry! He was the one who should be sorry. She pretended to be looking through a medical report on her desk when Roger looked in through her open door.

"I'm going to go out and get some exercise," Roger said. "I'll be back soon."

I'll bet you are, bastard. "I'll go to the gym with you," Olivia said cheerfully. "I could use a break."

He looked at her, surprised. They never went to the gym together; it was one of the few things they liked to do separately.

"I thought I might just take a long walk," he said.

"You don't want company?" She hoped her voice wasn't shaking.

"You have patients soon," Roger said.

"You'd rather be alone." Not accusingly, just adding up another crime.

"I need to clear my head."

"Of course."

As soon as Roger left she went to the front window that overlooked the street. He walked to the corner briskly, without his gym bag, and then he hailed a taxi and got into it. Olivia grabbed her coat and ran outside and got into another cab.

"Roosevelt Island Tramway," she said to the driver.

She had passed it and seen it, but had never been on it. She never had any need to go to Roosevelt Island. She wondered if Roger went there, or if the tram was simply a rendezvous. There were stairs leading up to a place where you could wait for the little red commuter tram that traveled on its cable high over the water like a dangling plaything. It was a slow time for commuters, and she knew if she climbed the stairs to wait for the tram with him he would see her. Or maybe he wouldn't.

She went up cautiously, keeping far back.

She saw him standing there, his back to her. There were a couple of old men, an old woman, a teenage couple, and a young woman, very pretty, with light hair. She looked familiar. The young woman and Roger glanced at each other and looked away. Olivia moved closer to the stairway wall, hoping they couldn't see her, still able to see them. When the tram stopped, Roger and the young woman got on with the other people and sat together although there were many empty seats. They did not appear to speak or even to know each other, but that made it just as obvious she was the one he was meeting.

When the tram moved away, Olivia went quickly down the stairs to the street. Maybe that woman lived over there. Who was she, anyway? She knew the face.

Brown Abyssinian cat, very high strung. Gregory. New patient, come for a checkup. Wendy . . . Wilton. Yes! So the woman Roger was seeing had become a client. Now she could look up the records, and soon she would be able to know everything. For the first time Olivia felt the strain lifting in the exhilaration of the quest. Soon the wondering would be over. And then, of course, the nightmare would begin, because it would at last be too real to ignore anymore. All the evidence she needed would be in.

Back at the office Olivia went through her patient files and found Wendy Wilton's home address and phone number. She called to hear her voice on the answering machine. It was the same as on the phone today, not that she needed any more corroboration. But there was one more thing she had to do. She took a blank piece of paper, folded it, put it into an office envelope and wrote Roger's name on it.

She saw patients for an hour, her mind on automatic pilot. The adrenaline was pouring through her bloodstream, but at the same time she felt strangely calm. Roger wasn't back yet, but she hadn't expected him to be. She checked her watch. Then she told Terry to tell the rest of the patients she would be running a little late, and she took a cab to Wendy Wilton's apartment building.

It was a nice building, with a doorman, on the East Side. Obviously the woman had some money. Olivia told the cabdriver to wait and gave the envelope to the doorman. "This is from Dr. Hawkwood's office," she told the doorman. "He said he would be dropping by here today. To see Ms. Wilton."

"They just went up," the doorman said. "Shall I ring?"

They just went up. It hit her like a blow to the heart. Olivia flashed him her brightest smile and handed him a five-dollar bill. "Could you please send it up?" she asked.

"Of course."

She got into her waiting cab and told him to take her back to the office. All the way there she couldn't stop shaking, as if she had the worst kind of flu. They were in there, the two of them, in Wendy Wilton's apartment. But she'd had to know for sure. And now Roger would know she knew. She held her arms tightly around her body to try to stop the trembling, and she had never felt so alone in her life.

* * *

The part of her that was strong kept her looking and acting sane while she saw the rest of the afternoon's patients. How good and loving they were, these furry dogs and cats with their sweet eyes. If you sent your pet away it tried to come back to you. They did not deceive or lie or look for someone they would rather be with. Once they had committed, they were yours, a member of the family. You could trust their loyalty. You could grow old together. No wonder some people finally gave up on relationships with people and just had pets. She had always thought it was somewhat pathetic, but now for the first time she could understand.

After a while she heard Roger come into the office and begin to attend to his own patients. Her nerve fibers responded as they always had to the sound of his familiar voice, filling her with warm reassurance, and then her mind took over and she was cold with rage. Be dignified, she told herself. Walk tall, be calm. She decided she would pretend to know even more than she did without being specific enough for him to know when she was faking.

At the end of their day she passed him in the hall. "I'm going up to the apartment now," she said. He looked frightened.

"I'll be right up myself," he said.

Upstairs in the welcoming rooms she had once believed were a refuge, Olivia repaired her makeup and poured herself a glass of wine. One sip, and then she put it down. She wanted full control of her faculties.

The door opened and Roger came in. He didn't say anything, he just looked at her.

"So you're having an affair with Wendy Wilton," Olivia said.

"I . . ."

"I know about the gym clothes, the phone calls, the meetings, the lies, the fact that her doorman knows you. Don't lie any more now because then I'll hate you."

"You'll hate me anyway," Roger said.

"At least you didn't say: 'It's not what you think.' "

"It's not."

"I'm sure it's worse."

He closed his eyes. She thought he looked very pale.

"Why did you need someone else?" she asked.

There was a long pause. "Why are you asking me a question that is so hard to answer?" he said finally, softly, sounding beaten.

"Is it?"

"Yes."

"Hard for you to answer or for me to hear?"

"Oh, Olivia . . ."

"I want to know," Olivia said.

"I don't love her," Roger said. "Not at all. She knows that."

"She must feel very used."

He sighed. "For what it's worth, I've never done this to you before," he said. "Never in all these years."

"Really."

"I promise."

"Then what makes her so special?"

"I don't want to talk about her," Roger said.

"Then let's talk about us. Why now?"

"I don't know. I don't know . . . she . . . I don't know."

"Obviously she had something you needed that you couldn't get with me."

"I love you," Roger said. "It's you I love, I want to spend my life with you. I can't imagine life without you."

"You wanted both of us."

He sighed again.

"Is she better in bed than I am? No, forget I asked that. I don't want to hear it."

"An affair is exciting and dangerous," Roger said. "That's the only thing she and I had that you and I didn't have. It has nothing to do with you. You're my heart. She's like a stranger."

"And you had sex with her twice a week and could hardly ever bring yourself to make love to me. What does that mean?"

"I'm too old to satisfy two women," Roger said.

"Oh, sure, when it suits your purpose to say it."

"I am."

"Then why couldn't you have tried to work it out with me? If you don't find me exciting anymore, is that the end of it? Ten years is all it can last?"

Roger poured himself a glass of wine. His hand was shaking ever so slightly. "Olivia, I'm not going to leave you."

"You already did."

"Don't say that. It isn't true."

"Everything's different now," Olivia said. She couldn't believe how calm she was. It was as if she were watching herself from one step away. "I might have to leave *you*."

"Don't."

"Then you can be with her all the time."

"That's the last thing I want. If I had wanted that I would have done it."

"Will you stop seeing her?"

A pause. "Yes."

"Because I want you to?"

"Because that's the way it is."

"Not because I want you to, or you wouldn't have started with her in the first place. And not because you want to. It's because I found out and you're afraid I might go. Life stinks."

"But I do want to, Olivia. I wanted to for quite a while, but I didn't know how."

"And now you'll find a way."

He didn't answer. She supposed his silence meant she had been right. He would have kept both of them as long as he could, drifting along, selfish, weak, needing Olivia to force the break.

The image floated into her mind of her second husband, Stuart, who had cheated with all those women. What was wrong with her that she had such bad luck? Was it her fault? Did she pick men like that? Did she drive them away? Or was that what you had to expect? No, Stuart had flaunted it. He was not Roger. But this Roger wasn't Roger either.

"I want you to sleep in the den until this is all settled," Olivia said. "I can't have you coming home from her to me."

"All right," he said quietly.

"And I'm going to have an AIDS test. There are no free rides anymore. I think you should have one too."

"She did," he said, sounding embarrassed. "She's fine."

"Where did you meet her, anyway?"

"It doesn't matter," he said.

"I want to know."

"At the gym."

Of course, why not? All those cute little things with their makeup on, and their jewelry, and their perky ponytails, and their designer workout clothes with the thong in back showing off their tight little buns. . . . "What does she do for a living?"

"She's a stockbroker."

Smart, too. And wanted Roger, who was taken. And had gotten him. Olivia didn't know what to believe in anymore.

"I thought if you and I didn't get married it would stay romantic," she said sadly. "I thought this time it would work. We were so happy."

"We are happy," Roger said, his eyes pleading. She almost melted at that look on his face, but she looked away until she had herself under control again.

"We might as well have been married," she said. "We have all this community property. The house, our practice. It would be like a divorce. Dividing everything up. The lawyers. Selling the house, dividing the patients. Would we keep the clinic and work together as friends—such a modern divorce—or would we have to lose it along with all our other dreams? At least we wouldn't have to fight over the kids."

"Wozzle and Buster," Roger said fondly, trying to win her. "They're our kids."

He had his way of pulling her apart and she hardened her heart against it. "I want you to end it with Wendy Wilton now," Olivia said. "From here on in, every day it gets worse."

"She's very neurotic," Roger said. "She's emotional, unpredictable. I have to handle the breakup carefully. I don't want her coming to see you."

"The way she already did?"

He paled again. Of course she had meant Wendy's office visit, but Roger didn't know that was all there was. "Did she tell you she tried to kill herself?" he asked.

"No. Did she?"

"She pretended to. It was a cry for help. I don't want to drive her to do it again more seriously."

So Wendy wanted Roger so much she was willing to do anything, risk anything to keep him. While Olivia was trying to act controlled and strong.

"Do what you have to do in the way you think best," she said. "I'll get out the linens for the den. You can use the bathroom in there. The shower's good."

He was silent as she laid the folded guest linens on the sofa bed in the den. Then he went into their bathroom and took out all his things. She felt her heart scream.

16

WHEN YOU HAVE LOST your lover there is no season so sad as late spring, when the lengthening days with their pastel twilights and softening air remind you of romantic beginnings and hopeful continuances that are not for you. Now that Olivia and Roger were sleeping in separate rooms under an uneasy truce, she felt she had the worst of both worlds. Sometimes it felt as if they were living miles apart, and yet they were in the same house with its closeness that made it hard to have secrets. But as he had once said jokingly to her cousin Nick, she had such separation anxiety that she couldn't even leave a bad hotel, so how could she push him further out of their life together?

She knew he had not yet made a clean break with Wendy.

"I can't just drop her," he said. "She's too fragile."

"Most men do it," Olivia said.

"I'm not most men, and she's not most women."

"Neither am I," Olivia said.

She waited for him to tell her he had finally ended the affair forever, but he didn't, and sometimes he went out saying something ambiguous, knowing avoidance was not so heinous as a lie or as insulting as the truth. He went to the gym only two or three times a week, so she supposed he really went. Once in a while she did a check on his gym clothes and they were always used.

"She asked me to try to be friends with her," he said. "There's something sad about that."

"Friends!"

"I feel as though I've messed up her life."

"What about mine?"

"But you have me."

Olivia didn't answer, because anything she could have said would have cut.

Every evening she and Roger still had dinner together. He always asked her first if she was free, as if she too had another life. She thought perhaps she should start to have one. When they had dinner together they tried to pretend nothing had changed, which was impossible, so they gently talked about safe things: the news, patients, movies. He even asked her if she had heard from her cousins and what they were up to, a subject that had never interested him before.

"Charlie the Perfect is going to run the New York Marathon with his son again next fall," Olivia told him. "Remember it was in the newspaper last year when they did it together and they both finished at the same time? He's fifty and Tony is twenty-five. Charlie trains six days a week. And he's a vegetarian. But I couldn't decide if he finished the same time as his son because he's such a good athlete or because they're so symbiotic."

Roger laughed. "You talked to him?" he asked, surprised. Charlie the Perfect ran the store with his father, Uncle Seymour, but other than that his life never touched most of the rest of the cousins.

"Of course not. Aunt Myra told me. And she said Charlie got cows for the summer again."

"Cows?"

"They have this estate in Beaverkill. A hundred acres. Cows look very picturesque grazing and lying around, and you don't have to pay to cut the grass, but they're hard to take care of during the winter, so every spring Charlie and his wife buy a herd of cows to decorate the estate, and then in the fall they sell them."

"Not to a slaughterhouse!"

"Of course not. To a dairy."

"Do they make a profit?"

"I don't know," Olivia said. "For a used car you don't. Used car, used cow? Don't ask me."

Roger laughed again.

Look how funny you think I am, Olivia thought. How well we get along. Has Wendy got anything for you besides sex? I doubt it. Maybe fear. How much obligation do you have, and for how long, to a suicidal mistress? Get rid of her. But maybe you think I'm boring. Maybe you're only laughing because you're fond of me.

She thought perhaps sex with her was boring compared to sex with Wendy. Maybe it had been boring all along, and that was why he had looked elsewhere. Maybe she had been too complacent. If he came back she would try again, make it more exciting. But then she realized that she was too angry with him to try at all. They didn't touch each other anymore; they were both too afraid of her rage.

At night she let Wozzle sleep on her bed. Buster slept in the den with Roger, confused the first night and then quickly getting used to it. Watching the large blond dog walk calmly into the den behind Roger, seeing Roger shut the door behind them, Olivia felt as if they were truly separated and torn apart, and that Roger had taken with him all his worldly goods.

"Oh, Wozzle," she murmured, dropping tears into her dog's soft black fur, "Wuzzy, Wuzzy, what's going to become of us?"

She had a hard time getting to sleep. She watched old movies on television late at night so she could have another excuse to cry. Sometimes, when there were patients staying over in the clinic, she wandered downstairs to look at them. Everything was so clean. The sleeping animals breathed quietly in their cages. Everything she and Roger had—this practice, their house, their life together—had been the fulfillment of their dreams. Maybe it was true that when you got what you wanted, the trouble began.

Her old friend Alys called. "I haven't seen you since Thanksgiving," Alys said. "This is a disgrace."

"I know," Olivia said. "Everyone gets so busy."

"Can you have lunch with me next week? No, dinner. Let's have dinner. Will Roger let you out?"

"As in out of jail?" Olivia said dryly. She knew Roger would rush to dinner with Wendy if he knew she had made plans of her own. "Lunch would be easier," she said. "Things are a little hectic right now."

They met at Alys's new favorite Italian restaurant. It looked just like Alys's last favorite Italian restaurant, and as always Alys ordered a salad with no dressing—a spare handful of torn-up greens on a plate for six dollars—and dry grilled chicken, and as always the salad annoyed Olivia, and by extension so did Alys. Olivia ordered just the chicken. The waiter looked disappointed. Alys had had her hair cut very short since Olivia had last seen her and she looked younger and quite attractive.

"You look great," Olivia said.

"I have found the new best hairdresser in New York," Alys said. "You have to go." Every six months Alys found the new best hairdresser. Her life was a constant search for better beauty.

"How's your job going?" Olivia asked, passing it off. Alys was an editor on a women's magazine, and sometimes wrote an article when no one else wanted to do it, for which she claimed she was unfairly meagerly paid.

"I hate it just as much as always," Alys said, "but they're cutting down the staff and firing people right and left because of the recession so I don't dare leave." She sipped from her glass of their seven-dollar bottle of Evian water. Olivia thought about the people who were hungry and out of work.

"You're lucky to have this job," she said. "You have great perks."

"Yes, I get on screening lists. And I still have an expense account, so lunch is on me. You did Thanksgiving."

"Thank you. So how's life?"

"It's seven months since I've been to bed with a man. I'm ashamed to tell anybody."

"That's not so long these days," Olivia said.

"I take a certain grim satisfaction in thinking I'm working on my first celibate year. I hardly ever meet men anymore. They're married or taken or gay or just hopeless. I'd settle for the hopeless ones, but there seems to be a waiting list."

"You'll find someone," Olivia said.

"You always say that. You're so lucky you have Roger."

"*You* always say that."

"It's true."

"Roger is having an affair," Olivia said. As soon as the words came out she felt better. It had been hard keeping the burden all to herself.

"No! What a rat! How did you find out?"

"It's a long story." Olivia told her most of it.

"How old is she?" Alys asked.

"Late twenties, I'd guess. No more than thirty. And pretty. Roger's almost fifty."

"Do you remember when we were that age and going out with older, sophisticated married men? We thought their wives were some old bat. The old bat was probably in her mid-forties. What we are now."

"Don't even say it."

"We couldn't understand why those guys wouldn't leave their wives for us. And sometimes they did leave them for somebody else—young, of course. It's come full circle. When we were young they cheated *with* us, and now they cheat *on* us."

"I never went out with a married man who wasn't already separated," Olivia said.

"Well, I did."

"Fairly recently, as I remember."

"What are you going to do about Roger?"

"I'm afraid to think about it," Olivia said.

"He'll give her up eventually and then you'll reconcile and forgive him. People don't throw a relationship away when they have as much together as you two do."

"I don't believe it can ever be the same again," Olivia said.

"You know," Alys said thoughtfully, "ever since I was a kid I wondered what real life was. I kept waiting for it to happen to me. I looked at other people, their families, what they did for fun, and I wondered if that was it. What did they do when I wasn't there? When I was a grownup, I mean actually *now,* I even used to look into the windows of the big apartment building across the street from me—everybody keeps their blinds up in New York like no one else exists—and I would watch people's lives. Who's watching television, who's alone, who's found someone, who's out for the evening. I'd watch them cooking. I'd look into people's shopping carts at the supermarket. I wondered how often people had sex. What their everyday conversations were."

"Because you're a writer."

"No. And I always wondered what your life with Roger was really like."

"You were curious about my life?"

"Yes. Because I thought I was the only person in the world who didn't have a real life. And then do you know what happened? The other day I was walking along the street, and it hit me. I realized this *is* my real life. Every day of it. This is all there is. This is it."

"How could you not know?"

Alys shrugged. "I didn't."

Olivia thought about her cousins who loved danger. They said it made life worth living, but now she suddenly wondered if they needed to risk everything in order to know they were alive. And Roger: did he need his affair with Wendy for the same reason? Push it to the limit. Be ready for that one moment to be caught, to lose. Know you had won, until the next time. Did that mean it was not her fault after all?

They finished lunch and had cappuccino, which always seemed like dessert.

"Now this Wendy, if she's thirty," Alys said, "she's going to want to get married. She's probably thinking about when she's going to have a child. At least a husband. And Roger's not budging. Eventually she's going to move on."

"She's threatening to kill herself over him, Alys."

"He's got to be hating it."

"Did you ever do anything like that when you were young?"

"Once," Alys said. "The guy would never see me again."

"He wasn't Roger," Olivia said.

They parted in the street outside the restaurant with a hug and promises not to wait so long before they saw each other. But Olivia knew they wouldn't keep them. "Call me and tell me what happens with you and Roger," Alys said. Was it possible? She seemed almost pleased. She had always been jealous when Olivia was happy and she wasn't, even though she pretended not to be.

"I will. Thanks again for lunch."

Olivia took a cab back to her office. She didn't even like her oldest friend. Alys was superficial and self-indulgent. She always had been. That was why Olivia hardly ever saw her.

But who else could she have told about her domestic crisis? So many of her friends were hers and Roger's friends together, and this was still a private matter. She couldn't tell her family, even Jenny, with whom she felt particularly close. She had pretended on the phone with Aunt Myra that everything was fine. She could just imagine the grapevine, the criticism, the I told you so's. The last thing she wanted was for her family to know she had another failure.

She realized with a wave of the most intense sadness who was the one she used to tell when something was bothering her, when she was unhappy or upset, when things were not right. Who had always been the one she went to: her confidant, her best friend. It had been Roger.

17

"I CAN'T BELIEVE you and I are having lunch together on a Saturday like normal people," Wendy said. She was happy and bubbling. She was wearing a black bodysuit under tight jeans with a hole in the knee. Roger smiled indulgently. He wished he weren't there. He had told Olivia he was going out to do his "things," but it hadn't fooled her. He felt as if Olivia were sitting in the restaurant watching them, and at the same time he was wondering where she was and what she was doing.

Wendy had chosen a small new trendy place in the Village that her friends liked. He was sure Olivia had never heard of it and he would be unlikely to run into anyone they knew. The restaurant was not crowded because people were already starting to go to the country for the weekends. Next weekend would be Memorial Day, and after that the summer exodus.

"I've taken a house in East Hampton for the summer," Wendy said. "It's a share with three other people, but I get every weekend. It's a much bigger house than the one we had last year. And it has a pool. There are lots of parties to go to."

"You'll enjoy it," Roger said. "You should be with people your own age."

"They're not all my age." She tilted her head. "You could come visit me."

"You know I can't do that."

"Just dreaming out loud."

"I wish you wouldn't," Roger said.

"Let's order," she said.

He looked at the menu. Everything was greasy and fatty and full of cholesterol. Three-egg omelets. Hamburgers and french fries. Macaroni and cheese. Old-fashioned meatloaf with gravy.

"This stuff looks like what my mother used to make," he said.

"It's the new trend in food," Wendy said cheerfully. "Comfort food. Don't you love it?"

"I didn't like it much the first time," he said. "But except for fabulous chocolate chip cookies, my mother was a terrible cook."

"I didn't know that."

"I didn't know it either. I thought that was what food was supposed to taste like." He waited for her to laugh, but she didn't.

"Does Olivia cook?" she asked.

"I don't want to talk about her, Wendy," he said uncomfortably. Ever since they had been caught, she had started asking more questions about Olivia, and whenever she did he felt as if she were intruding on something private.

"Does she know you're with me today?"

"Probably," he said. Talking about Olivia made it even worse.

Wendy had begged him to have dinner with her in a restaurant, so he had compromised on lunch. He was trying to break off with her slowly, wean her away, not just for her but for himself. But ever since he had told Wendy that Olivia knew about them, there had been a shift in their relationship. Wendy seemed to think that now that the thing he had most feared had happened, and the world had not ended, he hadn't gone anywhere, she had a chance to win him for herself.

He had told her that if Olivia found out about them the affair would be over, but here he was. Of course that exposed his weakness. It only fed her optimism and her stubbornness. He had stopped pretending he loved her; he said nothing. But she attributed that to nervousness on his part. He had stopped seeing her on their regular schedule, but she could understand why that was wise. He did still see her.

They ordered hamburgers and beer. When their food came they sat there for a while in silence while he tried to think of something neutral to say. "You're not eating," he said finally.

"I'm not very hungry." She smiled at him. He supposed she was thinking that next they would go to her apartment, but he had no real enthusiasm to go there; he just wanted to get away. He felt unaccountably lonely. They had never had a conversation that wasn't either a highly charged prelude to sex or a discussion about their relationship, and now over a simple lunch he didn't even know how to talk to her.

"You can do a lot better than hanging around with me," Roger said. "You're so pretty and bright. There must be men falling all over you."

"Oh, yes. There always were. But it never worked out."

"I'm wasting your time," he said.

"I love you."

"I wish you didn't," he said.

"But I do."

Why don't you just strangle me, he thought. "Do you want coffee?" he asked.

"Sure."

The waiter took away their barely touched food. "Something wrong with this, folks?"

"No, it was fine."

"Deep-dish apple pie with ice cream? Rice pudding?"

"Just two coffees."

The waiter left. "Are you having sex with her?" Wendy asked.

He didn't answer.

"Has she forgiven you? Is she pretending I don't exist?"

"You exist, all right."

"I'll bet the sex with her isn't as good as with me."

"This is an inappropriate discussion," Roger said.

"I want to know."

"There's no sex," Roger said. "I sleep in the den. We try not to step on land mines."

Wendy brightened. "Is she going to leave you?"

"That makes you happy, doesn't it?"

"Of course. Then you and I could be together."

"I don't want to start with anyone again," Roger said. "I want what I have."

"I don't understand," Wendy said, frowning.

"I know."

"I realize you and I never had a chance to really know each other," Wendy said. "It was all so passionate and so much fun. It was even romantic in a crazy way. But we were always rushing. Now you could stay with me longer. She doesn't know when you come home. You could stay overnight with me. If you knew me you might want me more than you want her. Just give me a try."

Poor Wendy, he thought. "You and I could never live together," he said lightly. "Gregory would scratch me to death."

"You'll win him over. I'll win you over. You'll see."

He was rescued by the arrival of the waiter with the coffee. For a minute or two they pretended to concentrate on it. He wondered if he was the only man in the world who didn't know how to get rid of a woman. If he didn't watch out, Olivia would be the one who left him. He knew he should be more forceful with Wendy, but he was afraid to because a part of him still wanted her. His ambivalence was his worst enemy.

"I don't have much more time," he said, looking at his watch.

"Come to my apartment," she whispered.

"I . . ."

"Just for a minute. I have something to show you."

"What?"

"It's a surprise." She ran her fingers through her thick shiny hair and smiled at him coquettishly. He wished she weren't so pretty. "You have no idea what it is, but you won't be disappointed."

He paid the check and they left.

In the cab Wendy put her head on his shoulder and her hand on his thigh. "I'm your biker babe," she murmured. "Your motorcycle mama. I belong to you."

Her doorman greeted them, as always. Roger wondered, as he did now every time he saw him, what he had said to Olivia. He thought how hurt Olivia had been and he could hardly bear to look at the man, not that it had been the doorman's fault.

As soon as he and Wendy entered her apartment, she started taking his clothes off. "I'm going to ride with you," she said, "and do anything you want." She was kissing him and rubbing up against him, and then she was taking off her own clothes at the same time. "Any bitch tries to put her hands on you, I'm going to kill her. You're the best. I'm yours. All yours."

She led him into the bedroom. In spite of his resolve and the reluctance he had felt in the restaurant he realized he desired her almost as much as he had before getting caught. Her body was as enticing as ever; it was only her emotions that frightened him away. Wendy lay on the bed on her back, her pale skin nacreous in the soft afternoon light.

"Look," she said.

Right above her pubic hair she had gotten a tattoo. In the middle of a small red heart and green and purple flowers it said *Roger.*

He was suddenly impotent.

She thought it was temporary and was all over him, fondling, coaxing, taking him in her mouth, but he pulled away. It was hopeless. He thought that if his frightened, shriveled dick could dive right up into his body cavity it would have, testicles and all. He stared at the tattoo of his name on her belly and he felt so invaded that he could hardly breathe. He sat up and retrieved his clothes.

"What is it?" Wendy asked.

"I have to go."

"You'll be all right soon," she said.

"How could you do that?" he asked, gesturing accusingly.

She smiled. "It didn't hurt much. I did it for you."

He was at the door, dressed, fleeing. She followed him, still naked. "Don't do anything else for me," he said. "Do you understand? I don't appreciate that."

"Oh, Roger, you're so silly."

"I mean it."

"I thought you would think it was sexy."

"Not to me," he said.

"Oh," she said. "Well." Then she started to laugh.

"What's so funny?" He had always suspected she was crazy, but now he was sure of it.

"It's just a *stick-on,*" she said. "It will come off in two or three days. I didn't think you'd freak out."

He thought he was probably on the verge of freaking out about everything lately. He felt like an idiot, humiliated. He had never been impotent before, and he had no interest in trying again to see if he wasn't. He only wanted to escape. When he left Wendy's apartment her laughter followed him down the hall.

"Come back!" she called, and then he heard it turn into tears.

He kept on going.

18

It was summer, hot and unbearable in New York, and almost time for Olivia to take Roger on his significant-birthday trip to the Plaza Athénée Hotel in Paris. The idea that had once seemed so sentimental and generous now seemed to her like a silly charade. Maybe she should call it off. His way of dealing with it had been to avoid talking about it, but she still had the tickets and the reservation. How were they supposed to travel—as friends? To be his friend or his lover was the same thing in her mind, so both had betrayed her. Why should she give him this reward? She didn't want to pay for Roger's half. She didn't want to go with him at all.

Now she remembered how hot it was in Paris in the summer, how in many places there was no air-conditioning, and wondered why they hadn't thought of that in the first place. When she had planned the trip she had told the travel agent to be sure their room had a double bed. Now, if they did go, she would have to ask for twin beds, an embarrassing change, letting a stranger know more than he should about them, but a suite was too expensive in a place she didn't want to be in the first place.

He would remember his fiftieth birthday for the rest of his life. It should have been wonderful; she had wanted to make it that way. It was his fault, not hers, that he would remember it as something strained and sad.

In the time that had passed since she had confronted him she had managed to put a kind of protective coating over her wounded spirit. There were hours that she was without pain, even hours that she didn't think about him. She knew there were other women who could put something like Roger's affair with Wendy out of their minds and say, Oh, well, that's just the way he is; but she wasn't one of them. She wondered if she would ever again be the relaxed and happy person she had been before.

"We should talk about Paris," Roger said, finally, over dinner.

"I know."

"I'd like us to go, but I don't want you to pay for it. You shouldn't give me a present. I want to pay for both of us."

"You really still want us to go?"

"I thought . . . maybe . . . we could use the trip as a chance to start over," he said.

"Reconcile?"

"Yes."

"I've never fought with another woman for a man," Olivia said. "I don't know how. It's not in my nature. Why should I have to do it?"

"You wouldn't be." He looked injured. "This has nothing to do with Wendy."

"What does that mean?"

"I'm not sleeping with her anymore," Roger said. "It's completely finished between us. I'm just doing a little final persuasion to get her to realize that."

"Not sleeping with her is a good hint," Olivia said.

They looked at each other. "I wish none of this had ever happened," Roger said.

"So do I." But that doesn't mean it didn't, she thought.

"Think about Paris," Roger said.

"Like a second honeymoon, or a blind date?"

"Like a courtship. There's no one in the world I'd rather spend this birthday with than you."

"I'll think about it," Olivia said. How could she not? It was on her mind all the time anyway.

Kenny called. His cheerful voice seemed like a greeting from another, almost forgotten, life. "What are you doing next weekend?" he asked.

"Nothing much. Where are you?"

"Santa Barbara. Pam and I are eloping next weekend. We just decided. You have to come to the wedding."

"Congratulations!" Olivia said. "I'm glad. But if you're planning it and inviting people, it's not eloping."

"We like to call it that." He chuckled. She had never heard him so upbeat. "Should I put you on the list?"

"I don't know if I can come to California on such short notice," she said reluctantly. The tension she had been living through these last months had left her feeling exhausted and drained.

"We're getting married in New York," Kenny said. "We want the family there, and New York is closer than Santa Barbara."

"That's really sweet, Kenny," she said, touched. "But the whole family's away. Why do you have to elope?"

"We want to. And they're almost all coming. Jenny and Paul, Melissa and Bill, Nick and Lynne, Uncle David, Uncle Seymour and Aunt Iris, Aunt Myra, even Taylor."

"Taylor?" Taylor had always hated New York, which she called New York City—there were too many people, too much traffic, it was big, ugly, dirty, dangerous. She hadn't been there since Aunt Julia's funeral, and when she and Tim went to Sam's bar mitzvah in Cambridge they had taken a flight that didn't stop in New York.

"Taylor and Tim have to see Uncle Seymour about the store. She's inherited all Grady's stock. Now you and Taylor have more shares than anybody else in the family."

"I didn't realize that."

"You're rich. You should enjoy yourself."

"I'll try," Olivia said.

"I'll put Roger's name down too," Kenny said. "The dinner and dancing after the wedding will be at the Rainbow Room, on the sixty-fifth floor, and the ceremony itself will be at the Radio City Suite on the floor below. I was lucky we could get so many people into the Rainbow Room at such short notice, but it's summer, and also I know somebody. Next Saturday at five o'clock."

"I'm looking forward to meeting Pam," Olivia said.

"She wants to meet you too. See you then."

When Olivia told Roger she would appreciate it if he came with her, he agreed immediately. Of course; he was on his good behavior. She hoped the family wouldn't notice they were different together, and then she realized that they had seen him so seldom they would never know.

The Radio City Suite was Art Deco, cozy and elegant, decorated with Bakelite radios from the 1930s. Huge windows overlooked the city spread out below, simmering in the late afternoon sun, but in here it was cool and nice. There was the main room for the ceremony, where Kenny and Pam had had them put up a *chuppah* made of white silk with flowers wound around the poles, and there was another room where the bride could dress. Waiters were walking around with trays of champagne. The cousins were all happy to see each other again, and hugged and kissed. They didn't seem to mind having been pulled away from their summer country vacations to make this unexpected trip, or if they did they were hiding it well.

Kenny, beaming, was walking around introducing Pam. She was an attractive blonde: fresh and trim and active-looking—a tennis player marrying Winnie the Pooh. There was also an air of great sweetness about her. She was wearing a white suit with a little veil and carrying a bouquet of flowers, but she didn't seem like a timid bride meeting his family for the first time; she seemed like a warm and happy hostess who wanted them all to enjoy themselves.

"I'm so glad to meet you," she kept saying, "Now you go on and have a good time."

"She's perfect for Kenny," Olivia whispered to Roger.

It was a small wedding. There was most of the family, Pam had invited three people and that was it: twenty in all. Kenny's son Jason was there, the only nonadult who had been included, wearing a suit and tie with a flower in his lapel and a big smile. He was probably relieved that his stepmother-to-be was old enough to be his mother, not his sister, unlike the stepmothers of most of his friends.

The ceremony was short, and when the bride and groom kissed they were so attracted they couldn't let go. Everybody laughed good-naturedly. Kenny had lipstick smeared all over his mouth, and when he finally wiped it off everyone laughed again.

I remember when Roger and I were like that, Olivia thought, getting depressed. Except I never even bothered wearing lipstick.

It seems so long ago, before we settled down and thought we knew what life would be like forever. She glanced at Roger and looked away.

They all went upstairs to the Rainbow Room. It also was elegant and Art Deco, but vast, with enormous windows for the spectacular view, a circular dance floor and tables set on two tiers. She and Roger had been there before; the other cousins hadn't. There were two big round tables with place cards, in their own little area, for the wedding party. Olivia was delighted to see that she and Roger were sitting with Jenny and Melissa and Taylor, and their husbands; and they looked glad and relieved too. They would always be the girl cousins from Mandelay. . . .

They talked about their vacations and their kids; they said they were pleased to see Kenny settled down with what seemed like such a nice woman; they basked in their small circle of closeness and familiarity, and drank champagne and ate, and when the orchestra came they danced with their husbands. No one danced with anyone they were not married to. And as the evening went on and the sun set and the city started to twinkle, they began to seem like couples on a date in this romantic place, on this sentimental occasion, away from the responsibilities of their normal lives.

Olivia danced with Roger because they didn't want to look different from the others. She had not been this close to him physically for two months, and part of her yearned for him while another part of her wanted to push him away so she wouldn't need him so much. She and Roger never danced together; he didn't like it because he said he wasn't good at it. But tonight he was courtly and she was gracious, and it didn't matter that he couldn't dance very well. They didn't speak.

Then they all went back to their tables and Pam and Kenny cut the first slice of their wedding cake. Jenny looked at her watch. "We're driving back tonight," she said. "I don't want to leave the kids too long with the housekeeper."

"But it's such a long trip," Olivia protested.

"I know," Paul said cheerfully. "It's a horror. And I'm the one who has to drive."

"We're going back tonight, too," Melissa said. "Jake has a

swimming competition tomorrow. Besides, I miss them when they're not around."

"I want to have a baby," Taylor said.

They looked at her, surprised. Taylor had always said she never would.

"Soon, when I'm off Prozac, we'll try," Taylor said. She glanced at Tim, who smiled at her. "I don't have to be a bad mother like mine was. I can learn." She paused. "I knew Grady would never have children. Now I need to before it's too late. A family shouldn't just stop."

There was a silence. Olivia knew they were all thinking about Grady's suicide. She was sure that despite her protestations of ignorance, Taylor on some level had understood that Grady was gay. Or had she really believed him when he said he couldn't trust anyone enough to marry, that like her, he was only afraid to carry on the family mistakes? Why would he have tried to fool her anyway, the only person he did trust; his sister, his soul mate? Taylor must have known he wasn't straight . . . hadn't she?

A family shouldn't just stop. Olivia thought about herself. She had never wanted children, still didn't, but Taylor's words hurt. She hoped the rest of them weren't thinking about her: the maverick, the disappointer. She knew Taylor was only thinking about herself and Grady.

"You would have an adorable baby, Taylor," she said.

Pam came back in a black linen dress to say goodbye and she and Kenny left. The party was breaking up. Aunt Myra came over and gave Olivia a kiss. "I didn't even get a chance to talk to you," Aunt Myra said.

"I know."

"Hello, Roger, how are you?"

"I'm fine."

"They're going to China on their honeymoon," Aunt Myra said, and giggled. "I wouldn't want to go to China, would you? I hear the living conditions are just terrible."

"I would," Olivia said.

"Oh, you. You're going to Paris, that's what you like."

Roger put his arm lightly around Olivia's shoulders. "We're just sybarites," he said, and smiled.

"Sounds sensible to me," Aunt Myra said, and moved on. Roger dropped his arm.

I wonder if any of the others is as big a fake as we are, Olivia thought.

"We're going to Cape Cod tomorrow," Taylor said to her. "I want to see the Atlantic Ocean. Can you have brunch with me before we go?"

"Of course. Do you want to come to the house?"

"Too much trouble for you. You pick a restaurant."

"There's a nice little place near your hotel," Olivia said, and gave them the address.

"Noon," Taylor said.

"Do you want me to come with you tomorrow?" Roger asked when they got home.

"I don't care," Olivia said. She was very tired.

"You like to be alone with your family," he said.

"And you can run to see Wendy."

"I told you that's over. Besides, she goes away every weekend. You're perfectly safe. Not that you aren't already. I thought I could go to the gym."

"The gym."

"We're going to eat a lot in Paris," Roger said.

"If we go."

"If we go. I hope we do. Hoping, I'm going to try to get svelte for you."

"All right," Olivia said. "You were nice enough to come to the wedding. You don't have to go to the brunch."

"I enjoyed it," he said.

"No, you didn't."

"I sort of did."

"All those years, were we together too much, you and I?" Olivia asked. "Was that the problem?"

"It was never your fault," Roger said. "Don't ever think it was."

"Sometimes I wonder. I have to."

"You mustn't blame yourself," he said.

Then I have to blame you, she thought. That almost makes it worse, because then what can I do to keep you from having another affair with someone else? "Goodnight," she said softly, and went to her room.

The restaurant where she met Taylor and Tim looked like the dining room of a small English country inn. There were pots of strawberry jam on the tables, and a waitress brought big, warm, fresh popovers. "Remember these from Mandelay?" Olivia said, tearing one apart.

Taylor smiled. "You always pulled the inside out and ate it first," she said. "And left the outside. You still do."

"It's the best part."

"Not to me."

They had hot, strong coffee and scrambled eggs. "We saw Uncle Seymour," Taylor said. "I have Grady's stock now."

"I know. You and I have more stock than anyone else in the family. We could get together and run things."

"I don't want to run a store."

"Neither do I."

"Grady liked to watch over things," Taylor said. "But I think they're doing a very good job."

"Grady didn't seem to think so," Olivia said. "He seemed . . . upset."

"He was hurt," Taylor said. "He asked Uncle Seymour to give him a job in the family business. He didn't want to be a stuntman anymore. He had lost his nerve. I knew that. Grady couldn't get work for a long time. He wanted to learn about the store. Uncle Seymour and Charlie said there was no place for him. That means they didn't want him. They were keeping it all for Charlie's son Tony. But they could have hired Grady too. There were lots of things he could have done. Grady was very smart."

So that was what Grady had been thinking about when he came to the house for lunch with me so soon before he died, Olivia thought. It was what he had seen Uncle Seymour about, and why he seemed so bitter.

"It was a waste," Tim said. "It was all a waste."

"I'm still stuck with his house," Taylor said. "I can't sell it. I have to pay the mortgage every month. I haven't disposed of his ashes yet. Why do people die and leave you these things to do?"

You mean, why do they kill themselves, Olivia thought.

"Grady left me and I can't even grieve in peace," Taylor said, as if reading her thoughts. "I'm still angry at him."

"Of course you are."

"People think you'll be sorry when they kill themselves, but you're not. You're too angry at them."

"It's the same thing," Olivia said.

"I wish you had learned to sign better," Taylor said. "Talking makes me tired."

"I wish I had too," Olivia said. Taylor does all the work, she thought, and we do nothing. She signed *I'm sorry,* and *I love you,* some of the few signs she still knew, and then she leaned over and put her arm around Taylor and kissed her downy cheek. "I love you. You'll always be my little brat cousin. I miss him so much."

They drank more coffee in silence.

"The week before Grady died," Taylor said, "he sent me a tape of the movie *Torch Song Trilogy.* And he sent me a script of it so I could follow the words. He wrote a note with it. It said: 'I used to be Matthew Broderick, now I'm Harvey Fierstein. Ain't life a bitch.' "

Poor lonely, conflicted Grady—his regrets, his yearnings, so different from the way he presented himself. He couldn't have been much clearer about his secret life, Olivia thought. And he didn't want to get old. Not being young and cute anymore must have changed the tenor of all his relationships. So Taylor knew.

"Did you watch the tape?"

"No," Taylor said. "I threw it away, and the script, too. I didn't want to see a movie about some old drag queen."

"It wasn't about some old drag queen," Olivia said. "It was about a man who only wanted his family to love and accept him. You shouldn't have thrown it away."

"Well, I did."

"And he never asked you about it?"

"No. We never said a word."

19

WHENEVER OLIVIA AND ROGER were on an airplane together he would reach over and hold her hand during takeoff. She didn't know whether he did it because he thought she was afraid or because he was; and it was one of the few things she had never asked him about, because she didn't want to know and because it seemed too fragile an issue to mention. It seemed so sentimental, so protective, that she preferred to think he was taking care of her, even though she had never been afraid of flying. So now, beginning the night flight to Paris, their plane hurtled along the runway and Roger covered her hand with his without even thinking about it. They lifted safely into the air, and she was suddenly filled with such unexpected excitement and hope that it was as if they had left more than the earth behind.

Their plane was a closed-off and protected capsule to adventure. Roger let go of her hand, as he always did when it became apparent that once again they would live. They adjusted the paraphernalia of comfort and drank champagne.

"Happy birthday weekend," she said, and lifted her glass to him, smiling.

"To us," he said, and smiled back.

After dinner he slept, and she tried to. She thought about the past and edited it to remember only the happy things. Whatever happens, she thought, we've always loved Paris, and we'll have a good time there. Then she dozed, and they woke up to coffee, dawn and France.

The Plaza Athénée Hotel was legendary to her. They had never actually stayed there before, but on their trips they always tried to have a drink at the Relais Plaza bar and watch the people. A large, elegant limestone building, with tall French windows giving way to tiny metal balconies with red awnings above them, overlooking Avenue Montaigne with its expensive shops, the limousines parked in front, the imposing lobby, the well-dressed guests, the feel of money—it was definitely a hotel for grownups. Rich grownups.

The hotel was quieter in the summer, though, and there were lower-priced summer special rooms, one of which they had. The furniture was antique, there was air-conditioning and a television set and a mini-bar. The two beds were separated with a night table in between.

They unpacked. "A shower and a walk, or a nap first?" Roger asked.

"Oh, I'm not tired," Olivia said. "Let's hit the streets."

They walked until it got too hot, wandering the way they used to in their happier days, and stopped for lunch in a little cafe they happened to come upon, where they had sandwiches and beer. There was a long line of people trying to get into the Louvre. She was relieved that they had been there several times before and that today they didn't even have to pretend to seek out culture. The winding little streets were culture, and the old houses, and the wide avenues, and the statues, and the huge, beautiful, historical buildings whose facades were kept so clean, unlike the ones in New York.

It was nice to relax with nothing to do but find things that seemed like fun, and after lunch they went to the Left Bank to look in antique stores and finally walked along beside the Seine, watching people, most of whom looked like tourists watching them. Roger wanted to have a drink in an outdoor cafe, so they did that. Olivia had mineral water, Roger had a small carafe of wine, and they looked at the view over the river.

He was her favorite companion. She couldn't imagine anyone she would rather wander around with. And yet the thought nibbled at the edge of her mind that all this was a temporary dream.

Something else had happened. It wasn't really like old times. It was more like a date with someone who had been her love a long time ago and had been away. If that was the case, she should be asking him what he had been doing; but of course she knew.

"What are you thinking about?" he asked.

What indeed? "That I have to buy you a birthday present," Olivia said.

"I don't want a present."

"I saw something you'll like."

"You're my present," Roger said. "Being here with me."

"Well, then, a souvenir."

Of course she should buy him something. She had been ambivalent about buying him anything at all, which was why she had waited so long. Now she felt sentimental about all the years they had been together, and touched that he was trying to recapture their closeness, and she wanted to. There had been a funny old microscope in one of the antique shops they had browsed in and Roger had liked it. She would go back tomorrow and if it wasn't too expensive he could have it for his desk.

"A souvenir," he said, and smiled.

He ordered another carafe. I wonder if he's nervous being here with me, she thought, or if he's just on vacation. In the old days, after so much walking and wine they would have gone back to their room to rest and make love. It was so different now. At least they could rest, and she could worry about the other possibility later. She was, finally, exhausted.

"I'd like to take a nap for an hour," she said when he had finished his wine.

"Did you get any sleep on the plane?"

"Not much."

"You know how you are with jet lag," Roger said. "If you lie down this late in the day I can never get you up. I made reservations tonight at a brasserie called Benoit that's supposed to be very fashionable. Nine o'clock. Will you be able to wake up?"

"I promise."

When they went back to their room they each automatically headed for the bed that was on the side where they usually slept in their big bed at home. We're like two comfortable old animals, Olivia thought. We didn't even discuss it. Roger set the alarm and then suddenly went to sleep so fast she wondered if he was pretending.

She looked over at his familiar form under the covers. It had been a long time since they had slept in the same room, and just having him there made her feel safe. But strangely she wasn't actually attracted to him. What she felt for him was more a deep and abiding love than a real sensuality. There were, of course, a number of reasons: exhaustion and self-protection came first to mind. She had always enjoyed sex with him, they made each other happy, but it had been a long time since she had regarded him in that haze of lust they had shared in their early years. She had always assumed it was the normal progression of things and not worth worrying about. Their love had developed and grown. They had always remained affectionate, which was more than she could say about a lot of other couples she had observed.

This faded passion is the same way Roger felt about me before he met her, Olivia thought sadly. And it's how he still feels. I know him so well. No matter what he's done to make him seem a stranger, I still know him. I acknowledged those subtle changes so casually, but they must have concerned him a lot. I didn't think lust was that crucial. He apparently did. What are we going to do about our lives? What will become of us?

The brasserie where they had dinner was warm and cozy and very French in an old-fashioned way. They had reserved at the other restaurants where they would dine for the next two evenings and left the rest to spur-of-the-moment decisions. Because it wasn't August yet the places they liked or wanted to try were still open before France's summer vacation overtook the city with a vengeance and closed almost everything as the Parisians fled.

They had fish and shared a bottle of wine, facing each other across a small table. Olivia wondered if this reconciliation they were attempting was supposed to involve lovemaking too, and when Roger ordered another bottle of wine she was sure he was thinking about the same thing. He seemed as nervous as a honeymooner.

"We'll get drunk and sick," she said and immediately was

sorry she had said something so unromantic, although it was true.

"We won't drink it all," Roger said.

"Let's take everything slowly."

He looked at her. "Of course."

"My feelings are so complicated," she said. "I don't even know what I feel from hour to hour."

"That's normal."

"Do you feel that way?"

"Sometimes. Oh boy, do I!"

They smiled at each other. "I love you so much," Olivia said. "You're my best friend."

"And you're mine."

"Are you having a good birthday weekend so far?"

"Very."

They were lowering the level in the second bottle, he more than she. "Let's pretend we just met," Roger said.

"Then I'd have to tell you my life story."

"Or make it up."

"I'd probably just omit the things you shouldn't know."

"I'd try to impress you," he said.

"Of course. I'd flirt with you."

"I'd like that."

"How could I tell you about my past?" Olivia said. "So much of my past is you."

There was a silence while he seemed to be taking this in. Then he took her hand across the table and held it. "I'm glad you and I didn't just meet," he said. "I don't want to have missed anything we had together."

By the time they finished dinner he was quite drunk. Then he insisted on having a *poire* to finish the meal. They got back to their room and looked at the two beds, which seemed very small, and at the distance between them, which seemed very large, although a few years ago it would never have been an issue. "I think I drank too much," Roger said.

"I did, too."

He put his arms around her like a cuddly bear and put his head on her shoulder. "We're going to have a great weekend," he said.

"You'll see," and then he got into his bed and pulled up the covers and was asleep.

The next morning he had a hangover. She wasn't surprised. She didn't feel so great but at least she was functioning, and she felt much better after a big café au lait from room service. "You sleep," she said to him. "I'm going out to get your birthday present."

"I'll be fine in a few hours," he murmured.

"I'll come back and we'll go to lunch at about one o'clock if you're up to it."

"Okay."

The sun was shining, and as soon as she started walking through the fresh morning streets Olivia began to smile. She noticed a few men smiled back at her, as if she had meant it for them instead of for the nice day in Paris, and she was pleased because it meant she was still attractive, still desirable, still a force to be reckoned with. She walked briskly all the way to the Left Bank, to the antique shop where she had seen the old microscope the day before, and to her delight it was still there and what was more, it was even affordable.

"I hope you'll take a traveler's check?" she asked the proprietor.

"Of course."

She filled it out and handed him her passport for identification.

"Miss . . . Oak-ren?"

"Okrent. Although Oak-ren is a lot prettier," Olivia said. "Would you wrap it, please?"

"Of course."

"Is that *you?*" an American-accented voice said. A young man came toward her through the gloom, emerging from behind crystal chandeliers and tapestry-covered chairs, glimmering a little in cream-colored linen Armani pants and a white T-shirt, his skin city pale, his long, straight black hair hanging on a slant over his forehead, his gray eyes gleaming like moonstones. "Dr. Okrent?"

Even though he was out of context, she realized in an instant who he was. Nobody else she ever saw looked like him. He was her client Marc Delon from New York, whose sturdy dalmatian she had been treating for two years. He had endeared himself to her by having named his dog Spot, because it was so silly, and also because he obviously loved Spot so much.

"Marc!"

"So this is where you come for your summer vacation," he said.

"Not exactly. It's just a long weekend. How's Spot?"

"He's fine. How's Wozzle?"

"She's great. What are you doing here?"

"I'm buying a birthday present for my grandmother."

He's so young, Olivia thought. He has a grandmother. I don't even have parents. "I mean in Paris, not this store."

"Well, I came to visit her. And you?"

"It's Roger's birthday."

"Cool."

Cool, she thought with a twinge. *That's what Wendy said.* "I bought him an old microscope," she said. "What are you getting for your grandmother?"

"I thought this box. Do you like it?" He held it out to her earnestly, hoping for her approval. It was small and perfect, made of fitted mother-of-pearl pieces.

"It's lovely," Olivia said. "Does she collect them?"

"She collects everything. There isn't an inch of any surface in her apartment that doesn't have little things arranged on it, and no dust at all. It's terrifying."

"Do you like her?"

"Yes, I do. I love her. Do you still have your grandparents?"

"No, I'm afraid not. You're lucky."

"I think so. We're having a big family dinner tonight."

"Is it a significant birthday?"

"Every birthday is significant at her age," he said, "But no, she's seventy-eight. It's a chance for the family to get together. I see my cousins, whom I hardly ever see now that I've been living in New York."

"I know," Olivia said. "I like seeing my cousins too, and we never get together unless it's an occasion."

"Are you having a party for Roger?"

"The two of us are going to the Tour d'Argent. He wants the view and the duck."

"I've never been there," Marc said.

"Is it too touristy?"

"Oh no, just too expensive. I'll go when I sell my book."

"You've written a book?"

"I'm writing one." The proprietor handed them their wrapped packages. "Would you like to have a coffee with me, Dr. Oakren?" Marc asked.

"Only if you call me Olivia. We're on vacation."

"Okay, Olivia. I know a place right near here."

He took her to a small neighborhood bistro with round marble-topped tables and straw chairs set outside on the sidewalk. The street was narrow, and a boy was playing with his dog, throwing it a ball. They ordered two coffees and watched the boy with his dog for a while.

"I miss Wozzle," Olivia said.

"I miss Spot. Do you want me to tell you about my book?"

"Yes, please!"

"It's about how children's stories influence our lives as adults, and what their messages are. Some are inspiring and allay fears, *but* some of them have actually warped and corrupted our self-esteem and sense of adventure, as they were probably meant to. Cautionary tales—you wonder what kind of people wrote them! My research goes back over almost two hundred years—it's quite historical. I cover some classic children's stories and also books people remember having read or had read to them as kids. I ask people: What's your favorite story from childhood, and then: What's the worst one you remember? Usually the horrible ones are the ones that sent the message that lingered. The stories they wrote for girls were even more threatening to individuality than the ones for boys, although the boys' stories were certainly about conformity in their own way."

"How strange," Olivia said.

"It's not strange really when you see how the stories reflected what society demanded of its children and its adults during each period. A bedtime story is basically written as a learning tool for a malleable little child. Some of them can make you very angry."

"That's so interesting."

"I was originally going to write the book with my girlfriend. She was going to do the girls' stories and I was going to do the boys' stories. But we weren't getting along and then we broke up, and she didn't want to write it at all. By then I'd gotten interested in her side of it too, so I decided to research and write the whole thing."

"I'm impressed," Olivia said. She wondered why he and his girlfriend hadn't gotten along. He was so unusually attractive, and so bright, and had such a sweet way about him, that if she were his age, which she guessed to be no more than thirty, she would have had a tremendous crush on him. Maybe he was hard to live with. Maybe the girlfriend was difficult. Maybe he cheated. Certainly he would have opportunities. You never knew about people's private lives. No one would suspect what hers was like.

"Would you like a croissant?" Marc asked. "They're good here."

"I'll share one with you."

"And another coffee?"

"My head will fly off. French coffee . . ."

"Put hot water in it," Marc said. "A lot of people do." He ordered the croissant and coffee and hot water.

What a very nice body he had, she thought; the hard, smooth muscles under his T-shirt, the slim waist. She wondered if he worked out or was just lucky. He probably liked sports—maybe skiing in winter, rollerblades in the park in spring. Here in the sunlight he was not as pale as he had always seemed indoors; his skin had a fresh, fair color to it.

He put some hot water into her coffee for her and cut their croissant neatly in half. "I'm so glad we met here," he said. "I always wanted to know you better. You fascinated me every time I came to your office."

"I did?"

"The beautiful doctor in the white coat. It's your domain."

"And rightly so," she said lightly.

"Exactly."

"Well, here I am," Olivia said. "What do you want to know?"

"Tell me a story your mother or your father told you or read to you as a child that influenced your life." He fixed her with his beautiful moonstone gray eyes and a mischievous expression. "Inspired you or warped you, either one."

"You're bad."

"No, I'm not."

"Well, my mother read to me a lot."

"What sticks in your mind?"

"I don't know," Olivia said. "Let me think. Meanwhile, tell me what got you interested in these stories in the first place."

"You're evading."

"I thought you would find it flattering," she said teasingly. "Most men like to talk about themselves and their work." I'm flirting with him, she thought, surprised. But also she was reluctant to reveal too much about herself. After all, she was the authority figure back in New York. What he was asking her to remember and share could turn out to be very visceral.

"I'll tell you how I got interested," Marc said. "Two years ago when I came to Paris with my parents to visit my grandmother, my mother began reminiscing about the books her mother had read to her as a child. There was one that had always upset and frightened her, and she said it still upset her to think about it. It was the story of a little girl who accidentally knocked over a vase that belonged to her parents, and broke it. When her mother asked her if she had broken the vase she was afraid of being punished, which she knew she would be, and she denied it. So every day her mother asked her again to confess, and when she wouldn't, her mother gave away one of the little girl's dolls.

"Day after day her dolls were taken away, until finally the only one that was left was the little girl's very favorite one, a humble and ragged and much-loved doll she had owned since she was a baby. No punishment could be as bad as losing that one last doll. So she confessed to having broken the vase.

"My mother couldn't remember how it ended. She thought that since the little girl had already been given her punishment, for breaking the vase, and for lying, and all her other dolls were gone, the ending was that she got to keep the one. She said it also might have ended where the mother returned the dolls to the little girl, but she couldn't remember. To me that sounds more logical, since cautionary tales had so-called happy endings. But all she did remember was that the book made her miserable, and that her mother read it to her often, and that for the rest of her life she always told the truth."

"What an awful story," Olivia said. She was upset for the little girl in the book and for the child who had been his mother. She thought of her own mother, and of Grady and Taylor and Big Earl. "Children are so helpless," she murmured.

"My mother asked my grandmother about it, and she didn't know what the fuss was about. She told my mother: 'But you always loved that book.' "

And Grady never fought back when his mother hit him, Olivia thought. "How did the book end?"

"We don't know. Their copy is long gone, and they don't remember the name of it. It's probably out of print—this happened over fifty years ago. If I decide later that I really need to know, I'll go dig it up somehow. But my book will be written with anecdotes and case histories as well as actual text, so it doesn't matter. What matters is how it affected her as an adult. She always remembered the fear and the lesson. You understand my grandmother didn't mean to torment her. My grandmother was probably a little crazy, but so were all the mothers who read that book to their children and expected them to learn from it how to be good little girls. In my grandmother's house you didn't break the rules. You still don't."

"I'll tell you mine," Olivia said.

He leaned forward. "Good or bad?"

"Bad. My mother made this story up. She said it was my favorite, and I remember asking her to tell it to me. I couldn't have been older than four. It was the story of Spindle Legs the cow."

"Spindle Legs?"

"Well, you know cows have skinny legs." As she started to tell it she could picture herself again as a four-year-old in her pajamas, her mother a comforting presence in the lamplight, explaining to her what life was about.

"Spindle Legs was the best milk cow on the farm. She gave more milk than any other cow there. From time to time she would see the boy cows, and the girl cows who didn't give any more milk, being put on a cattle car to go away to see the world. 'I want to go too,' she told the farmer, 'I want to go away to see the world,' but the farmer wouldn't let her. Then she noticed that the cows who were allowed to go away to the city were the ones who couldn't give milk anymore. So Spindle Legs stopped giving milk. Just stopped. And finally, sure enough, she was put on a cattle car to go to the city. How exciting! But when she got there she discovered that they had all been taken to a slaughterhouse, where they were going to be killed.

"When she realized they were going to kill her she was very frightened and she begged: 'Please, don't kill me, I promise I'll give milk again. Lots of milk!' So her life was spared, and Spindle Legs went back to the farm, where she gave more milk than any other cow for the rest of her life."

Marc looked aghast. "Who wrote that story, Ilse Koch?"

"No, my mother."

"Wow." There was a pause while he looked at her with renewed interest and sympathy. "I can see how it must have affected you."

"In more ways than I can imagine," Olivia said.

"What was your mother like?"

"Afraid of everything."

"Conventional?"

"Very."

"Wanted you to take your preordained place in society and be an overachiever at it?"

"Exactly," Olivia said. "She never dreamed I'd become a vet."

"She didn't like that?"

"Not much. She didn't like animals."

"She didn't seem to like people much either," Marc said.

"I never thought of that," she said. She realized that she hadn't ever told Roger the story, it just hadn't occurred to her. "How did you get to speak English with such an American accent?" she asked.

"I've been in New York ten years."

"Still . . ."

"In the summers, when I was a teenager, my parents sent me to stay with a family in Iowa. They felt it was typically American. Plus, I have a good ear."

"Ah. And can you actually support yourself as a writer?"

"Miraculously, yes. I write for magazines. And I have simple tastes at the moment."

"I should read more magazines," she said apologetically.

"You haven't missed very much. I'll send you some tear sheets of my better pieces."

"I'd love to read them." She glanced at her watch. She hadn't realized it was so late. "Uh-oh, I have to get Roger for lunch."

He put some money on top of the bill in the saucer. "Thank you for spending some time with me. It was interesting and fun."

"It was for me, too." They looked at each other. It had been so long since she'd had an exciting conversation with a new person —a new man—that she didn't want to leave. She felt different: more alive. "I wish I could stay longer," she said reluctantly.

"I wish you could too. Maybe we can meet in New York sometime. Have coffee. Talk some more."

What would that be, she thought, a date? No, it's not possible. He knows I'm taken, and he's so much younger than I am. He'd probably like to become friends. I wouldn't mind that at all. There's something about him that's like fresh air. And I do love looking at him. "Maybe we can," she said.

She and Roger had lunch at the Relais Plaza in their hotel, watching the chic and elegant people. "So what did you do while I was sleeping off my excesses?" he asked pleasantly.

"Bought your present. And I ran into a client of mine in the antique store, so we went for coffee."

"Who?"

"Marc Delon. The dalmatian."

He thought for a moment. "Oh, the French kid."

He's not so French and he's not such a kid, Olivia thought. "Yes."

"That's nice," Roger said. There was something in his tone that was almost condescending, and it annoyed her.

He said I fascinated him, that I'm beautiful, that he wanted to know me better, she thought. He's writing a book. And he knows something about me that you don't know. "Yes," she said, "it was," and her tone was as casual as his.

In the afternoon they walked, stopped for an apéritif at Ma Bourgogne in the Place des Vosges, a cafe they had always liked, overlooking the little square park and the picturesque old houses that were now apartments, and came back to the hotel to get ready for dinner.

Olivia put on a sand-colored linen dress that looked wrinkled because it was supposed to. "I wonder what Aunt Myra would have to say about this," she said.

"Didn't you bring a travel iron?" Roger said, mimicking Aunt Myra's voice. "Don't they have pressing at your hotel?"

"Oh, is that the new look?"

He had ordered a bottle of champagne sent to their room, and Olivia gave him his present. She had wondered what to write on the card, and finally settled for a very banal *All my love, Olivia.* He was pleased with his gift and kissed her fondly, not passionately. They drank a toast to future birthdays, to be spent together in interesting places, put the rest of the champagne into their small refrigerator to drink later and took a taxi to the Tour d'Argent.

Looking at Roger across the table in the golden light, and out at the view of Notre Dame's illuminated stone gargoyles, and at the Seine moonlit below, Olivia thought how lucky they were. They had enough money and they were healthy, they could go where they wanted and do whatever they wanted to. They cared about the work that made it possible for them to do these things, and she had funds of her own besides. They had loved each other so much. Why couldn't he have left well enough alone?

"What are you thinking?" Roger asked.

"That we'll never have to worry about winning the lottery," Olivia said.

They had a lovely wine with the famous duck, and a bottle of champagne with dessert. Their dinner was very expensive, but Roger insisted on paying for it himself even though it was his birthday. At the next table there was a man a little older than Roger, with a woman Wendy's age and obviously not his daughter. They were looking at each other seductively, the young woman's long fingers playing with the stem of her wine glass in a way that seemed erotic. Olivia looked away.

Would things always remind her of his betrayal, even when they were trying to get close?

They went back to their hotel, and got ready for sleep, although neither of them was sleepy. They were both a little nervous. The night maid had closed the drapes, turned down their two beds and made the room lighting soft. Roger opened the bottle of champagne they had started before they left. "You looked very beautiful tonight," he said.

"Thank you."

He came close and put his arms around her, but this time it was not as a cuddly bear. "I love you," he said.

"I love you."

He took the glass out of her hand and put it on the table, and then he began to kiss her. They hadn't kissed like this for such a long time, and so much had happened, that there was something about it both familiar and strange. He slipped her robe off her shoulders, dropped his and, still kissing her, led her into her bed.

My bed, not his, Olivia thought. There must be some symbolism to this. But then, he always liked to do it on my side.

How long I've wanted this, and now . . .

Roger was kissing and stroking her, ready; and she caressed him, but not so ready; and then unexpectedly the image of Marc Delon slid into her mind. The body in her arms was Marc's, taut, slim and strong, and the face she saw behind her closed eyelids was his, fresh and young, his long black hair hanging down over his forehead and touching her breasts like gentle feathers. She was suddenly, instantly, aroused. The fingers exploring her were Marc's, and the tongue, and when he entered her she was wet and throbbing, trying to pull him further into her body, straining against him, wanting more, more. . . .

Two thrusts and Roger was out, finished. She wasn't even aware that he had come, so fast and mild was his ejaculation. She felt frustrated and angry, lost between her passion and her disappointment, waiting. He held her for a moment, but he seemed embarrassed. She realized he wasn't even going to try to take care of what he had started. He was probably nervous, she thought. He probably drank too much. Maybe he's not really attracted to me anymore. Then he kissed her forehead and went into the bathroom.

She lay there holding on to her fantasy, thinking about Marc Delon.

20

After Labor Day the city came back into its own. It was the start of a new season, no matter what the calendar and the thermometer said. There was excitement in the air again, things to do. Roger had lunch with Wendy.

He had been avoiding her during the summer as best he could. They had met for drinks three times, and lunch once, always platonically. Getting out of the office for lunch was as difficult for her as it was for him, she had said, since she was working very hard, hoping to get a promotion. She had not complained that he hadn't taken her to dinner, so he knew she was dating new men, probably ones she met in the Hamptons where she had rented her summer house. He was a little surprised that this woman whom he had known as a hysteric was getting herself together so well and so quickly, but he was relieved. Since he had run away from her apartment in impotent disgrace, he had been less than eager to try again.

They met at a steak house in midtown, where, she told him, she sometimes took clients. In her chic little corporate work suit she looked like she was playing another role for him, but he knew this one was real. Still, it was strange and therefore somewhat alluring.

"My boss likes me now," she said cheerfully.

"I didn't know he didn't," Roger said.

"He used to complain that I would leave the office for too long.

That's when I was meeting you. Of course, he's sort of a tyrant. Wants all us little serfs to be right there."

"You have to be, to produce," Roger said. He felt like her uncle, not her former lover.

"I know," Wendy said. She picked at her Caesar salad. "How are you and Olivia getting along?"

"All right," he said.

"Made-up and happy?"

"Sort of," he said. He supposed that was an accurate answer. They were back in their bedroom together, they treated each other affectionately and even had sex from time to time, but it had never gotten any better than it had been that unsatisfying night in Paris. He was too nervous. The more he worried about how it would be, the more it stayed the same.

"You could have had me," Wendy said. "Too bad."

He didn't answer.

"Men and guilt," she said.

"It isn't guilt," Roger said, annoyed. "It's loyalty. And I love her."

"You used to say you loved me."

I wish I had never said that, he thought, but he didn't respond.

"Men and lies," Wendy said, and smiled.

"You wanted me to lie," he said.

"Did I? Did we ever discuss it?"

"It was understood."

"I guess you're right."

The conversation had made him lose his appetite. Wendy always knew how to make him feel guilty. "I shouldn't have said that," he apologized. "It was cruel."

"But truthful. I knew it was pretend."

Pretend. What a childlike choice of words. She looked so vulnerable he wanted to kiss her. She looked like a little girl dressed in a stockbroker's suit. Did clients actually trust her? "You deserve a man who doesn't play-act at taking care of you," Roger said.

"I know."

"Did you ever consider going for professional help?"

"A therapist?" she asked.

"Yes."

"Because I was crazy enough to go out with you?"

"In a way."

"I've been in therapy for two years," she said sweetly. "I told her everything you and I did together."

"Oh, God." He hated the idea of her telling a stranger about him and all his weaknesses . . . about his fantasies, his secrets! He felt exposed and ridiculous.

"You're freaking out."

"Of course I am. What we did was private."

"Not always so private," Wendy said, and laughed. "Remember Julia's?"

"You told her that, too?"

"It's what a therapist is for. Do you want to know what she said?"

"I'm not sure."

"She said you were lucky I was so inventive."

He let that sink in. Absolution. Praise. He felt a pang of loss. "I *was* lucky," he said.

"My mistake was wasting it—and me—on you," Wendy said, in that same sweet, matter-of-fact tone. Her eyes were wide open and innocent. How blue her eyes were. They would never cease to surprise him.

"I told you that," he said, trying to regain control. "I could have saved you a pile of money on the shrink."

"You told me that to get rid of me. You didn't believe it."

"Is that what she said?"

"I'm not going to talk about this anymore," Wendy said, and went back to her salad.

"So . . . how was your summer?"

"Great."

"The house was a success?"

"Absolutely. I went to lots of parties and met lots of men."

"Anyone you liked?"

"Mmm-hmm." She put down her fork. "I'm in love."

"In love?"

"Yes, and he loves me, too." Her face lit up. "He's a wonderful man. Handsome, kind, sexy, very intelligent, rich, older. All the things I like. He treats me so well . . ."

I thought you couldn't live without me, Roger thought. "Sounds great," he said.

"And he's divorcing his wife for me."

"Well."

"I don't need someone to pretend to love me anymore," Wendy said. "I have a man who really loves me."

"I hope you don't get hurt."

"Oh, you sanctimonious pig."

"I just meant it's sudden."

"People always know right away."

He thought back over his own life. "I suppose so."

"It's not like I'm a homewrecker," Wendy said. "He and his wife weren't happy. It's just that I'm the only woman he was ready to change things for. He wants to marry me."

"And you?"

"I always wanted to get married," Wendy said. "I just never thought I'd meet the right man."

"And he's it."

"Yes, he's it."

"I'm happy for you," Roger said. Now that he was completely free of her he felt released, weightless, like a balloon sailing up into the sky. He also felt strangely sad. This other man, whoever he was, would have all the joys of Wendy's body and imagination. He could show her off. He would never be bored.

But he would be bored, eventually. He would have to talk to her. Would he notice she had nothing to say? Would he care?

"How do you see the two of you in ten years?" he asked.

Wendy ran her fingers through her hair, in the gesture he knew so well. A faraway look came over her face, and then she smiled. "Best friends," she said. "Good sex. Two kids."

"Best friends?"

"Of course," she said. "That's essential. Didn't you know that?"

21

It had been six weeks since Olivia had seen Marc Delon in Paris, and now she felt foolish for having had fantasies about him. If he had really been interested in seeing her again, he would have called. She told herself it might have been uncomfortable for him —even awkward and odd—to call her when she was at home with Roger, but he could have phoned her at the office. Nor had he sent her the promised tear sheets of his articles, which would have given her an excuse to call him. No, she was sure he had forgotten her, and it would be best for her to forget about him too. Their meeting had been a moment out of time; it was what it was.

She thought his life was probably filled with such highly charged moments. How interesting it must be for him, and how interesting it would have been for her. But she didn't want an affair.

Roger had been on his best behavior, but the barrier between them remained. She wondered if things would ever be the way they were before Wendy came into their lives. He told her it was completely over between him and Wendy now, that she had actually fallen in love with another man whom she was planning to marry, and that he was rid of her. But you're never really rid of anyone, Olivia thought, because you remember. She wondered if Marc Delon ever thought of her—not that it was the same.

Melissa had called to tell her that she and her brother Nick were giving a seventy-fifth birthday party for their father, Uncle David, to which she and Roger were of course invited, and that everyone in the family had to find a memento from Uncle David's past and send it to her because they were going to make a commemorative scrapbook. Olivia went through the old family photographs—the ones her father's second wife Grace had tried to destroy—and found a picture she liked of Uncle David when he was a young man. How handsome he had been! Nick looked just like him. She found a photograph of herself as a toddler, squinting and beaming under a sun hat, at about the same time the other picture had been taken, and pasted them side by side on a sheet of paper.

What should she write on it? What memories came up? Except for herself, they had been wild and happy children who during the long summer days at Mandelay paid no attention to the adults, but the adults had always been there, a comforting framework for their lives. She remembered Uncle David playing croquet on the lawn beyond the formal gardens, under the huge old trees, with Aunt Hedy and his friends. Even now she could hear the click of the wooden mallet on the balls, Uncle David's cheerful tenor voice and Hedy's deeper, authoritative one ringing out in the middle distance.

They took their croquet games seriously and always wore white, and when the games were over they went back to the house where Uncle David made drinks on the terrace. She had found that sophisticated. He also did magic tricks, good ones, for the entertainment of the children. She remembered him taking an egg out of her pocket. No matter how she cajoled, he would never tell her how he did it, even when she was grown up. And he was always laughing and smiling. Uncle Seymour, his older brother, worried and fretted—he had an ulcer, he had migraines, and when he came to visit there was always something important about business to discuss. Uncle Seymour smiled when he spoke about the improvements he was making on his own summer place, or when he could tell them how well Julia's was doing, but Uncle David would whistle a little tune just because it was a nice day.

Olivia found another photograph of herself as a tall and gawky teenager, and pasted it beside the two others. Next to it she put a photo of Uncle David, still a handsome man, taken at about that time at some Mandelay party. Then she went through her recent scrapbooks and found a photograph of herself in her office, seated in front of her framed diplomas, holding Wozzle. She pasted that alongside the others. She didn't add a recent picture of Uncle David, because he knew how he looked, he saw himself in the mirror every day, and this was a tribute to the past. Below the pictures she wrote: *Dear Uncle David, Thank you for the magic. But don't you think I'm old enough to know how you got the egg into my pocket? And also how you stay so young?*

Actually, the last line was pure flattery. But if you weren't nice to someone on his birthday, when would you be? *Love, love, Olivia,* she wrote, put the paper on cardboard in a big envelope, and mailed it to Houston, to Melissa.

It suddenly occurred to her how strange it was that her mother had never given a birthday party for her father, although she always gave one for herself and for Olivia. Was it because he was only a son-in-law, not a Miller, an outsider? Her father said giving a party for him would be silly. He had been cagey about his age for years, but when he was finally seventy-five he decided longevity was an asset and began bragging about it. But Lila had cancer by then, and probably she hadn't been up to celebrating. Then, later, Grace had planned to give him an eighty-fifth birthday party, but he never made it; he got sick and then he died. At least he'd had a happy life in spite of everything. He always said how lucky he was.

Uncle David's party was going to be in New York, at Nick and Lynne's big new apartment, which most of them had not seen. Roger had agreed to go with such alacrity that you would think he had always gone to every family function as a matter of course. Luckily they didn't have to worry about a present, because the family was all chipping in to send Uncle David on a cruise around the world. It had been Nick's idea. Usually the family bought some large silver thing, but Nick believed his father should have some last adventures before it was too late, and Melissa agreed. Olivia wondered if Uncle David was still seeing his woman friend, and if he was going to take her along on the cruise and just not mention it. Did seventy-five-year-old people still have sex? She remembered when she was a kid talking to her cousins and discussing whether or not people in their forties still had sex. And then one afternoon in the office, when she was least thinking about Marc Delon, she looked up to see who her next appointment was with and there he stood with Spot.

She was a little embarrassed to see him in the flesh after her fantasies about him, but she smiled warmly. "Hello," she said. "How nice to see you again. Is it time for Spot's checkup already?"

"No," he said. He seemed almost bashful.

She stroked Spot's silky ears. "Well, how are you both doing?"

"I'm okay, but his paw hurts, I think."

"Which one?"

Marc lifted Spot's right front paw and Olivia inspected it thoroughly, looking at it, pressing it. "He's not complaining," she said.

"He was."

"I don't feel anything." She tossed a dog biscuit and Spot bounded after it. "Not limping."

Marc shrugged.

"When did you notice it?"

"Last week."

"It seems to have gone away."

"Well . . ."

"I could take an x-ray if you want, but I honestly think it's unnecessary." She looked down at Spot who was standing before her wagging his tail. "This is not a dog in distress."

"I know," Marc said mildly. He paused. "I have to make a confession. I really came here because I've been thinking about you and I didn't have the nerve to call. Could we make a plan to have lunch together, or a drink?"

He was afraid, she thought, surprised and pleased. He didn't forget after all. "Of course," she said.

"What about this afternoon when you're finished?"

Here is a man who makes plans to do things within the next moment, she thought, amused at how young he was. That afternoon was one of Roger's gym days after work. Even if it weren't, she was entitled to see a friend; it was harmless. "I could do that," Olivia said.

"Should I come and get you, or should we meet?"

"I'll meet you," she said, and immediately felt guilty because she realized she was hiding him. But it wouldn't be right to have him show up again; it would cause talk in the office. "Six o'clock. Tell me where."

"The bar at the Carlyle?"

It was expensive, and he'd said he didn't have much money. "Are we celebrating something?" she asked.

"No. I just wanted to go somewhere nice."

How sweet; she was touched. "That would be lovely," she said.

The Bemelmans Bar at the Carlyle had playful murals on the walls, and little tables with bowls of nuts and baskets of homemade potato chips on them. It was flatteringly dim but bright enough so you wouldn't go there if you were hiding. A pianist was playing rather loud background music. They both ordered white wine.

"Spindle Legs is in my book," he said.

"Lila is immortal at last."

"Cheers." He raised his glass.

"To your success." She raised her glass and touched his lightly as their eyes met and held.

"What have you been doing since I saw you?" he asked. He was still fixing her with his moonstone gaze, looking really interested, as if her life were something exotic and strange.

"Working," she said lightly. "Trying to re-enter real life. You never sent me those articles you wrote."

"I brought them," Marc said. He looked away finally and took some tear sheets out of his briefcase. "Here. I hope you read them."

"Why wouldn't I?"

"Too busy."

"I'll read them."

"Good."

She put the tear sheets into her handbag, and when she looked up at him he was staring at her again. "Why are you looking at me that way?" she asked, to make him stop. He made her feel like blushing, and that unnerved her.

"You're so beautiful," he said.

"Well, thank you."

"Roger must tell you that all the time."

"Of course he does."

"He's lucky."

"Terribly lucky," Olivia said with a little laugh. "Have you found a new girlfriend yet?"

"No."

"You will."

"Maybe."

For some reason right now she didn't want to think about his finding a new girlfriend so quickly. "You know what I never asked you?" she said. "Which books influenced you when *you* were a child?"

"I was spared gruesome fairy tales," he said. "I liked adventure stories. The ones I felt comfortable with strangely enough had an adult figure in them, a kind of mentor. I always liked the idea of traveling through life with someone who knew the terrain."

And do you still? she thought. "Sort of like *Star Wars*," she said.

"Sort of."

"And what have you been doing since you got back from Paris?"

"Just my book. And thinking about you. I didn't call because I felt stupid. I thought: What does she want with me? She has a life, a husband."

Roger isn't my husband, she thought, but she said nothing. He might as well have been. What *did* she want with this beautiful young man who apparently had a crush on her?

"Anyway . . ." Marc said.

"Anyway what?"

"Here I am."

"So I see."

"I was so overwhelmed by that story you told me," he said. "I thought: Here is a woman who was told as a little girl that she had to stay home and give her mother everything she had, forever, or go out and be killed. But she went out bravely and made a life for herself. I admire you."

"Thank you," Olivia said. "My family still thinks I'm a little odd. Two divorces, unusual clothes."

"I like your clothes."

"Thank you. We do have a few other mavericks. I had two cousins who were stuntmen."

"Stuntmen!" he said, pleased.

"Unfortunately they both died before their time."

"I'm sorry." He obviously assumed it had been in accidents, and she didn't amplify. Now she remembered dating, it was all coming back to her—the revealing of interesting tidbits of information, the holding back of anything that sounded too neurotic, such as a history of family suicides.

"I had a cousin who was a ballerina," he said. "She could have been famous, but she died, too."

"Of what?"

"Anorexia."

Suicide, Olivia thought. We do have something in common. "How tragic," she said.

"I know. She never had a sense of her worth."

"It's easy to lose," Olivia said.

"But you have it."

"I try."

"I'm trying too," Marc said. "At this stage of my life, still in the struggle, sometimes it's difficult."

"It's supposed to be."

"Well, I'll be famous one day, and then I'll come back and impress you."

"You impress me now," Olivia said.

"Do I?" He smiled wickedly. "Do you think we could fall in love?"

Only if I were completely crazy, she thought. "I'm taken," she said gently.

"Just kidding."

"I know," she said.

"Maybe."

"Maybe what?"

"Maybe I'm just kidding," he said. His eyes were innocent, his mouth turned up at the corners, he was adorable. She remembered Alys saying once, bitterly, that she was thinking of pretending to be married in order to attract a man, because married women were safe.

She looked at her watch. "I'll have to go soon."

"Would you like another glass of wine?"

"I think I'd better stay sober with you."

"I'm flattered you think I'm so dangerous."

"I'll read your articles and call you," she said. "Thank you for the drink."

On the street he offered to hail a cab for her but she said she'd rather walk because it wasn't far. His lips brushed her cheeks, soft and sensuous. "Thank you for seeing me," he said, and then he was gone into a taxi, off to his evening. She walked away, toward home.

And then she realized that she was completely, unaccountably euphoric. What does that say for my sense of self-worth, she thought, that I need him to flirt with me to make me feel this way? And then she was sorry that he wasn't there so she could say it to him. But of course it was just as well that he wasn't and that she couldn't.

She got home before Roger did, and began to prepare dinner. She remembered the softness of Marc's lips on her face, and imagined what they would feel like on her mouth. When she closed her eyes he was there. If she had just turned her head, a little bit . . . It wouldn't be sensible to say anything to Roger about her drink with Marc. She didn't know what to say about it anyway. She would have to make it sound like it had been nothing, and that would ruin the fantasy. But of course that was all it was going to be.

She read Marc's articles in bed because that was the only time she had to herself. "What are you reading?" Roger asked.

"Marc Delon was in the office today with his dog. He left me these. He wrote them."

Lie number one, she thought. Is this how these things happen? And I didn't even do anything with him.

"Any good?" Roger asked.

"Actually, yes." They were essays mostly about feelings, social mores and what it was like to be a young man like him in the world today. One was about problems with a girlfriend he was living with, an affair that seemed doomed. She looked at the publication date and figured this was the one he had recently broken up with. Why had he given her this particular piece? He obviously wanted her to know him better, unless it was a favorite of his. She recognized the sadness of knowing that something that had been briefly radiant was over, that nothing was right anymore and all that was left was closure. She had felt that way herself in her series of ill-fated romances between husbands and before meeting Roger. It was interesting to read it from the man's point of view.

She remembered the cleaning woman who had worked for her years ago, who had formerly worked for her family. They had been looking for a way to get rid of her, and offering her to Olivia as a favor was a good excuse. The cleaning woman was a friend of the woman who worked for Uncle David and Aunt Hedy. "Your family is saying bad things about you," she reported, having heard the household gossip from her friend. "She keeps telling him that you're a slut. He tries to defend you but . . ." The *she* was Hedy, the *he* Uncle David. Olivia had been deeply hurt.

"Tell her it's very painful being a slut," she had said cheerfully, and the cleaning woman had laughed. She knew how hard single life was, even if Hedy had forgotten.

Olivia waited two days to call Marc. "I read your articles," she said. "You're very talented. I loved them."

"Thank you."

"Some of the things you said reminded me of myself."

"Really?"

"Especially the one about how hard it is to go on being with someone when you both know you've made a mistake. I mean—not Roger, of course. I'm talking about the past."

"Your two marriages."

"And a few other errors."

"But I don't like being alone either," Marc said. "Did you?"

"No. But I was good at it."

"I'm not even very good at it, unless I'm with someone. Then I love my private time. I like to go off by myself and write, or just think."

"The comforting framework," Olivia said, remembering Mandelay.

"Yes, exactly."

"You must need these tear sheets back."

"I do. We could have a drink together next week and you could give them to me then."

She was glad he hadn't said she could just mail them, but she hadn't expected him to. "All right."

"Monday?"

"That would be fine." Monday evening Roger would be at the gym. It seemed ironic that now she was using his former cheating hours to do something secret of her own. She refused to let herself feel guilty; it was only a drink in a public place.

"The Carlyle again, at six?" he said.

"All right." Just don't say *It's our place,* she thought, or I'll cancel.

"It's our place," Marc said ironically, and then he laughed.

She smiled. She had underestimated his charm. She didn't intend to cancel.

22

UNCLE DAVID'S BIRTHDAY PARTY was on Saturday night. Nick and Lynne's new apartment, which they had spent so long renovating, was a duplex, with a large, curving staircase, a wraparound terrace overlooking all of Central Park, a Lichtenstein, a Jim Dine and a Botero in the living room and three Warhols in the dining room, which had been set up with round tables and spindly gilt chairs for the party. All the other furniture was modern but very comfortable, and the painted walls were so shiny you could ice-skate on them. Everyone was very dressed up. The adults were walking around inspecting the new apartment, complimenting everything. The children were gathered in Amber's room, which was actually a suite, waiting impatiently for turns to play her pinball machine. Next to Amber's suite was another one, furnished but without any toys in it yet, waiting for the second child Nick and Lynne hoped to have someday.

While Nick and Lynne showed off their apartment, Melissa and Bill were showing off the Uncle David commemorative scrapbook, which was huge and reposed on the living room coffee table. A tuxedoed waiter brought around glasses of champagne and sparkling water, a maid passed hors d'oeuvres. Someone had been hired to play the piano, and cocktail music tinkled quietly behind the familiar voices as the Miller family gathered again. The cousins greeted each other with hugs and kisses. Uncle David was beaming.

Almost everyone was there: Uncle Seymour and Aunt Iris, Aunt Myra, Jenny and Paul, Taylor and Tim, Kenny and Pam, even Anna the Perfect and her husband, and a young man who looked oddly familiar until Olivia recognized him as Charlie the Perfect's son Tony, there with his preppy-looking wife. There were also over a dozen older people, who were longtime friends of Uncle David's.

"You have to come visit us," Pam said warmly to Olivia and Roger. "We're moving into our new house next month. It has lots of rooms for guests."

And no unheated water bed, Olivia thought, remembering. Kenny has someone to take care of him now. "We'd love to," she said, although she knew that was the last thing Roger would ever want to do on a vacation.

She wandered away and looked into Amber's bedroom suite, admiring her little cousins. They all seemed so much older, bigger than when she had seen them last. They changed so fast. She felt a kind of sadness wash over her. I'm missing their lives, she thought. They were much too busy to notice her, and she went back to the living room to join the grownups.

"Those kids are something," she said to Jenny, who was standing at the window gazing out at the view.

"I know," Jenny said. "Did you see how tall Sam has gotten? All the girls at school are crazy about him."

"Does he have a girlfriend?"

"Two or three." She preened. "Do we look like parents of a teenager?" She obviously expected Olivia to say no.

"No."

"And Max is the next teenager coming up."

The maid came by with her tray. "Sushi," she said.

They took some. "Do you still eat this stuff?" Olivia asked Jenny in a whisper.

"Why?"

"You know, pollution."

"Not usually, but this is such a fancy party, I'm sure it's fresh."

"I guess." They ate it. "Nice apartment, isn't it," Olivia said.

"Amazing. Expensive, though."

"I can just imagine. Funny to see Charlie's son here all of a sudden. I didn't even recognize him."

"He wants to get to know the family better, I think," Jenny said.

"Ah. But of course Charlie isn't here. He never comes to anything."

Jenny's eyes opened wide with shock. "You didn't know?"

"Know what?" Olivia said.

"Charlie's dead."

Dead? "How could Charlie be dead?" she said, feeling as if they were talking about some other family. "How could I not know? When? What happened?"

"His plane went into a mountain in July," Jenny said. "He was at the controls, as usual. It wasn't his fault, it was structural failure. You and Roger were in Paris. I thought somebody would have told you."

"Nobody told me."

"Well," Jenny said, "it was a pretty big shock."

Olivia was so numbed by the news that she didn't even know how she felt. Charlie the Perfect had always been the golden boy. Although she had hardly known him, she had known about him. He had been the family genius in business, on the board of many charities: well-dressed, handsome, charming. Charlie dead in a stupid, pointless accident. And he had been so healthy! For this he needed to be a vegetarian, she thought; to work out instead of eating lunch, to run the Marathon and finish at the same time as his son?

The name Charlie the Perfect, which she had given him years ago, was partly ironic, because like his sister, Anna the Perfect, to the older generation he could do no wrong. But she had always felt that he had been too competitive. She remembered an incident years ago, when he had visited Mandelay. He was already an adult. Olivia had told the family proudly that she had finally swum fifty laps in an Olympic pool. It was a particular triumph for her because she was so unathletic. They were impressed.

"Single or double laps?" Charlie had asked briskly, his eyes narrowing.

"Single."

"That doesn't count," he said. "You did twenty-five laps. I do seventy-five double laps in an Olympic pool at my gym. Where did you do yours?"

"Here."

"Mandelay doesn't have an Olympic pool," he said. "An Olympic pool is the size of a football field. You'd know it if you saw one."

He had left her feeling embarrassed and silly.

"Uncle Seymour is teaching Tony about the store," Jenny said. "He was a lawyer, but now he has to give it up. He always knew someday he would run Julia's, but he didn't think it would be so soon."

"Even Aunt Myra didn't tell me," Olivia said. Now she was beginning to feel left out and insulted. "I would have said something to them."

"It's very strange," Jenny said quietly. "Uncle Seymour and Aunt Iris never mentioned Charlie again."

She imagined their silence. "It must be so painful for them," she said. "They can't even talk about it yet."

"Of course. At their age, to lose a child. They expected to go first."

"Everyone must think I'm terrible not to have gone to the funeral," Olivia said. "But no one told me."

"It was a huge funeral," Jenny said. "He was a pillar of the community. It was in the New York *Times*."

"We didn't get the New York *Times* when we were in Paris."

"Well, don't worry about it. Nobody's mad at you."

"They're always mad at me," Olivia said.

"No, no," Jenny said calmly, soothingly, like a good mother. Olivia thought how lucky Jenny's children were. Lila would have told her the family was angry and upset.

She glanced over at Uncle Seymour and Aunt Iris. Suddenly they seemed very frail. They were smiling at Tony, their grandson. His little boy had come out of the room where the children were playing and was clinging to his mother's side, asking for hors d'oeuvres. Aunt Iris leaned down to pat him and handed him a cheese puff. Their great-grandson: the chain of life. This was how they could go on.

The pianist stopped playing. Nick came forward to make a toast. "To my wonderful father," he said, raising his glass. Olivia wondered if Charlie's recent tragedy would make Nick think again about continuing to risk his life helicopter skiing. She hoped so.

Nick began to reminisce. He told of fun-loving Uncle David's youthful adventures that had been handed down as family anecdotes, and then of the good times they had all had together as Nick and his sister Melissa were growing up. Olivia had heard these stories before. She let her mind wander. She looked at Roger across the room, so familiar and solid and kind—and yet burdened by secrets—and then she thought about Marc Delon's soft lips against her face.

Melissa came forward then, slim as a waif in her narrow black dress with the little rhinestone straps, and raised her glass. "To my darling father," she said. "Happy birthday, and thank you all for coming here to help celebrate his special day."

There was applause. Uncle David stood up. "I want to thank my children for this wonderful party," he said, "and for just being them. I couldn't ask for better children, or nicer grandchildren. And I thank my beloved wife Hedy for the many years of happiness she gave me, gave all three of us. She was the best of wives, and the best of mothers. I have had a happy life."

He always thought Hedy was a paragon, Olivia thought. This marvelous Hedy he was thanking was not the sharp-tongued, critical Hedy she had known. Somehow it seemed strange to hear him talk about Hedy, as if she shouldn't be there anymore, should just disappear, because nobody else had liked her. I wish I were that important to someone's life, she thought. I used to think I was to Roger. But Uncle David never looked at another woman in all the years they were together.

They went into the dining room for dinner. Olivia and Roger sat next to Taylor and Tim, at a table with Jenny and Paul and Kenny and Pam. "It's nice to have a family," Taylor said. She looked wistful.

"You have all of us," Olivia said.

"I mean parents and children."

"I don't have parents or children."

"I have my *mother,*" Taylor said, and made a face, as if that didn't count. But it did count, that was the trouble.

They ate cold lobster and drank a crisp white wine. "Isn't this a lovely party?" Pam said. "I'll give you one, Kenny, when you're old." She smiled flirtatiously. The idea of Kenny's being seventy-five seemed light-years away.

" 'Will you still need me, will you still feed me, when I'm sixty-four?' " Kenny sang. "Do you remember how ancient that seemed? You'd have to be fed."

"I'm off Prozac now," Taylor said. "I can start trying to get pregnant before I'm too old."

"The child will feed you," Kenny said, smiling.

"The child may have to," Taylor said. "I'm still paying Grady's mortgage. No one wants to buy his house. I need to get his deck fixed."

"I wanted to fix it myself," Tim said, signing. "It would have been kind of fun. But she won't let me."

"You have better things to do," Taylor said. "You're an artist. Grady is my responsibility."

Is she being possessive or guilty, Olivia wondered. Perhaps both. Taylor had to be aware that Grady had never felt secure enough to come to her directly to talk about his life, and she had been the closest person to him in the world. Neither of them had ever mentioned the videotape he had sent her; they obviously felt it had been an overture best forgotten. Perhaps now Taylor was sorry about that.

They ate tender, rare filet mignon with baby vegetables, and drank a velvety red wine. "How was Paris?" Paul asked cheerfully.

"Wonderful," Roger said. "It was a perfect vacation."

Except that you weren't really attracted to me, Olivia thought, and I met someone I can't seem to get out of my mind. "It was fun," she said.

"There is something to be said for not having five children," Jenny remarked dryly, but they all knew she didn't mean it.

They ate field salad with brie with the rest of the velvety red wine, and then there was sorbet, long-stemmed strawberries, champagne and a huge chocolate birthday cake which Uncle David cut to applause from the guests. "Your uncle is going to drop dead from this meal before he even gets to go on his cruise," Roger said.

His saying that annoyed her; she felt it was ill-advised and morbid. Dear old Uncle David. Why couldn't Roger behave himself; what was wrong with him? She didn't want to think about one other person dying. But of course, Roger didn't know about Charlie yet.

23

WHEN OLIVIA MET Marc again at the bar at the Carlyle, "their place," this time he was waiting for her at a table in the corner, more private than the one where they had sat the first time; they could now sit side by side. In spite of her good intentions, she felt a little thrill of anticipation that she would be so close to him. Across the room she could see a couple sitting together on the banquette in what had been a seat for one, almost on top of each other because the tables were so small, kissing vigorously. She turned away quickly and handed Marc his tear sheets.

"Well," he said brightly, smiling at her with the pleasure of seeing her again, his face so unguarded that she was suddenly afraid she could hurt him.

"Well," she said back. They sat there beaming at each other. Then the waiter came and they ordered white wine.

"I want to know what you're thinking," Marc said to her. "Right this minute. Tell me."

"That you're even more attractive than I remembered," Olivia said, and then was embarrassed. It was only a compliment, she told herself; nothing wrong with that. Men loved compliments. And this particular man was probably used to them. She knew that if she weren't so aware of her infatuation she would be flattering him without a thought.

"What have you been doing?" he asked. He drew a little closer, looking in her eyes in that anticipatory way he had before, as if he was fascinated by her life, as if it was not like anyone else's. Well, maybe he was really intrigued. She was more than curious to know what he did on a typical day, if only to place him in reality for her fantasies. He would probably think her life was ordinary if he knew, but she didn't care if his was.

"Working," she said. "You know what that's like. And I went to my uncle's seventy-fifth birthday party." Why didn't I say *we* went? she thought.

"Was it fun?"

"Actually, it was very nice. But I found out one of my cousins was killed in a plane crash. That was quite a shock."

"I'm sorry."

"It happened months ago and we weren't close. But it was still a shock."

"Of course," Marc said. "In a big family there are more tragedies. That's the way it is."

"I think ours has had more. Maybe not."

"Maybe not," he said. "Life is dangerous. You just can't think about it."

"But I do."

"Of course. So do I. So we have to enjoy it."

"That's how he got killed," Olivia said. "Enjoying it."

He suppressed a smile. "You're funny."

"Tell me what you've been doing," she said. And who you did it with, she thought.

"On the weekend I went to a party. Some old friends. Afterward we went downtown to a club. I don't like that sort of thing as much as I used to. I feel like I'm reliving my life over and over."

"Already!"

"If you went to clubs, you'd know what I mean."

"I did," Olivia said. "I remember."

"And I worked on my book. Ran in the park. Ate a lot of takeout."

"Alone?" she asked lightly.

"Were you?"

"No," she said. "But you know that."

"I was alone," he said. "And now you know that." He gave her his most appealing grin. "Run away with me while I'm still single. I want you."

"You're very good for my ego," Olivia said, and laughed.

"Tell me how you see me," he said, suddenly serious. "Tell me how I seem to you."

"As . . ."

"The truth."

She looked at the line of his neck, both strong and vulnerable, and suddenly, in flashes, she imagined she was seeing him when he was five years old, and as a teenager, and now. This continuum of people was endearing but also rather frightening—it made her feel wistful and soft. She wanted to be kind to that little boy, advise the adolescent and fall into the arms of the grown man she saw before her. She felt guilty, not so much because of Roger, who was not there, but because Marc seemed so real, so *human* when she thought of him this way. The fantasy had been easier.

"Well," she said slowly, "I see a very sexy man I want to flirt with, and at the same time I see the little boy you used to be. I think it's because you're so much younger than I am."

"I'm not so much younger," Marc said. "And that's exactly the way I see you. I see the feisty little girl and the sophisticated, beautiful woman. You've read enough to know that the child never really goes away. That hidden child is part of what makes you so interesting."

"And so nutty," she said, and laughed.

He reached over and took her hand. His fingers were neither warm nor cool, and his touch jolted her and traveled through her body, leaving her silent with surprise. "Flirt with me," he said. "I dare you."

"You dare me?"

"Yes." His cool eyes looked into hers. Young men do that, she thought, they stare at you, they're so intense. She felt saved by the waiter, who came over to see if they wanted another drink, but Marc said yes without asking her or releasing her hand, and the waiter went away. "You did want another?" he said.

"I can't stay very long."

"You don't have to drink it. I just don't want you to leave."

"I don't want to either," she said.

He turned her hand over and looked at her palm. "You have a star in your hand," he said.

"What's that?"

"It means you're very lucky."

She looked at her palm. There it was, a seven-pointed star. She had never paid attention. "It's very unusual," he said. He ran his thumb over it, lightly, and she felt the same electricity. She looked at his mouth.

"Do you read palms?" she asked.

"No," he said. "Someone told me that once." He showed her his hand. "You see, I have one too."

"Do you believe in it?"

"I'll believe anything that says I'm lucky."

"I guess I will too," Olivia said.

The waiter brought their wine. The room had become crowded and smoky. Now, with all the voices chattering, the piano did not seem so loud. She looked around to make sure there was no one there whom she and Roger knew. She had already decided she wasn't going to mention meeting Marc, but she didn't know what she would say if Roger found out and she had to explain it. The couple opposite them who had been kissing disentangled and got up and left. She and Marc watched them go.

"I wonder if they're going to have dinner or sex," Olivia said.

"Probably sex first, then dinner," Marc said.

"Or the other way around. Maybe they're hungry."

"But definitely sex."

Under other circumstances it could have been us, she thought. She imagined what it would be like to be free again and in love with someone when it was all fresh and new. No, not *someone:* Marc Delon.

"Is Roger romantic?" Marc asked.

"Why are you asking something like that?"

"I'm jealous. I want to know."

"You can't be jealous."

"But I am."

"We've been together almost twelve years," Olivia said.

He looked pleased. "Is that the answer?"

"Of course he's romantic," she said. She thought of their shared Jacuzzi, the hot bubbling water, the scented candlelight, the music playing, the food on the rim of the tub, the dogs dozing on the floor, Roger rubbing the tension out of her back . . . Romantic? No, just therapeutic. Our relationship has turned into goddamn Canyon Ranch, she thought.

"But you're here with me anyway," he said softly.

"Yes," she said. She thought what it would be like to have him at home in the Jacuzzi with her. His body would be so beautiful, and he would be so intense. To dwell on it for even an instant more was unbearable. "But I have to leave now," she said. "He'll be waiting."

"Will you tell him you saw me?"

"I hope it . . . doesn't come up."

He smiled, triumphant. "Will you meet me again?"

"Yes," she said.

"When?"

She thought. "Next week," she said. A week away seemed safe.

He paid the check, like an old-fashioned date, and they went outside to the street. It was dark. She was deciding that when he moved to kiss her on both cheeks, this time she would turn her head to meet his mouth; but before she could he had kissed her very gently on the lips. It was exactly as she had imagined it. She stood there, stunned.

"Yes," he whispered. "Wow."

On the way home there were Halloween decorations in the store windows. Olivia looked at them happily, smiling with joy. She felt like a kid again.

Safe in their house, with the warm chaos of the welcoming dogs, the last of the nightly news on television, the arrival of Roger, virtuous from the gym, the discussion of what to order sent up for dinner, Olivia knew she was glowing with lust for Marc. She wondered if this was the way Roger had felt with Wendy. She hoped not. It hurt her too much to think of Roger being this alive because of another woman, and she didn't want to think of it at all. She thought of the duplicity of people, herself included, and of how territorial they were. She wanted both Roger and Marc.

They ate mystery burgers from a vegetarian Indian restaurant on the couch in front of the television set, watched a mindless docudrama, because it was her turn to pick, and discussed their day briefly during the commercials. Roger's arm was affectionately around her shoulders.

"I love you," she said.

"I love you too."

They were always so kind to one another.

As the week went by she both looked forward to and dreaded her next meeting with Marc. Where could this infatuation go? Each possibility seemed worse. But it didn't have to go anywhere, she told herself. She should just enjoy it. Roger had finally shaken off the sexual malaise that had hung over him since their reconciliation, and now when they made love, although it was still not frequent, at least he tried to be passionate. As for herself, she thought of Marc and became wild, the way she had in the old days. Roger thought it was for him, and responded. So the result was that they were getting along quite well. Did it matter why? It seemed such a long time ago that she had believed everything to be perfect.

When she called Marc she told him that they should choose a new place, because she didn't want them to become known as regulars, a couple. He suggested another bar, not so chic or public but pleasant, around the corner from his apartment on the Upper East Side. As before, she could walk there and back from her office and not have to deal with gridlock while Roger was busy at the gym. The fact that their moments together were so rushed and secret made them even more exciting. Never enough, she thought, but never too much either. She was still afraid that all this would disappear.

His neighborhood place had a hail-fellow-well-met look about it: dark wood walls, leather booths, a big television set over the bar with a sports event on it, young men in business suits waving bottles of beer and cheering their team. The women were all in their twenties, suitable for the young men and hoping to find one. Marc led her to a secluded booth in the back, sat across from her and pretended to pull a curtain protecting them from the world. They sat there smiling at each other as if they had been parted for a long time.

"So this is where you hang out," Olivia said.

"It's convenient. Do you hate it?"

"No, I like it."

Her left hand was on the table. He reached over and ran his finger lightly between her fingers. She felt that streak of light again. She was wearing a ring, as she almost always did, and Marc moved his finger over it, stroking it, obviously thinking it was her wedding ring.

"Did you think about me this week?" he asked.

"Yes," she said. She was picking up flirting very fast for someone who was out of practice.

"I thought about you, too."

When the waiter came over for their order, Marc ordered beer. "I have to warn you," he said to her, "the wine here isn't great."

"Perrier, then."

The waiter went away. "What did you think about me?" Marc asked.

"You would only be flattered."

"So would you."

"You're not still alone?" she said, hoping he was. I shouldn't have asked that, she thought. But I want to know.

"I didn't go out with anyone who overwhelmed me," he said.

"Just checking."

So he went on dates. Of course he would; why should he stay home and wish he were with her? He was horny and free. She wanted to know about his private life and yet she didn't. Reality had to disappoint. He liked that she was taken, he thought he knew just where she was; but she didn't like that he was available because that meant soon he wouldn't be. If she didn't ask, it would be better. She could pretend.

"You're the woman I really want," he said.

She smiled.

The waiter brought their drinks and left. "I have some superior wine in my apartment," Marc said.

"Really!"

"I live practically next door."

"I know."

"We can't do anything so bad in an hour."

"Oh, yes we could."

His eyes were glistening; she couldn't tell if he was still flirting or giving it a real try.

"No, I don't think so," Olivia said.
"Just checking," he said, imitating her.
"You're outrageous."
"Now you know what I was thinking all week."
"Thank you."
"Do you think I'm terrible?"
"I know you are," she said, and laughed.

He was playing with her hand again, his touch delicate, almost thoughtful. She wondered if that would be the way his fingers would move over her body. "I'm going away next week," he said.

"Oh? For how long?"

"Till after Thanksgiving. I have some friends who have a house in the Berkshires, and they're lending it to me to write. Actually, I'm house-sitting for them, so we're all happy."

She felt both disappointed and reprieved. No decisions, no guilt. The safe, sweet longing of separation. "I think I'm going to miss you," she said.

"I'll miss you. I wish you could come with me."

She pictured them making love under a feather comforter, in a room with wooden beams on the ceiling. There would be a window overlooking green and orange hills. She wondered if the leaves would have fallen by then. But this was her fantasy, and so the trees would be forever in full flame. "So do I," she said.

"Nature, fresh air, long walks. Get in the car and explore. But if you were there I wouldn't get much work done."

"And Roger would never understand."

"Is it all right if I send you a postcard?"

"Only if you write something really boring on it."

"Don't worry. Boring writing is my trade."

"Your book is going to be wonderful," Olivia said.

"Thank you. I hope so. Will you read some chapters when I finish them?"

"I'd be flattered."

They looked at each other across the table. She saw the child again in his face. "Will you have to be all by yourself on Thanksgiving?" she asked.

"I'll make friends," he said cheerfully. "Someone will be sorry for me and invite me. They always do."

"Your family doesn't get together?"

"Yes, but you know, they're French, so it's not really their holiday, even though we always enjoy it."

"I love Thanksgiving," Olivia said. She remembered how he had said he didn't like being alone, how he needed someone so he could wander away and come back, knowing she was there. That person wasn't herself, so maybe he would find her in the Berkshires. She hoped not.

When it was time for her to leave, Marc kissed her goodnight in the street in front of the bar. This time his lips were not so tentative. She felt her head reel, and she kissed him back. They stood there kissing for a few moments and then they both pulled away. It was, after all, a public place and this was not a casual goodbye. But before he moved she felt the unmistakable hardness of his attraction to her. She felt giddily happy, irresistible. *I could live for a month on this,* she thought.

"Goodbye," he whispered. "I'll call you as soon as I come back."

"Do."

She wanted to run after him to kiss him again, but she also wanted to go on to her orderly life, carrying this confidence with her. She began to walk home. She felt a little guilty toward Roger, but it made her feel as if she were at last as in control of their situation as he was. And then, as she walked through the streets that had become so comfortably familiar to her, she remembered her single days, and what she had always dreaded about an affair—it was the waiting, the imagining, the longing. It was, most of all, the obsession. She would have to be careful.

24

THAT THANKSGIVING Olivia gave her annual feast for their friends. Alys, who had passed her first adult year of celibacy and was depressed about it, got drunk as usual, but not disorderly. Her single friend's adopted baby was a year older and running around. One couple had broken up, so only he came to the party. Another couple, who had broken up but remained friends, each arrived with a different partner, and the four of them acted as if it were perfectly normal to be there chatting happily like a long-standing quartet. It was a year since Olivia had seen the cat scratch on Roger's thigh and had let him delude her into thinking that it was nothing.

She had received a picture postcard from Marc. It was of scenery, and as he had promised, his inscription was boring . . . but not to her. She put the card on her desk among a pile of papers and mail so it would look unimportant, and once in a while she ran her fingers over it, feeling her lips burn. She already knew it was possible to lust after him more when he wasn't there than when he was. The feeling was safe but confusing.

She kept asking herself what exactly she wanted from him. He made her feel confident, sensual and desirable again. He made her feel alive and silly. He wanted her, and she withheld what he wanted as if it were a game. She wondered if part of the excitement of their flirtation was that her still lurking anger made it a way of punishing Roger. She knew she liked her guilt because it made her feel strong. It made her love Roger more in a way, and want to protect him. She had always thought she was above such perfidy, but wouldn't it be ironic if her anger had simply freed her to think of doing what Roger had already done?

Marc came back between Thanksgiving and Christmas and they met for a drink. They sat side by side in a back booth in a small, dark bar and kissed. His hand was on her leg. They talked and kissed and kissed again, like teenagers with no home of their own to go to, and she had difficulty breathing.

"Come to my apartment," he whispered. "Please."

"You have no idea how much I wish I could."

"Then do."

"I can't," Olivia whispered, and sank again into his soft lips.

"Get away from him and have dinner with me," Marc said. "A whole evening. Think of it. . . ."

Roger's not a *him,* Olivia thought, defensive and offended for Roger, whom she loved and who had often been so good to her. She shook her head no, and smiled.

"You could tell him you're helping me with my book," Marc said. "Giving me research material."

"Oh, right. I'm such a source of information. He'll be bound to believe it."

"But he will. People believe almost anything. And you would be helping me, you could."

"Help you?"

"Yes. You said you'd read some chapters."

"I will," Olivia said. "Alone. Not with you, you'd distract me."

"I want to distract you."

"I know." They smiled, and kissed smiling. He rubbed his face against hers like a cat, put his head down and she massaged his neck.

"You don't know what you're doing to me," he said.

"I have to go home now." She looked into her compact mirror at the damage he had done to her mouth, and put on lipstick.

"I can't get up," Marc said. "I have a hard-on."

She was flattered. "The semi-permanent affliction of the young," she said lightly.

"No, because of you."

"You make me happy," she said. Their eyes locked. She knew she was glowing.

"I could make you happier."

She looked away. "I know. I'm leaving now."

"What am I doing out with a married woman?"

"I have no idea."

"You could become very dear to me," he said. She smiled. What a nice way of saying he could fall in love with her without committing or saying that overused and threatening word.

"I'm fond of you, too."

He held her hand and tapped it gently, pensively on the table. "Will you meet me next week? Then I'm going away skiing for Christmas."

"Are you!" She was both disappointed and relieved. Again the reprieve, but it seemed too soon. What did she expect? They both had lives of their own. "Where?"

"The French Alps. And the whole family is going to spend Christmas in Paris with my grandmother."

Safe and far from here, she thought. She wondered if he would be going away if they were having an affair, and thought he would. "All right," she said. "We'll have a little pre-Christmas celebration."

I must never, never fall in love with him, she told herself.

They met for their holiday drink in a different darkened bar. She felt like a spy, covering her trail. She had brought him a silly present: a tiny paper bag on a magnet, with a tinier toy bear inside it, wearing a Santa Claus cap. He gave her a CD of rock stars singing Christmas carols. It might have been something she would have bought for herself. He also gave her a manila envelope.

"The first three chapters of my book," he said.

"Thank you!"

"You have to call and tell me what you think before I go."

"Of course I will."

They drank champagne and looked into each other's eyes. She wondered if he would be sleeping with a woman, or many women, over the holidays. She didn't dare ask, because he could then reply that she would be sleeping with Roger. She didn't want to part on a note like that. This was their own private place, their fantasy. But the question tormented her anyway.

"Why do you have that odd look on your face?" he asked.

"I was wondering if you were taking a date with you."

He smiled. "No."

"I guess there are lots of women there to . . ."

"Go to bed with?"

"Yes."

"Would you care?"

"Of course I would," Olivia said lightly. "It's selfish, but I would."

"Well, there are, but that doesn't mean I will."

"I'm glad."

"An intelligent person would have to be crazy to be wild these days," Marc said. "I'm very prudent."

"Good."

"You would be completely safe with me," he said. "I can promise you that. Are you tempted yet?"

"I'm always tempted," she said. "I'll miss you."

He inhaled her neck. "I'll miss the way you smell."

"My perfume?"

"Your skin. I can tell the difference."

"What do I smell like?"

"Pure sex," he said. She laughed.

They fell upon each other's mouths quite naturally by now—this was what they did. "I'm not going to ask you to come to my apartment," he said. "I'm going to make you suffer."

"And ask *you*."

"Yes."

"I like that arrangement better."

"You won't. You'll think about me more than you expect when I'm away."

"I know I will."

"Do you want another postcard?"

"Yes," Olivia said. She stroked his silky black hair, his smooth cheek. He had always obviously shaved just before he met her, and this touched her. He wanted to look nice. He didn't want to leave marks. If he had left a mark it would have been a disaster. Knowing he was leaving soon, she allowed herself to feel very tender. There was something about him that was strangely moving, and she felt a little flutter in her heart, like a leaf falling.

"What are you thinking this minute?" Marc asked.

That this is almost as bad as fucking, she thought guiltily: or worse because it's so intimate. She was achingly aware that she was betraying Roger. "Nostalgic," she said, thinking of Roger's happy, welcoming face.

"Good," Marc said. Of course he thought she meant she was nostalgic only for him.

They said goodbye in the street, as always. But by now their arms were wrapped around each other, under their open coats. He felt so thin. As always, he had an erection for her, so hard she felt it was an intrusion to be so close to him and do nothing about it.

"You see what you could have?" he said.

"I would be so sad if you didn't feel that way about me."

"You're a terrible woman."

They kissed again, lingering, and finally she pulled away and left. On the way home she thought he was right; she was a terrible woman. She couldn't figure out why he put up with her, why he still wanted her, what was in it for him. Maybe he was a masochist who wanted only what he couldn't have: something wrong with him, a little off. Or maybe it had become a contest he was intent on winning. Or perhaps he was secretly madly in love with her, which would have been such a nice thing to believe.

When she came home, Roger was lying on the couch. She was startled to see him; he was supposed to be at the gym. "Where have you been?" he asked.

"You didn't work out?"

"No. I felt like I was coming down with a cold this afternoon so I thought it wouldn't be a good idea."

"Oh," she said. "I'm sorry you're feeling sick." She went over and felt his forehead.

"No fever," he said.

"What about if I send out for chicken soup?"

"Where were you, anyway?" He didn't sound suspicious or angry, just curious.

"I had a drink with Marc Delon," Olivia said. She could hardly believe this was her own voice coming out so calmly. She held up the manila envelope. "Remember I told you that he was writing a book? Maybe I didn't tell you. Anyway, this is the first three chapters he wanted me to read."

"Why you?" Roger asked. He didn't seem jealous, just surprised. She was hurt by his tone, which clearly implied she was not anyone to be consulted for her literary opinion. Well, maybe she wasn't, but Marc cared what she thought of him.

"He interviewed me that time when we had coffee in Paris."

"About what?"

"Stories I read as a child."

"Oh," Roger said.

She went into the bedroom to change. She was relieved that he wasn't jealous of Marc, and at the same time, she was a little annoyed.

25

THE HOLIDAYS WERE OVER, another year gone. Discarded Christmas trees lay on the sidewalk waiting to be collected, shreds of tinsel still clinging to them—what had been so coveted and delighted in was now just garbage. Huge plastic bags lay there too, the green ones loaded with wasted food from celebrations, to be gotten rid of; the transparent ones bulging with glass and plastic bottles and aluminum cans from boozy parties, to be recycled. Snow fell and covered all of it, leaving only large, white, mysterious lumps that quickly turned gray, then icy black. The cousins had returned from their vacations, some from the cold of mountain ski trails, others from the warmth of tropical beaches. Marc would be coming back too, which made Olivia nervous and excited. But she was also filled with a lingering sadness, because it was soon to be the first anniversary of Grady's death.

Then, unexpectedly, she received a letter from Taylor. Taylor never wrote to anybody in the family, but there it was:

Dear Olivia—I finally scattered Grady's ashes in Mexico. It was in a pretty place near the Sea of Cortez, where he had wanted me to do it. I hired a bus and driver to get there, and invited all his stuntman friends and their wives. We had a mariachi band on the bus, and lots of food and liquor. We partied for four days. Everybody had a good time, which he would have liked. It cost me a lot of money, but that's okay. We had a memorial service at sunset when

I scattered the ashes, and that night in Mexico, after the memorial, is the night I got pregnant. I consider it a sign.

That was in November, so now I'm two months along and doing pretty good. Please tell the family. Pregnant! Me! Imagine!!

Love,
Taylor

Olivia pictured Taylor and Tim and their celebrating group on the bus, drinking and joking and having fun, making the best of what could have been a sad occasion. She thought of the mariachi band Taylor couldn't hear but only feel—swaying to the vibrations with their hearing friends, alone again in her deaf world. Their straight friends—Grady had been alone too, all those years.

She was delighted at the good news about the forthcoming baby. It was interesting that Taylor had disposed of Grady's ashes in what amounted to secrecy, since she had not mentioned it until two months after the fact, but her pregnancy had galvanized her into action and made her write a letter. It was as if Grady belonged to Taylor, but becoming pregnant was an event that had finally catapulted Taylor, the self-proclaimed neglected half-breed, into the family.

Olivia called Aunt Myra, knowing she would be good at spreading the word. "Oh, I knew that," Aunt Myra said.

"You did?"

"Sure. She wrote to me last week."

"And you didn't call?"

"I was going to."

"And she told you about the ashes."

"What about the ashes?"

"She scattered them, finally."

"No," Aunt Myra said. "She only told me she was expecting."

"Then she didn't tell you about the sign."

"What sign?"

"Never mind. It's just Taylor."

"Well, I was going to call you anyway," Aunt Myra said. She giggled nervously. "I've been getting over a big shock."

"What was that?"

"Uncle David is getting married."

"Uncle David?"

"Yep."

"To that woman he's supposedly been going with forever? But then I thought they broke up."

"Oh, who knows about her, that was so strange. I think they were just friends. No, no. To a woman he met on the cruise the kids sent him on. Apparently all the widows and divorcees were chasing him on the ship, and he met one he liked."

"But that wasn't even three months ago," Olivia said.

"I know," Aunt Myra said, sounding half exasperated, half embarrassed at the precipitousness of it. "He says he's seventy-five and life is short."

The way he raved about Aunt Hedy at his birthday party I thought he'd never marry again, Olivia thought, but she didn't say it. "He's right," she said.

"I guess he was lonely," Aunt Myra said. She sighed. "Melissa and Nick went to Florida to meet her. They were surprised, too. She isn't after his money, anyway. She has a home in Key West and a house in Tuscany. They said she seems like a nice woman. At least she's not too young. He's happy." Aunt Myra, however, did not sound happy at all. In an instant she had lost the company of her brother, who would now be a newlywed.

"He'll live longer this way," Olivia said to comfort her.

"Oh, I'm not passing judgment. It's his business."

"Did they set a date yet?"

"Next month," Aunt Myra said. "I told him: 'What's your rush? *She's* not pregnant.' He said at their age a long engagement is silly. They want to move in together, and travel."

"You should get married again," Olivia said. "You're still fit and youthful."

"Well, thank you. But I don't want to get married again. I had a long, wonderful marriage and that was enough. I keep busy."

"It's great about Taylor, isn't it?" Olivia said.

"Yes, sure. You know these old widows, they'll do anything to get a man. There's a woman who lives in the penthouse in my building, whose husband died. There was an old man who used to deliver the clothes from the cleaner downstairs. He had heart trouble, he was pale and skinny, he looked half dead. His wife had recently died. So this widow in the penthouse, she invited him up to commiserate, I guess to feed him, and the next thing you know, they got married! Well, you should see him now. Nobody can call him by his first name anymore. We have to pretend we didn't know him when. He's got a good belly now, he gets all his suits made in England, he wears a coat with a velvet collar. She's happy."

"Who are we talking about here?" Olivia asked. "You or Uncle David's fiancée or what?"

"Neither one," Aunt Myra said. "I'm just telling you a story."

Olivia wrote to Taylor.

Dear Taylor—I'm thrilled that you're having a baby. I know what you mean about a sign. The births and the deaths, the giving and the taking—how interesting life is! Please stay in touch.

Love,
Olivia

She wished she had someone to talk to about her feelings for Marc and for Roger. She couldn't tell her cousins. She wasn't sure even Jenny would understand. And she didn't quite trust Alys not to tell anyone. If this situation were happening to someone else, she could easily have dispensed sensible advice, but it was happening to her, and all of her good sense seemed to have vanished.

She met Marc at yet a different dark bar, and they sat in the back. She thought she should write a book of her own someday called *Places to Sneak Around In.* He had a gently healthy glow from his skiing holiday and looked very young and fresh and appealing. He wound his fingers around hers and looked into her eyes. Then he kissed her, and she melted helplessly again.

"Remember the couple who were devouring each other at the Carlyle bar when we were there?" he said.

"Yes."

"Now that's us."

"We'd never be so ostentatious," Olivia said.

"No, never." They smiled at each other and he ordered drinks. As soon as the waiter went away Marc kissed her. "Did you get my postcard?" he whispered.

"Yes. It was perfect. It was so boring."

"Tell me the news. What did you do while I was away?"

"Some Christmas parties. We always have a quiet New Year's Eve. What did you do?"

"Skiied, saw my family, went to a big New Year's Eve party. I was faithful to you."

"The entire time?"

"Yes."

"Why?" she asked, happy and flattered. "It seems such a waste."

"Because I knew you'd want to know. And besides . . . it's very romantic being faithful. Very alluring. It makes me want you more."

"You're like a cavalier from another century," she said. "Or maybe I mean knight. Anyway, it's lovely."

"No. I'm just me."

She glanced around the room to make sure there was no one who could recognize her. The waiter brought their wine and they sipped it and looked at each other with such intensity she was sure anyone who saw them would see everything about them—and more—in an instant. She wished they could have the whole evening. She suddenly hated watching the time, leaving things unfinished, parting with longing. She had forgotten how much she needed the high of his desire for her, but now that he was back again she remembered.

"I had an uncle who had an affair with a married woman for twenty years," Marc said. "She was the love of his life. He became a friend of the family. People who didn't know about them wondered why he never married. I always found it interesting."

"Your family sounds as eccentric as mine," Olivia said.

"You don't find the concept appealing?"

"Twenty years? No, if I were the woman, I'd have to choose one or the other."

"Which one would you pick?"

"It's too theoretical."

"I didn't mean I'd do that myself," he said. "I'm just teasing you."

"It must have been awful for that woman's children," she said. "Did they have any idea?"

"They were very fond of him."

"Anyway, we're not having an affair," Olivia said. "We're having a drink."

"Of course."

She would not want Roger to have such a drink with anyone.

The winter wore on. Invitations arrived for the forthcoming spring bar mitzvahs of Jenny's second son, Max, and Melissa's oldest, Abe, who had been named Absalom in homage to their dead grandfather, Abe Miller. Olivia accepted for herself and Roger. Uncle David and his fiancée were married in a small ceremony for only their children and grandchildren at her house in Key West; and went on their honeymoon to the South Sea Islands, which they had enjoyed very much on the round-the-world cruise where they had met. This time, however, they took a plane. And Taylor, who was beginning to show, sent Olivia a photograph of herself in front of her house in Topanga Canyon, proudly holding her dress out at the sides to reveal her rounded stomach.

Dear Olivia—Here we are! Isn't it amazing? I've been going to a support group for abused children, to be sure I don't make the mistakes my mother did. I really want to be a good mother.

Love,
Taylor

Olivia wrote back.

Dear Taylor—Thank you for the early family picture for the album I now intend to start. I know you'll be a wonderful mother. I remember when you and Grady were little, how protective and sweet you were with him.

Love,
Olivia

She continued to meet Marc once a week, and they tormented each other in private corners of public places while Roger was at the gym. She was constantly aware of the irony of it. Marc gave her two more chapters to read. She was impressed by his writing and flattered that he was showing it to her, but she didn't mention him or his book to Roger again. She thought about Roger's lack of jealousy, and realized that it wasn't that he took her for granted or thought no one else would want her, but that he completely trusted her. This made her feel guilty, of course. But there had been a time when she completely trusted him.

She remembered once discussing marital infidelity with Jenny and Melissa. "My husband would never cheat," Melissa said. "He can't live without me." How comforting, Olivia had thought at the time, to be able to be so confident, so without fear. But so had she been. She wondered now if any of her cousins' husbands cheated on their spouses, and she decided that if they found out they would never tell, just as she had not. You told only if you broke up over it. They were not sisters; they weren't that close. You kept humiliation to yourself. They hadn't even mentioned the possibility that they might cheat on their husbands. It had probably never occurred to them. But there had been a time when it had never occurred to her.

Then one night Roger came home looking distressed and grim. "I have to go to dinner with my brother on Wednesday," he said. "He doesn't want to pay his half of our mother's old-age home anymore. He says he has two adult unemployed children to support, and his wife doesn't work, so it's up to me to pay it all because you make a living and we have no children. I can't believe that guy."

"Lawyers make a lot of money," Olivia said. "What's his problem?"

"He hates me and wants to make my life miserable," Roger said.

"Oh, Roger," she said sadly. She put her arms around him. "I'm sorry you two have such a bad relationship."

"I thought if I never saw him I wouldn't have to deal with it," Roger said.

"If you need money, I'll help."

"No, sweetheart, you shouldn't have to. She's his mother, too. He should pay *some.* It's his attitude of complete entitlement I resent, not just the money. He's always been like this. That's why we never got along."

"I wish you two would find a way to make up," Olivia said.

"It's a good thing Mom doesn't know he thinks she's a burden," Roger said. "She never wanted to be a burden to anybody. Maybe I can get him to contribute a part of it. God, I hate having to negotiate with my own brother. You're lucky you're an only child."

Wednesday. On Wednesday she was meeting Marc for a drink. When he called to confirm and to tell her where, Olivia said casually, "If you want to have dinner too, I can."

26

ROGER MET HIS BROTHER at a midtown steak house. It was, as always, Michael's choice. It was also across the street from Michael's office, which made it convenient for him and inconvenient for Roger. He was a successful corporate lawyer, and lived in a large cooperative apartment with his wife and two sons. In the summers they had for many years rented the same house in Sagaponack where the rent for one summer would have made a tidy down payment—something Roger liked to mention to annoy him. They did not choose to have any pets. The two brothers bore a definite family resemblance, but while Roger looked pleasant and accessible, Michael always looked as if he were smelling something slightly offensive. Roger used to say it was himself. He could not remember any time, even as small children, that they had liked each other. He did remember Mike leaving him tied to a tree for an entire day, an event of such betrayal and cruelty that it had traumatized him for years.

When he got to the table Michael was already there, which made it unnecessary for them to shake hands, hug or make any other pretense of affection. Roger slid into his seat. A frosty martini was in front of his brother's place.

"If you want the charcoal-broiled chicken you'd better order it now," Michael said by way of greeting. "It takes a long time. I ordered mine."

"I think I'll look at the menu first," Roger said, picking it up.

"I always have the chicken."

The waiter came over and Roger asked for a glass of white wine and, annoyed at himself for it, the chicken.

"He wants it very crisp," Michael said to the waiter. "No salt and no butter."

"I'll have it the way it comes."

"My doctor says I have to watch myself," Michael said.

"Don't we all."

"How's Olivia?"

"Fine, thanks. How is Norma?"

"She's fine."

They sipped their drinks. "I think Mom's deteriorating," Michael said. "Last time I was there she thought I was a little boy again."

"She does that sometimes."

"Didn't know Norma."

"Norma's not from her past."

"So." He tapped his fingers on the table. "As I told you on the phone, I have ongoing financial pressures. Two kids still at home, still unemployed. Norma does a great job taking care of all of us, but she can't contribute money. It's up to me, and frankly, I don't think it's right that you, with an easy life, aren't taking on more of the responsibility of Mom's upkeep."

An easy life. How resentful he sounded. "When we wanted to put her in a nice place we knew it would be expensive," Roger said. "We agreed to share."

"You don't have two grown children at home."

"Why is that different from when they were in college?" Roger said. "It cost more then; you had to pay for school."

"You wouldn't understand. You have no kids."

On the few occasions he had seen his brother's sons—he thought of them as that, never his nephews—they seemed like two hostile, unkempt louts with attitude. They behaved as if they were stoned, did not speak unless spoken to and when they did answer they acted as if they were doing you a favor. "What I do understand," Roger said, "is that they're adults and they should work."

"It's hard to get a job."

"Let them do *something*. Work in a record store. Get an MBA. Anything."

"Even people with MBAs can't get jobs these days," Michael said.

Especially if they lie in their rooms all day smoking dope, Roger thought, but he said nothing.

How could this have happened? What had gone wrong? They were probably spoiled. He wondered what kind of father his brother had been, and if that would have mattered. Their own parents had been well meaning, and look how he and Mike had turned out. Why do you hate me? he wanted to say. Why did you have such terrible jealousy of me? Mom and Dad loved both of us the same, they were proud of both of us. Why did you always wish that I had never been born?

The waiter arrived with their chicken. Michael's looked burned to a crisp and he apparently liked it that way. He cut into it enthusiastically. Roger's looked burned too, but he had very little appetite at the moment and didn't want to make an issue of it. He'd be out of here soon and could find something at home where he could eat in peace.

"Unless you want to take Mom out of there," Michael said, chewing. "Unless you're that kind of person."

"She's happy there!"

"So. Your move."

"What does that mean?"

"I can't afford it."

"You seem to be able to afford all the other things you do," Roger said.

"What does *that* mean?"

"Just what I said."

"You know nothing about responsibilities," Michael said.

"Setting up my own practice wasn't a responsibility?"

"With a rich woman?"

He wanted to punch that pinched and sneering face. "Leave Olivia out of this."

"Nothing wrong with money," Michael said. "I don't know why you don't marry her."

The man in front of Roger was a stranger. He always had been, always would be. "She's too good for me," Roger said lightly. "I think we should get on with our discussion. You don't seem able to pay half at the present time, so I would accept your paying a third."

"That's too much."

"You can manage."

"I can't."

"A fourth," Roger said. His stomach turned over and he pushed his untouched food away. This was his mother they were talking about. A sweet old woman who offered him milkshakes, who sang little songs. He wondered what would happen to her if something happened to him and she was left to his brother's mercies. Roger was glad he had thought to put her in his will.

"You like to be in control," Mike said.

"No, you're the one who always has to win."

"I could never figure out why Mom liked you better than she liked me."

Better? She had loved them both equally. Never in his entire life had Roger gotten the feeling that their mother had played favorites. Her only flaw was in not noticing that his older brother was terrorizing him, but then he hadn't told her, for reasons that now seemed pathetic and ridiculous. He had hoped that somehow, if he didn't tell their parents, that his brother and he could turn out to be friends.

"Yes," Roger lied, "she did like me better. Because I was nicer to her than you were."

There was a long silence. He watched the rage play over his brother's face. "I'll pay a fourth," Michael said finally. "Only to keep you from having control. I don't want you thinking you can move her without consulting me."

"Thanks for your gesture of filial love," Roger said. "I know she'd appreciate it if she knew."

There was nothing else to say. They decided to forego coffee and called for the check, which they split on two credit cards.

When they left the restaurant Michael took a taxi without offering to share, and Roger decided to walk for a while, even though it was cold, to clear his head. His father was dead, his mother lived on another planet, his brother was a hostile bully. He had no feelings for his two nephews at all, nor had they for him. His family, such as it was, was an accident of birth and a casualty of time. He was alone.

But he was not alone. He had Olivia. When he thought of her—her love and comfort, her warm, sensual body, her child's smile, the way she could make him laugh, the safety he felt just by knowing she was in the same room with him—he realized she was all the family he needed. And that was good, because she was all the family he had.

When he remembered how he had hurt and betrayed her with Wendy, he felt saddened. There would be other temptations, he suspected, because what he had discovered about his secret self would never change, but he was not so interested anymore, and determined not to give in to them. The destruction wasn't worth it. And maybe, after a long while, his fantasy of the seduced stranger would let go and disappear, and he would just be happy: with Olivia, the way he was now.

He stopped at the Korean market on the corner, the only place still open, to buy Olivia flowers. He never brought her flowers. He would bring them home to her and she would be so pleased. He was unexpectedly turned on by the thought of her waiting for him.

27

Olivia met Marc at a tiny, romantic French restaurant he had chosen near his apartment. She thought about how in each neighborhood there were these little places tucked away, known to only the local people, many of whom had become regulars, and felt a part of his private life. There were lace curtains on the windows, and small round vases of red and purple anemones on the crisp white tablecloths. He twined his fingers around hers and kissed her, and as always, she was lost.

"I'm going to order champagne," he said, and did.

She watched the waiter performing the ritual of uncorking and popping, pouring the festive bubbly liquid, and felt as nervous as a virgin bride. This is just dinner; I don't have to do anything, she thought, trying to reassure herself, but already she felt the damp throbbing that had become even more powerful than the guilt. She looked at Marc's sweet, eager face and dared to let herself fall a little in love with him.

"What are you thinking?" he asked.

"That we've never had a whole evening before."

"I've been thinking about it all day."

They held up their glasses in a toast and drank. She didn't want to get high, but she wanted to take the edge off her inhibitions a bit. Not her lust, her inhibitions. If it were lust alone from which she operated, they could have left the table now.

They looked at their menus. After all, they were here to have dinner. She couldn't have salad—bits of green might get in her teeth—no onions or garlic, nothing heavy, and nothing that could give you gas. The waiter assured them that the maigret of duck was very lean, very good, so they ordered it, although she doubted if she could manage more than a few bites. People should eat after lovemaking, not before, she thought—at least the first time.

Neither of them mentioned sex; it was too close.

"How did you manage to get away?" Marc asked.

"Roger had a meeting." She didn't want to think about Roger and feel guilty again. She smiled at Marc and cleared her mind of everything but him.

"I went to the museum by myself this afternoon," he said. "The Met. It's very relaxing. I like the Egyptian rooms."

"Yes, I loved to go there when I was growing up," Olivia said. "Those were my favorite. And the armor."

"The armor?"

"The men were so small. They were smaller than I was. Of course, I was a tall child."

"That's funny. I like thinking about you as a child."

"And I thought the Middle Ages were romantic," Olivia said. "I was particularly partial to the knights. All that love at a distance and longing. Being rescued."

"But they were so brutal," Marc said. "When they went away to battle they put their wives in chastity belts."

"I found out about that much later. What an appalling thing to do!"

He looked into her eyes rather mischievously. "It's lucky we live in the present time, isn't it," he said.

They were talking about sex anyway.

The waiter brought Marc's green salad and the sliced tomatoes Olivia had ordered. As she watched Marc eat she noticed he had those straight, even teeth that never got food caught in them; he was so fresh and clean and perfect she wanted to bite his neck.

"What?" he said.

"You're edible."

His knee touched hers under the table and his hand followed. "I'm yours."

She smiled.

"You know how much I want to make love to you," he said. "I've wanted you for so long. I said I wouldn't ask you again, I'd wait for you to ask me, but . . . I lied."

"I suspected you did," she said.

The hidden little packet of condoms she had bought secretly before coming here nestled in her handbag, seeming radioactive. They were just in case she gave in. It had seemed strange to buy them—when she had come of age, women were on the Pill; then, when unwanted pregnancy became the least dangerous thing about sex, she was already safely with Roger. They aren't a commitment, they're a precaution, she told herself.

"I'll be careful," he said.

She didn't answer.

"We would make each other so happy," he said. "You know we would."

They put on politely enthusiastic faces at the intervention of the waiter arriving with the duck. The small rare slices lay neatly fanned on the white plate, surrounded by pureed vegetables, and she was sorry about the obvious effort that had gone into something in which she had no interest at all.

"Red wine, or finish the champagne?" Marc asked her.

"The champagne."

He devoured his food with the energy of the young and healthy, as if he wanted to get it over with, and she picked and pretended.

"You're not eating anything," he said, sounding concerned.

"I'm fine."

"This is a pretty place, isn't it?"

"Yes, it is."

"Do you want coffee?"

"Only if you do."

"I'd like you to see my apartment. You never have, and it's right up the street."

I can say no, she thought. I always say no. Then I'll go home and wish I had said yes. She glanced at her watch. There was still time. The evening stretched ahead of her, tantalizing, sexually charged. Her heart began to pound and she could hardly breathe.

"Please?" he said. "Just for a minute?"

She nodded. She didn't trust her voice.

His apartment was on the second floor of a brownstone. The front room had bowed windows overlooking the tree-lined street; the back room, which was his bedroom, overlooked the small private gardens of his and the other buildings. There were books piled everywhere, and he seemed to be the only person in New York who had not yet thrown out his withered Christmas tree. That was all she saw, because as soon as they were inside his door they were kissing and tearing off each other's clothes as they headed for his bed.

His body was as lean and silky as she had fantasized and his lovemaking was even better. She knew how wild she could be, but he had not, and the look on his face was amazed rapture. In a few minutes she even surprised herself. There was no guilt, no hesitation, no outside world—only the culmination of everything she had been dreaming of for so long. It was as if all this time she had been celibate and longing, waiting for him.

"You are . . . amazing," he whispered.

"No, you are."

They lay kissing, stroking each other's skin, looking at each other with genuine affection, waiting to have the energy to start again. She touched the small crescent-shaped scar on his knee where he'd had stitches years ago, feeling somehow as if he were hers.

They knew each other's secrets. They would never be nervous with each other now. The affair they had started shimmered tantalizingly ahead of her—if she wanted it. She couldn't imagine not wanting it, for as long as it took to burn out. She felt trapped and doomed by her senses, and idiotically happy.

"Why haven't you gotten rid of your Christmas tree?" she murmured.

"I don't know. I thought it could be firewood."

"You'll burn your apartment down."

"I hope not."

"I'm going to worry about you."

"Then I'll put it out in the street tomorrow."

"Good."

They did not speak of love.

After a while they began again: insatiable, confident, new. When it was over she looked at the clock on his bedside table, and it was as if time had melted. She realized with a stab of panic that unless an unexpected complication with his brother had arisen, Roger had to be at home already. How had it gotten so late?

"I have to leave," she said, and moved quickly out of bed. There was no time to take a shower. She went into Marc's bathroom and splashed around at the sink, used his towel and comb, reapplied her makeup. She thought she had not looked so ripe and wonderful in a long time.

"You're incredibly beautiful," he said.

"So are you."

They rescued their strewn clothes and dressed quickly. "I'll put you in a cab," he said.

"You don't have to."

"I want to."

It was very cold out. A tiny winter moon hung in the black sky like a coin. "When will I see you again?" he asked.

"Soon."

"Sooner."

"Soonest." They kissed gently at the door of the taxi.

"Take good care of this woman," Marc said to the driver, as if the driver cared. He stood in front of the steps to his building, his coat collar turned up against the wind, his long black hair blowing, until her cab turned the corner and she couldn't see him anymore.

In the taxi going home she tried to collect her thoughts, to be again the Olivia she had been a few hours ago. But she couldn't be. Everything was different. She didn't know how she felt; she was afraid even to think about it. She had never cheated in a relationship—not in her two marriages, never on Roger and not even during those brief affairs of the distant past. For her, cheating had meant it was already over. But it certainly wasn't over with Roger, not at all. She knew he would be waiting for her and she only hoped she would be able to handle it.

* * *

Roger was in the living room in his bathrobe, watching television with the dogs. He looked unexpectedly vulnerable, or maybe that was only because she realized how much she could hurt him. She hoped she didn't look different from the last time he had seen her. "Hi," she said.

"Hello." He sounded happy to see her, and not suspicious. "You went out too," he said mildly.

"Yes."

"Where?"

"Dinner with Alys."

"How is Alys?"

"Complaining as usual." She went over to kiss him hello and then noticed there was a bunch of flowers in a glass vase on the coffee table. He had obviously put them there. "What's this?"

"For you," he said.

He never brought her flowers. She wondered why he had this time, but she was touched. "Thank you. They're lovely."

He smiled. "I wanted to come in with them in my hand like a suitor, but you weren't here, so I had to put them in water so they wouldn't die."

"It's even better this way. Such a nice surprise."

He turned off the TV, got up and put his arms around her. "You have no idea how glad I am to see you," he said.

Why? she thought in panic. "Oh?" she said.

"I feel like I'm back from the enemy and safe at home."

"Ah . . . your brother. Was it awful?"

"Mr. Milk of Human Kindness is willing to pay a fourth," he said wryly. He stroked her hair and touched her neck, as if he needed to feel the solidity of her. She hoped he needed only comfort and not sex; she didn't know how she could handle having sex with him tonight.

"At least you don't have to see him again for a long time," she said.

"Yes, there's that. This evening was a horror. Not unexpectedly."

"I'm sorry," she said.

"As far as I'm concerned I don't have a brother."

"As far as I'm concerned you never did."

"I love you," Roger said. "I don't know what I'd do without you. I realized tonight that you're my real family. You're what holds me together. You're what stands between me and that abyss, that cosmic loneliness. . . . I don't think I ever tell you often enough how much I love you."

He had never been so emotional. She loved him, she always had. She hugged him and fought back tears. She didn't even know why she was crying. "I don't want to lose you either," she said.

"But you won't."

He kissed her then, and she went numb. "Let's go to bed," he said.

"All right. I'll just wash up."

She changed into her robe and fled into the bathroom. She brushed her teeth, removed her makeup and again hurriedly washed away every trace she could find, real and imaginary, of Marc's body scent and her own from the past two hours. When she came out of the bathroom Roger was waiting for her in bed. She knew that look on his face. He held the covers up for her, welcoming her into their cave of delights. There was nothing she could do about it.

As soon as she got into bed he began to kiss her again. She knew if she turned away, if she refused him, this special moment he had started with his declaration would be gone and the damage might be irreparable. No matter what Roger had said, she would lose him. She was sure of that. She would just have to do the best she could, even if she had to pretend.

But then quickly, entwined with him, her need for him surprised her. Feeling the familiarity of his body, her desire came pouring back, and she wanted him more than she had in a very long time. He felt so *real.* They were the two halves of one whole. She knew what he liked, and he knew what she liked, and he made her feel safe and cherished. Their passion for each other had always been there, it had just been hiding for a while. Those things happened. She didn't have to fantasize about Marc, or even think of him. All she thought about was Roger.

Afterwards she lay there listening to Roger's breathing and thinking, stunned, about what she had done. She had made love with two men in the same night. She had never considered that in her life. She could hardly believe it had happened to her. Something to tell my grandchildren, as they say, if I had any, she thought, and smiled.

28

It was not until the next day that Olivia had second thoughts. And then they came moving in on her serenity, changing it to the feeling of being off balance, in danger. Part of her felt warm and loved, desired by two men, but another part of her wished none of it had happened. So this was what an extramarital affair was like—having to switch gears so quickly, having to pretend, being on the edge of disaster. No wonder Roger had avoided her when he was having sex with Wendy. He couldn't play-act the way she could. But what she had felt for both Roger and Marc had been genuine. She knew she could never look at Roger in exactly the same way again, because she had seen—no, *understood* how easily she could hurt him, the same way he had hurt her.

Snow fell, another winter blizzard, the thick, fat flakes pressing against their windows like fog. And it was cold. Wozzle and Buster went out to do their business and came back in quickly, refusing to play in what was out there, shaking the snow off their coats and making puddles on the floor. Clients who did not have emergencies canceled their appointments. It was good that it was an easy day because her mind was still on herself.

Marc called her at the office. "I guess I can't throw out my Christmas tree today," he said.

"Oh. You could try." She smiled, picturing him in his apartment calling her.

"I'm thinking about last night," he said. "It was wonderful."

"Yes, it was." Suddenly the phone seemed dangerous. "But be careful," she said softly. She did not mean about the Christmas tree, and he knew it.

"Of course," he said.

"I'm sorry if I sound strange."

"No, I understand."

"Such a snowy day."

"Nice to stay at home and write," he said. "And you don't even have to go out to get to work either."

"We're lucky."

"When can I see you?"

"Next week," she said. It seemed far away, it seemed too close.

"Call me," he said.

"I will."

"Soon, sooner, soonest," he whispered, and she felt him inside her again.

"Yes. I promise." When she hung up her heart was pounding too hard, but she didn't know whether it was from anticipation or fear.

In the afternoon, driven by restlessness and confusion, when she had no more patients to see and the sky was still light, she bundled up and went out into the falling snow. In an instant she was covered with it, even her eyelashes. The flakes stung and melted on her tongue. The dirty piles on the sidewalk from the last snowstorm were white again, temporarily. A single taxi groaned through the ice, trying not to fishtail. She was alone on the street and she liked it. She walked to Central Park.

The few blocks seemed endless against the wind, her boots sliding. She didn't know why she was going to the park, but it was somewhere open and empty, somewhere to go. The harshness of the weather calmed her. She needed to think.

She was not a woman who had affairs, and yet that was what she had just done. Last night's triumphant bliss had given way to today's questions. She had thought having an affair would make her feel guilty, but she had never anticipated the rest of it. She wanted them both, she wished they would both disappear. People do this all the time, she thought. What's so hard about it? But now she understood.

She was the only person in Central Park, and indeed it seemed as if she was the only person in the city who was out of doors. The flakes swirled in the white sky, and piled onto the branches of the trees until they bent. She had snow epaulets, an ice hat. Across the park the outlines of the tall apartment houses were gray and fuzzy. The blizzard was rough but also surprisingly serene. She stood there letting it hit her, letting all the images in her mind empty out.

All I ever wanted was an uncomplicated life, Olivia thought.

Then she realized her feet were cold and wet, and so was her coat, and she started to shiver. She could walk to Marc's apartment and surprise him; he would be so happy. Or she could go home, light a fire in her own fireplace and ask Roger to rub her frozen feet in his warm, capable hands. I can make love with either of them, she thought, pleased with her power. But I can't make love with both. Someone else could—I can't.

She turned away, bent against the wind, and walked slowly home.

When she got back Roger had already lighted the fire and had made tea. "Where were you?" he asked, in that same mild way he always did. She had never before realized how often they had to account to each other. It had made her feel safe, and then threatened, and now it would just be a part of their lives again.

"Playing in the snow," she said, and laughed.

"You're crazy," he said, chuckling, and when she joined him on the couch in front of the fire and poked him with her bare toe he warmed her feet without even being asked.

She thought how good it was to be back to her senses, but she knew it was not that easy. Marc would not turn ugly to look at just because she wanted to be free of her attraction to him. And although men she had cared about had disappeared often from her life with no explanation, she felt she owed him more than that. They were friends. He was her client. And she hoped they would stay that way.

She called Marc two days later because she couldn't wait any longer to clear her conscience and, if she was going to upset him, get it over with. "When can we meet?" he asked, and his eager, intimate voice made her feel both sad and a little trapped. I don't belong to him no matter how close we were that night, she thought; but how could he know that, and besides, when had he ever said she did?

The blizzard was over, paths had been cleared, Roger would be at the gym as usual. "Tomorrow afternoon," she said.

"My apartment?"

"No, I think we should meet at that bar on your street."

"Okay." Did his tone sound a little questioning, or was that her imagination?

As soon as she slid into the booth where Marc was waiting, he leaned forward to kiss her hello, and she moved away. He looked surprised, but then the waiter was hovering over them and Marc took her reluctance to be because of the waiter. They ordered their usual. As soon as the waiter left, Marc took her hand. He looked happy, and that hurt.

"I missed you," he said.

She looked at his mouth, and her lips throbbed. She forced the feeling to subside. Then she pretended his touch meant nothing to her, and after a few moments it was—surprisingly—easier to deal with, almost brotherly. She had not known her will was so strong, or perhaps it was her fear. When he tried again to kiss her she briefly let him and turned her head.

"We need to have a discussion," she said.

"That sounds ominous."

"I thought about you a lot," she said. That was certainly true.

"What did you think?"

"You're so attractive and bright and so nice, I'm really drawn to you and I like you so much, but . . ."

"But?"

She sighed. "I'm not able to handle this."

"What happened?" He looked very concerned. "Did he find out?"

You always call him *he,* she thought. "No," she said.

"Then what can't you handle? Tell me, I'll help."

"Us. I just can't cheat on Roger. I never did this to him before, and now I realize why. I'm not good at it."

"You're wonderful at it," he said softly.

"Not really." She was the one playing with his fingers now, but in a bemused way, as if he were her sweet child. Then she took her hand away. "I *have* thought a great deal about this, Marc. I think we shouldn't see each other for a while."

"How long is a while?"

"Until we can be friends again."

"We were always friends," he said. "I thought we were."

"I mean just friends."

"Oh." His voice was flat, but she could see how hard he was trying to hide his disappointment. It pained her to look into his eyes. He's young, she told herself; he'll get over it. Sooner than I think, I'm sure. "That's what you want?"

"Yes. Please try to understand."

The waiter brought Marc's beer and her Perrier and left. "Well," Marc said.

"Well."

They looked at each other. They sipped their drinks. This time he did not ask her what she was thinking "right this minute," because she was sure he didn't want to know.

"I guess I'll go away again for a month or two and concentrate on writing my book," he said finally. "Someplace warm. I have a friend whose parents have a house on Anguilla they hardly ever use. I've always had an open invitation, maybe I'll go there."

"I'm not telling you to leave town!"

"Nothing to keep me here, and it's been a hard winter. I'd be glad for the sun."

"That sounds nice," she said gently. "This *has* been a hard winter."

"Do you want me to send you a postcard?" Echoes . . . no, just a connection.

"Of course," she said. "As long as it's boring."

"They always are, aren't they?" he said, and smiled.

"Not to me," she said, and smiled back. "Never to me. Even as friends."

She left him earlier than usual because there wasn't anything more to say—and there was too much. And she didn't want to risk arriving home after Roger again and having to lie. Marc put her into a cab. He kissed her lightly on both cheeks in the French way, as he had the first time they had drinks together. They both noticed.

In this one bittersweet gesture the ending was the same as the beginning, but of course it wasn't at all.

29

SPRING WENT BY, and then a blastingly hot summer was full upon them. In the spring the cousins had met twice on happy occasions—the bar mitzvahs of Jenny's son, Max, and Melissa's son, Abe—and caught up on family news. Jenny's Didi, who was now eleven, was doing extremely well with her singing lessons and was determined to become a Broadway star. She had already won a local children's beauty pageant, which she entered herself with no help from her parents, and now she was looking for an agent in the Yellow Pages. Jenny and Paul intended to stand off and let her pursue her career by herself, but they were thrilled and a little surprised at what had blossomed in their midst.

"You know how at beauty pageants they ask all the contestants the same question," Jenny told Olivia. "The question is: 'Who would you go to for advice?' She said: 'My mother.' And then she went on and on about how I was her best friend and how she admired me so much. The woman sitting next to me was saying: 'Oh, you must be so proud,' and I was just sitting there laughing because Didi tells me seventeen times a day how much she hates me."

Taylor was hugely pregnant and happily obsessed with the coming event. She who had always been afraid to have a child now believed that motherhood was going to be the pinnacle of her existence. She seemed annoyed but not worried about the specter of Big Earl as Grandma. Somehow the guilt and fear that had allowed her to put up with Earlene's unwelcome visits had been pushed aside by her view of herself as an adult responsible for a tiny, vulnerable life. It was clear she knew who the mother was going to be in this new story, and it was not Earlene.

Nick's agency had mounted a fresh advertising campaign to update Julia's image, a concept he had decided upon with Charlie the Perfect's son, Tony. Suddenly the venerable old institution was going to be trendy.

"I suppose even Julia's has to keep up with the modern world," Aunt Myra told Olivia with a trace of regret in her voice. It seemed to be working; they had higher dividend checks this year.

Tony didn't come to family functions after the time they had seen him, just as Charlie had not. He devoted himself to his own family life and to the business, although unlike his late father, he used commercial airliners on his trips for the company. This was due less to a fear that something might happen to him than because certain family shareholders had complained about the expense of a private plane. It was the first time anyone had dared to criticize anything.

It was more than the store that had come into the modern world.

In August Olivia and Roger decided to spend ten days in Nantucket, something they had never done before. Somehow the memories of Paris lingered in a way that did not make either of them anxious to go back so soon. They stayed at an inn, read, walked, ate and made love. It was very romantic, although they agreed afterward that their next trip would again be to a foreign city; perhaps in Italy.

She hadn't seen Marc again, but he had sent her several picture postcards with innocuous inscriptions. The first was from Anguilla, the next two from New York—from bars where they had met, which was not so innocuous—and the last one from Paris. *My grandmother's birthday again,* he wrote. *So much changes, so much remains the same.* She was not sure what he meant by that.

At first she had thought about him often—every day. Sometimes it was just a flash of memory, sometimes a brief daydream.

She didn't allow herself to think about him with sexual longing, but with nostalgia and with fondness. What had been so intensely physical had diluted through her wish for peace into a recollection that was mild and, in a way, much sweeter than it had been when it was actually happening. And then, finally, there were days when she didn't think about him at all. She felt relieved about that, although she knew he would be a part of her life for a very long time.

In August, when Olivia and Roger were in Nantucket, Taylor gave birth to a healthy baby boy, whom she and Tim named Cody. Aunt Myra called on their return with the good news.

"Tim told me Taylor thinks the baby looks just like Grady," Aunt Myra said.

Olivia sent the baby a sterling silver teething ring with an imitation ivory elephant on it, from a catalogue that shared the proceeds with the campaign to save endangered wildlife. He would be getting things from Julia's soon enough. A month later a little card with a blue ribbon on it arrived, announcing Cody's birth, along with a note from Taylor and a photograph of the baby himself. He did look a little like Grady, which was nice.

Dear Olivia, Thank you for Cody's beautiful teething ring. He loves it. I can't wait for you to see him. He is exactly like Grady. He has the same smile, the same little expressions on his face. Do you remember Grady's friend Miranda? I think you met her at the funeral. She came to see the baby and she cried. She said, "That's Grady." I really believe my baby is Grady reincarnated. He has come back.

Love,
Taylor

Oh, Taylor, Olivia thought.

She remembered Grady's hidden lover, the young man who had seemed so out of place at his funeral, who had inherited her mother's crystal glasses and had become friendly with Taylor, telling her about his interest in reincarnation. She supposed that was how this had started. But at the same time, Olivia was rather taken by the idea. She thought about how much she had adored Grady when he was a child at Mandelay, and how much she had missed him when he grew up and changed and started to seem so uncomfortable with the family. How wonderful it would be to have him here again. As long as Taylor treats this baby as himself and not like a little returned Grady, it will be all right, she thought.

She propped up the baby's picture on her desk where she could see it. She had told Taylor she would start a scrapbook, but she realized she had so surprisingly few photos of any of her cousins that right now it seemed premature to get one for Baby Cody. She bought a frame instead.

Fall came, bright with changing leaves and a reviving crispness in the air. She and Roger talked again about how fast time seemed to be passing, how when you were young it had appeared endless, and now in a flash it was gone. And then one morning they woke up, turned on the television to watch the news, and saw the Santa Monica Mountains covered with towers of flame racing toward Topanga Canyon, where Taylor, Tim and Cody lived.

The sky on their screen glowed pink, the flames deep orange. The air was filled with thunderclouds of black smoke and raining white ash. Helicopters hovered overhead, dumping fire retardant and huge buckets of ocean water, but still the flames swept on. In the past few days Olivia had heard news reports that there were fires in California, but she hadn't realized how terrible they were or how close to Taylor until this moment with the film of them before her eyes. It seemed unreal, like something seen in a movie, but it was not. Taylor's house was now in the fire zone, but no one knew what was happening because the phone lines were down.

"What's she going to do?" Olivia asked frantically, not really expecting an answer. "She has a little baby, she can't even *hear*."

"I'm sure they've been evacuated," Roger said.

"Then they'll have no home. Where will they go?"

"Let's wait and see," he said.

Even though she knew there would be no answer, she called Tim; and there was none. She spent a nervous day worrying about their safety, and between patients she turned on the portable radio she had brought to work. It was "some nut with a match," the police said. But huge firestorms this year were "more probable than normal" in any case, authorities said. Six years of drought had left much dead vegetation in the canyons, a rainy spring had added thick new underbrush, there had been a long, dry summer and now there were the hot, dry Santa Ana winds fanning the fires, those winds that years ago, when she was a child, Stan had told her made people go crazy.

That evening Aunt Myra called. "Have you been watching the fires on TV?"

"Yes," Olivia said.

"I called, but nobody can get through."

"I know. I tried too."

"I guess Tim will call when they're all right," Aunt Myra said. She didn't say *if.*

"I'm sure," Olivia said, but that didn't help right now. She imagined Taylor grabbing her mementos if she could and running away like a deer; but of course she and Tim would be driving, and the deer would be screaming and dying in the flames that roared up the rock faces and sped crackling along the ridge in pursuit. I know Taylor thinks it's paradise, but who would want to live there, she thought. You never know what will happen.

The fires went on for a week, battled by increasingly exhausted fire crews, and then one day the winds stopped and they were over. Authorities said that the few fires that were still left seemed sure to be contained. In the Malibu area and the nearby canyons, more than thirty-five thousand acres had burned, and more than two hundred homes were gone. Tim called from his mobile phone.

"We're all safe," he said.

"Thank God," Olivia said. "Where are you staying?"

"We're still in our house. We were there all along, hosing it down. Fires are very arbitrary. The other side of our road is completely destroyed and we're fine. The wind changed direction. And also, when the fire hit the cleared area around our house, it just stopped. Those two things saved us. We're covered with ash, of course. Big white flakes, like snow, in everything, even the dishes. A whole mess to clean up. But Taylor's good, the baby's good, it's all okay."

Olivia sighed with relief. "I was worried."

"Well, Grady's house burned down," Tim said. "Completely gone. Nothing left but the brick fireplace, just sticking up there."

"At least *he* wasn't in it," Olivia said. "You have insurance for it, don't you?"

"Oh, yes," he said calmly. "To tell you the truth, Taylor's kind of relieved it's gone. She never could sell it. Now that worry is over."

"You're doubly lucky."

"Yes. Very lucky. A lot of our friends aren't."

"I guess not."

"Terrible thing," he said. "But that's nature."

"Can't live without it, can't live with it?"

"Sort of. Well, got to make some more calls. If you talk to anybody in the family tell them we're okay."

"I will," she said. "Tell Taylor I miss her, and give her my love."

Thanksgiving was coming, and now with Taylor and her family safe, there was something more to be thankful for. As usual, all the cousins and their immediate families had their own plans, for feasting or for travel, and it was time for Olivia to plan her annual Thanksgiving dinner for the waifs and strays. She made out her guest list, and then, in an impulse of goodwill, she called Marc Delon to invite him too.

30

"HELLO?" MARC SAID. Olivia had not heard his voice for nine months. She waited for her heart or her body to do something at the sound of it, but she felt only the anticipation you feel when about to speak to a friend after a long time. So she was safe at last.

"Hi, it's Olivia."

"Olivia!" He sounded extremely glad to hear from her.

"How are you?"

"I'm very well. And you?"

"I'm fine. I got your postcards. How is your book coming along?"

"It's almost done. I'm beginning to feel that it's finally real."

"I'm looking forward to reading it."

"I'll send you a copy when it's finished. I didn't forget."

"Good. Well, the reason I'm calling is that I give a big Thanksgiving dinner here at the house every year, and I'd be delighted if you could come."

"How nice," he said. "I'd love to."

"Come at five and then we'll eat and drink for hours."

"It sounds wonderful. I . . ." There was the smallest pause. "Can I bring someone?"

"Oh?"

"Well, yes, I have a girlfriend."

She wasn't surprised. She was relieved that he was in love again, and hoped he was happy. But, strangely, a part of her felt a little left out. What did she expect, for him to be available forever? "Then you must bring her," she said warmly. "What's her name?"

"Daisy. She's very bright. I'm sure you'll like her."

If he has to say she's very bright then she must be very young, Olivia thought. "I'm sure I will if you do," she said.

So there they all were again, gathered in her large kitchen, her guests chattering and watching her finish her festive preparations. Peggy was helping with the huge turkey, Roger was uncorking champagne. Last year's active toddler had become a dignified little girl, the man who had come alone last Thanksgiving because he had broken up with his wife was here with his new wife, and Alys had brought along an attractive and attentive man who was even younger than Marc. She had announced to Olivia on the phone that she was bringing someone special, but Olivia hadn't known what she was supposed to expect.

"If no one impresses you anymore then find someone you can impress," Alys whispered to Olivia, glowing. "After winning the world's record for doing without, I'm finally making up for it."

"I'm sure of that," Olivia whispered back, grinning. "You've never looked better."

Marc came late, bringing a bottle of good red wine and Daisy. He was wearing a beautiful overcoat and his hair hung over his cheekbone in that way that used to touch her so. She waited again to see if her body or her heart would betray her, but they did not. She observed him objectively: he was just as appealing-looking as ever. What a catch he is, she thought, congratulating herself for having had him for a while. She looked at Daisy.

She was pretty, with very short dark hair, big eyes and dewy skin. She seemed sweet. They were both in Armani, both in black. The black generation. Olivia wondered if they were late because they had been having last-minute sex. They were holding hands. Marc kissed Olivia hello on both cheeks, as he always did, but this time it seemed too formal: not as if their affair had never happened, but as if he was trying too hard to pretend it hadn't. She would have settled for a friendly hug.

"Olivia tells me you're a writer," Roger said, taking Marc into the kitchen to meet the other guests.

"So is Daisy," Marc said. "Unpublished as yet . . ." Olivia smiled. She stood there alone for a moment thinking about the family Thanksgiving dinners so long ago, at Uncle Seymour's and Aunt Iris's, when everyone was still alive; those luxurious, magnificent dinners filled with goodwill and tension. Had she been the only one who had felt it? There had been so much for her to live up to, and she had always thought she was disappointing and didn't fit in. Now she wondered if in fact it had been her mother who was concerned about her shortcomings, because Lila had to appear to be the perfect parent of the perfect daughter. For the first time, Olivia wondered if it had been her mother all along who had unknowingly driven the wedge between her and the others in those old days by making her think she was never good enough.

She remembered Jenny reassuring her: "No matter what, they will always love you. They will *always* love you." Now she considered if it still mattered so much if they didn't, because some of them had not. And some of them had. Family is not magical, but how much they can hurt us, she thought.

She went back into the kitchen. Marc, holding a glass of champagne, smiled at her from across the room, and then he came over. "You look wonderful," he said.

"Thank you. So do you."

"I think about you so often."

"I think about you, too," she said lightly.

"I'm glad we're friends," he said. "I hope we always will be."

"That's why you're here."

"Do you remember the last time we had champagne?" he asked softly, mischievously.

"You're not supposed to talk about that," she said, matching his tone.

"I know." He gave her a sip from his glass. She felt comfortable with him and glad he was here. "I want you to get to know my girlfriend," he said. He nodded at Daisy, who came to join them and took his hand.

"It was so kind of you to invite us," Daisy said politely. To her I'm just another adult, Olivia thought. If she only knew.

"I'm delighted you could come," she said. "Please make yourself at home. As you can see, everyone here does."

"Thanks."

"Time to put the turkey on the table," Peggy announced. "I need someone strong."

"Excuse me," Olivia said, and rushed away to help.

When everything was in place, someone snapped a picture of the spread, while the others gazed admiringly at the result of their communal effort. It looked as if it belonged in a magazine, and nothing was burned or undercooked: a miracle. Hungry, they all dove for their seats. Before Olivia and Roger sat down at the head and foot of their groaning board, Olivia nestled against Roger for a moment, feeling a rush of warmth and love.

Her Thanksgiving party was a success, as it always was. Near the end Roger got up and delivered his customary toast of appreciation to her. How old-fashioned and nice that is, she thought, appreciating him back. There is much to be said for traditions, especially the ones you create yourself.

"I want to make a toast, too," she said, rising and holding up her glass.

They all looked at her expectantly. "On this Thanksgiving," she said, "when I see again how solid and happy our life together is, how blessed we are with wonderful friends and too much food and a comfortable home, and good health, and helpful work we care about; when so many people don't have any of these things, or very few of them, I am in awe at our good luck. I really see the meaning of Thanksgiving." Then, unexpectedly, her eyes filled with tears and she choked up and sat down.

They all applauded, a little nervously. "Olivia always cries when she's happy," Roger said affectionately, smiling at her, and then they all laughed, relieved that he had cut the intensity.

At one in the morning, with everyone gone and the leftovers banished, the dogs dozing, their house in some semblance of order again, Olivia and Roger went to bed. They were holding each other in that near-trancelike state she loved and had once thought they would never achieve again. "We've survived another year," she murmured.

"Yes," he said, and then they slept.

* * *

Two days after Thanksgiving Jenny called from Cambridge. Jenny never called—Olivia always called her. She hoped nothing bad had happened. "What a nice surprise to hear from you," Olivia said. "Happy belated Thanksgiving."

"Same to you," Jenny said. She sounded odd, grim, as if her face and voice were clenched up into a ball. "I called to tell you about Nick."

"What about Nick?" she asked, her heart sinking.

"He was helicopter skiing. There was an avalanche. He was killed."

Nick gone? Not Nick too—there had been too many family tragedies already. "Oh, no," Olivia said. She remembered how concerned she had been about Nick's attraction to danger, and how she had put it out of her mind because there was nothing she could do about it.

"It happened the day after Thanksgiving. He went out alone the way he always does . . . did, and he never came back. Lynne and Amber waited and waited, and he just never came back to the lodge and then they heard about the avalanche."

Olivia imagined his wife waiting there, her anxiety building, and finally learning that what she had for so long feared and half expected had actually happened. She imagined Lynne's dread and grief. But as for herself, for the moment she felt only stunned disbelief.

"Melissa and Bill and their kids were there for Thanksgiving," Jenny said. "Everybody was skiing, but just normally. Everyone's in shock. At least Lynne has Melissa with her, she's not there with Amber all alone."

"Our family has bad luck with mountains," Olivia said. She thought of Kenny deserted on the Himalayas, Stan going off Mulholland, Grady's suicide, Charlie's plane and now Nick.

"Yes . . ." It was a sigh. "They'll have to wait for spring thaw next May to find his body," Jenny said. "If they ever do. What a mess. There's going to be a memorial service at the Metropolitan Club in New York next week, but no actual funeral right now. My mother will call to tell you what day. I still can't believe it."

"No body, no closure," Olivia said.

"I know."

"My God, there's no letup. What's wrong with our family, anyway?"

"Melissa and Kenny say our family is cursed," Jenny said. "I used to think so, but now I think they looked for trouble."

"Don't tell anybody, but so do I," Olivia said. She was relieved to be able to share this feeling that had made her feel so guilty.

"Nick had everything," Jenny said. "Everything. Maybe that was the problem. Money does bad things to people."

"He said the mountains made him feel peaceful," Olivia said.

"And risking his life?"

"Maybe he didn't think he had everything."

"Well, we'll never know, will we?"

"Maybe he didn't know either," Olivia said.

The Metropolitan Club was a large, dignified building that whispered of tradition. An iron fence shut it off from the street, and inside, the main hall was two stories high with an enormous chandelier hanging down and a wide staircase leading to the rooms above. The memorial service was at five o'clock. When Olivia arrived with Roger she expected to find the service in one of the smaller anterooms, but instead, to her surprise, it was in the main ballroom.

"I didn't know Nick knew so many people," she whispered.

They were pouring in, somberly, expensively dressed. People from Nick's ad agency, people who looked like his friends; his contemporaries and older people; none of whom Olivia had ever seen in her life. Their family, even with Hedy's side present, was vastly outnumbered. It was the biggest memorial *or* funeral that she had ever been to.

Rows of chairs had been arranged in the ballroom, and they were already almost all occupied. Olivia and Roger sat down in the section that had been reserved for the immediate family. She saw Uncle David, hollow-eyed and bewildered to have outlived his son, tears pouring unchecked down his face, being led in by his new wife. Nearby were Melissa and Bill with their three children, and Lynne in black, very pale, with an expression of complete shock, clutching little Amber's hand. Uncle Seymour and

Aunt Iris, reminded again of the loss of their own son, looked grave and almost uncomprehending at this repeated reversal of the natural order.

Behind them she saw Jenny and Paul, who had left their children at home for this hurried day trip, and Aunt Myra, Kenny and Pam, Charlie's son Tony with his wife, and Anna the Perfect with her husband. The only ones absent were Taylor and Tim. No one had really expected Taylor to leave her three-month-old infant at home after the recent terrifying fires, or to bring him all the way to New York for this, and besides, Olivia remembered, Nick hadn't gone to Grady's service anyway.

A man whom she didn't know, but whom many of the others seemed to, got up and began to talk about Nick. He spoke of Nick's philanthropy, of his good works: his help to the underprivileged and the handicapped, his efforts for the environment, his hours of volunteer work, the boards he had served on, the money he had given. Olivia was surprised. She had always seen the hedonistic, superficial Nick having fun, and this side of him, which apparently had been there all along, was completely new to her. He hadn't talked to her about it in their brief meetings at family functions, and she hadn't asked—why would she? But now she regretted it. She felt very sad.

She thought of Grady's funeral, his friends telling about a cheerful, joking Grady she had never known: the unexpected Grady, the side of him that had been hidden from the family. And here now was the unexpected Nick. How little we know about our own relatives, she thought.

Some other friends of Nick's got up and made similar speeches about his virtues, an opera singer he had used in one of his commercials sang one of his favorite songs and then it was over. Long tables had been set up at the back of the room with tea sandwiches, petit fours, coffee and wine. People milled around, and the cousins hugged and kissed each other. There was such a mob of solicitous comforters around Nick's widow and sister that Olivia couldn't even get to them.

Olivia put her arm around Jenny and they walked to a corner away from the crowd. "Poor Melissa," Olivia said. "She and Nick were so close."

"I told Melissa: 'Now you know what it's like to be an only child,' " Jenny said. " 'We have to stick together.' "

"You *said* that? About being an only child?"

"It's true."

"We're all only children now," Olivia said.

"I know. Isn't that weird?"

They thought about it for a moment.

"I wonder what's going to happen to Lynne," Olivia said.

"She'll be all right," Jenny said. "She'll get married again. She's beautiful and rich."

They thought about that, too.

"We do have to stick together," Olivia said. "We keep talking about Mandelay and being together, but we never do anything about it."

"Maybe someday," Jenny said.

"Maybe." She thought about what it would be like, and because she knew that with their jobs and lives all scattered around and settled where they were it would never happen, it seemed like paradise.

31

THAT YEAR THE WEATHER was a vicious antagonist to the entire country. Fires, floods, mudslides, hurricanes, blizzard after blizzard, apocalyptic and strange. People who remembered the old days said this was what nature used to be like, and what we had known more recently had been only a respite. And then the nation woke up and turned on the news one morning in January to discover that Los Angeles had been struck by the worst earthquake to happen in Southern California in this century.

Apartments collapsed, freeways fell down, buildings were condemned and lifelong possessions were shattered to bits. It was so soon after the fires, and now Olivia was glued to the TV and the radio again, worrying. There was no way to get phone service in or out, but the family eventually discovered from the news reports that the area where Taylor, Tim and Baby Cody lived was, although shaken, relatively undamaged. They and their home had come through again. As for Kenny and Pam in Santa Barbara, they were not close to the earthquake and they were fine. The epicenter had been in the San Fernando Valley, with what seemed to be a separate quake in Santa Monica. Kenny called to reassure the family, and eventually Tim called too. But for others who were not so fortunate, everything was gone.

"I wouldn't live in California," Aunt Myra said to Olivia, making her round of phone calls. "I'd be too scared."

"Taylor is very hardy," Olivia said. "She's a survivor."

"I feel sorry for her, with such a little baby to take care of. I like New York."

"You won't even go out in the street at night; you're afraid to get mugged," Olivia said, not unkindly.

"I take a taxi."

"So we do the best we can."

By February, a month later, there were reported to have been three thousand aftershocks. Boarded up, evacuated, waiting to be rebuilt, certain parts of Santa Monica and the Valley still looked like a war zone. But, Olivia thought, parts of the South Bronx looked—and felt—like a war zone all the time. No, it wasn't so great here, either. She was thankful again for her safe, comfortable life, and concentrated on it.

She received a note from Taylor with a current photo of Cody. He was six months old already, and he was adorable.

Dear Olivia—Being a new mother is a full-time job and I love it. I'm managing very well. We set up a system of lights so I can hear the baby when he cries. I worried so much about how my mother would behave, but it's working out fine. When he was born she came from Santa Fe and stayed a week. She was bored with Cody after the first day. She never liked kids. She only came once more, for three days at Christmas. So I can see she won't be a pest. She's not rushing back here so soon!

I wish you could get to know him. He is so much like Grady. Do you think you and Roger will ever get out this way? You're always welcome.

Love,
Taylor

"I feel bad for Taylor," Olivia told Roger. "Nobody from here has seen the baby. And he's our cousin, after all."

"He's only six months old," Roger said. "He has a lot of childhood yet to come."

"I know, but it disappears so fast. Taylor's always felt like an outsider. I think someone should visit her, and it seems I'll have to be the one. I'm going to go for a weekend."

"It's nice of you to do that," Roger said. "You're always so thoughtful and good."

"It's for myself, too."

It would only be for a weekend, but that would be enough. She was aware that the visit would be just as important to her as it was to Taylor. It had something to do with the closeness of their childhood and the mystery of the separate time between then and now, an attempted recapturing of their escaped lives. She didn't suggest Roger come with her, and he understood and didn't volunteer. And when they kissed each other goodbye, she knew that this time while she was away she could trust him.

Taylor and Tim picked her up at the airport. The baby was not with them; he was at home with their housekeeper, asleep. The California sun was warm on Olivia's face through the car window, and it was a surprise and relief to be away from the snow and here in such a mild and sunny place.

As they drove through the canyon, Taylor pointed out damage from the fires. "Look!" she kept saying. "Look! Look at that!"

There were twisted blackened trees on bare terrain covered with gray ash that looked like a moonscape next to underbrush burned brown, and next to that, places of untouched lush green. On the mountainside above the narrow road there were weathered sandbags that had been placed there to prevent mudslides after the rains. You could see the bricks where the foundations of houses were all that was left, a geometric design. On one burned-out home site there was a satellite dish, incongruous there among nothing else at all.

"Look what the fires did," Taylor said. "Look."

They finally reached the house. Olivia had been there only once, after Grady's funeral, when it had been filled with mourners. Now it had a happy feeling about it, the living room floor was covered with toys, and there were a high chair and a baby's carry seat in the kitchen. The furniture was very eclectic: partly traditional, partly modern, partly antique. It almost worked.

"Do you remember Grandma's paintings?" Taylor asked, pointing. "And her loveseat, and her tea set?"

"Yes."

"I like having things from the family."

"Do you have any of Grady's stuff?"

"No," Taylor said. "I couldn't bear to look at it. Now it's all gone in the fire anyway."

Tim took Olivia's duffel bag into the guest room. It was done in Santa Fe style, obviously with great care, as if Taylor had been dreaming of someday having a visitor she really welcomed, not just her mother.

"How pretty," Olivia said to her.

"Thank you."

"Now I want to see Cody."

Tim nodded. "I think he's up."

The third bedroom was the baby's room. I wonder if he really is Grady reincarnated, Olivia thought unexpectedly as she walked down the hall. The door was open and she went in, alone. Their housekeeper, a pleasant-faced, middle-aged Hispanic woman, was holding Cody in her arms.

He was a large baby, with pale, translucent skin and delicate baby features, his round head covered with a fuzz of straight dark hair. He looked at Olivia the moment she entered the room, and immediately his face lit up. He smiled and began to wave his arms and legs wildly, giving little sounds of recognition and joy.

I know him, she thought. *He knows me.*

She felt flooded with love and relief. She beamed at him. "Well," she said, "it's nice to see you again."

Apparently he felt the same way. She and the baby kept looking at each other, their eyes intently locked, smiling happily, communicating, and he kept making those excited little noises.

"I've never seen him like this before," the woman said, surprised.

"No?"

"No. He's usually very shy."

Olivia kissed him on the head. His hair was as soft as down and he had that wonderful, sweet infant smell that was partly baby powder and partly himself. How sturdy he was. She wondered if she was looking at a future stuntman, or if he would grow up to be something entirely different, a physicist, perhaps. He would get older, learn to speak and to sign, and he would forget that he had recognized her from his previous life. Do you remember your cousin Olivia? they would ask him, meaning from the last family event, but he wouldn't even remember that:

he would look blank and a little embarrassed. How would he remember, she would say, he was so young. She would never see his face light up in exactly that way again.

But she would love him, and he would grow to love her in return. She would just have to woo him every time until he got to know her. That was the way it was.

Taylor and Tim were in the room then, watching. "He's Grady come back, isn't he?" Taylor said.

Olivia nodded. "But this time you'll give him a happy childhood," she said.

Tim's hands flew, translating, and for the first time, Taylor smiled.

They had dinner at home. Tim barbecued swordfish and vegetables on the deck under the trees, and Taylor made the salad while Olivia watched Cody rocking on all fours and babbling.

"He'll know three languages: English, Spanish, and sign language," Tim said. "He's going to be a man of the world."

It was too cold to eat outside so they ate in the dining room. "Tim made this table," Taylor said. It was a free-form shape, of pale caramel-colored burled wood that had been polished to feel so satiny it was a pleasure to touch.

"It's lovely," Olivia said.

"He made the chairs, too."

The chairs, of that same wood, had pieces of metal set in them. It made them look like art. "You're very talented," Olivia told Tim. He smiled and shrugged.

After dinner they had coffee in the living room in front of the fireplace. Baby Cody was half asleep in Taylor's lap, sucking on his pacifier. Tim lit a fire. For an instant Olivia thought of the recent devastating flames, and then she looked at the fire, domestic and contained behind its screen, and thought how cozy it made the room look. Shadows danced on the beamed ceiling.

"I thought I would never see all this again," Taylor said.

"I know."

"I'll try to make my son happy," Taylor said. "I try every day. And I know he's Cody. I'm going to treat him like himself."

"That's wise."

They sat there for a while in silence, each with their own thoughts. Taylor was stroking the baby's hair. "There's something

I never told you," she said. "A few years ago, Grady told me he was gay. He had tried to go straight when he went with Miranda, but it didn't work for him. He said he'd had an affair with one of his male friends, one of the stuntmen, and it was the most satisfying relationship he'd ever had. He said he finally knew what he was. I was upset. I told him I didn't want to know about him being gay. I said he was never to mention it to me again. I said it's your life, you can live it the way you want, but I don't want to know about it. I feel very guilty now."

Olivia just looked at her. All Taylor's denials, the inconsistencies, the blank spaces in her memory, her calm acceptance and befriending of Grady's lover made sense at last. Of course Taylor had known. Olivia didn't know what to say that wasn't a reproach, so she said nothing, but Taylor read her expression.

"You don't understand," Taylor said. "You're sophisticated. The bulk of America isn't like you. The bulk of America thinks it's bad. I'm like them. I think it's bad. I can't help it."

How could she avoid being prejudiced? Olivia thought. She's Stan the Stuntman's daughter; the tough old cowboy, a macho man. And Grady was his son. Stan would have hated having a gay son, and Grady knew it. Sometimes the dead are as with us as the living.

"I wish I could undo that now," Taylor said. "I wish I had said something kinder."

That night, before she fell asleep in Taylor's guest room, Olivia imagined she could hear the whole household breathing. It was a sound of such security and comfort to her that she lay there for a while listening to it, thinking of Jenny and Paul and their five children, of Melissa and Bill and their three, of happy families sleeping everywhere and how few of them there were. She thought of Roger, and Wozzle and Buster, and breathed with them, and then she slept.

In the morning Taylor was in a good mood again. She made cranberry pancakes for breakfast and then they all went out sightseeing in the car, the baby too, strapped into his little car seat, flirting with Olivia. "Let's show her where Grady's house was," Taylor said. Tim headed up into the canyon.

It was gone, of course. There were what had been the rooms, outlined by the stones of the foundation; and the fireplace, the only part still standing, sticking up like a large tombstone. The view below was breathtaking. With so many houses burnt to the ground, you could see for what seemed like miles. Olivia could understand why Grady had wanted to build a deck in just that place.

Around the foundation, where the garden must have been, tiny fresh greenery was beginning to grow again, irrepressibly, pushing up among the white crust of ash wherever there was a space.

"It's too bad you never saw his house," Taylor said. "It was nice."

They drove past several horse ranches, behind split wood fences, and Olivia could glimpse horses through the trees. In his car seat Cody was babbling cheerfully.

"I ride here," Taylor said, pointing to one ranch. "I have a favorite horse. He's so great."

"She's good, too," Tim said.

"Don't sign when you drive," Olivia said. "You make me nervous."

Tim smiled.

"You never saw the house I grew up in," Taylor said, as if it had just occurred to her.

"No," Olivia said, surprised at the realization that she never had. She had imagined it so often the fantasy had seemed more real than the reality.

"Let's go see it. Tim, you know where it is."

They drove on through the narrow canyon road, past houses that had survived the fire seemingly untouched, and then Tim stopped the car.

"Well, here we are . . ." Taylor said. She seemed confused.

There was no need to get out—the house was completely gone. All that remained was the foundation; not even the ubiquitous tombstone fireplace disturbed the flatness. Olivia looked at what must have been the front doorway, and thought of Grady as a child being locked out that cold night by Earlene, and Taylor helplessly watching. This was the house where all those terrible things had happened, during all those years. Little patches of new growth moved in the wind.

"It's gone too," Taylor said. "Damn, ain't that a bitch!" She looked pleased and amazed. "Let's get out and look."

They climbed out of the car. Taylor took Cody from his safety seat and held him up so he could see it.

The past is over, Olivia thought. At least in this small way. It's a beginning. Tim put his arm around his wife and child.

"Let's go home now," Taylor said.

On the way back to their house Olivia closed her eyes, day-dreaming. She thought of the surprises and diversity of all their lives, down through the chain of generations. Next to her in the car the baby had her finger clutched tightly in his fist. Abe Miller's great-great-grandson, Julia Miller Silverstone's great-grandson, Stan the Stuntman's grandson, Taylor's son, christened Cody Bay.